Frédéric Latreille

The Lachine Canal Chronicles
The Luck of the Irish

BookLand press

Copyright © 2021 by Frédéric Latreille

All rights reserved. No part of this publication may be reproduced or transmitted in any form or by any means, electronic or mechanical, including photocopying, recording or any information storage and retrieval, without the written permission of the publisher. Names, characters, places and incidents are either the product of the author's imagination or used fictitiously, and any resemblance to actual persons living or dead, events or locales is entirely coincidental. All trademarks are properties of their respective owners.

Published by BookLand Press Inc.
15 Allstate Parkway, Suite 600
Markham, Ontario L3R 5B4
www.booklandpress.com

Printed in Canada

Front cover image by Lio2012

Library and Archives Canada Cataloguing in Publication

Title: The Lachine Canal chronicles. The luck of the Irish / Frédéric Latreille.
Other titles: Les chroniques du Canal Lachine. La chance des Irlandais. English
Names: Latreille, Frédéric, author.
Identifiers: Canadiana (print) 20210155787 | Canadiana (ebook) 20210155868 | ISBN 9781772311280 (softcover) | ISBN 9781772311297 (EPUB) | ISBN 9781772311303 (PDF)
Classification: LCC PS8623.A8155 C4713 2021 | DDC C843/.6—dc23

We acknowledge the support of the Government of Canada through the Canada Book Fund and the support of the Ontario Arts Council, an agency of the Government of Ontario. We also acknowledge the support of the Canada Council for the Arts.

Table of Contents

Between the Canal and the Aqueduct	5
The Lost River	97
Return of the Prodigal Sons	175
Epilogue	267

Between the Canal and the Aqueduct

I

"Ouch! Eamon ... Why the fuck did you punch me in the ribs? It friggin' hurts, you bastard!" said Tom – in pain.

"We're going to be late for work. God! I've been trying to wake you up, like forever. Where were you last night? Did you double dose your morphine again?" I asked – mad at him.

"Oh, shut the fuck up, Eamon! You sound just like my mother."

"Well, if she had done her job, rest her soul, you wouldn't be such a prick sometimes ... At what time did you come in last night?"

"I don't know! 'Must've been around 4:00am or so. I was out with this hot chocolatier and ..."

"I don't give a rat's ass about the girls you fuck! You knew we were working at 9:00am this morning. God! I used my influence to get you this job."

"Dude! We wash dishes and cut potatoes and vegetables at the Cage. It's not like you made me a business partner in a goddamn law firm or some crap like that."

"I don't care if it's a shitty job. You've been living on my couch for the past year, not making any money and leeching off me. It's your first day, for cryin' out loud. You look like hell and smell like a goddamn hobo."

"Yeah! I got pretty wasted last night. I'm telling you, this girl …"

"I don't have time for your shenanigans right now … Go wash yourself up and get dressed, like right the fuck now. I don't wanna be late."

"Yeah, yeah! I'm goin' … Mom! I just don't know why I gotta do this crappy job anyways. I have money. I have my pension as a war veteran …"

"You asked me to get you this job! Anyways, you spend your pension on booze and painkillers."

"You know I got injured in Afghanistan. Be respectful."

"Ah, come on! You shot yourself in your own goddamn foot to get the hell outta there … So don't you come cryin' to me!"

"You don't know what it was like out there. It was fuckin' hell. I couldn't sleep. I kept having these flashbacks of slaughtered civilians and soldiers blown up by IEDs … and I still do. It was too goddamn painful … I just had to get the fuck outta there."

"I told you that you weren't fit for the army. You're too free-spirited and sensitive."

"But I didn't think that they would actually send me in combat. I was prepared to be treated like shit like in *Full Metal Jacket* … but not this."

"Well … you did volunteer, didn't you? Anyways, go prep up fast and please try to do a proper job."

It had been a year since Tom had gotten back from Kandahar. He had nowhere to go and no place to live. His mother had passed away in 2009 – during his time serving at the Edmonton Base of the Canadian Army. He could have gone to live with his cousin Lisa, but she had hooked up with my cousin Andrew and they were now living together in a nice suburban home in Brossard – so he didn't want to infringe upon them – especially since they had a young child to take care of. They certainly didn't need another "child" to pick up after. I was the only "family" Tom had left. He rang my door bell on a rainy May evening in 2011. I temporarily let him crash at my place, but his stay has prolonged itself. I had gotten accustomed to his presence by then.

I had been living in a second story, three-and-a-half-room apartment, on De Biencourt Street – near the corner of Laurendeau Street – in Côte-Saint-Paul. All my life, I had never really left Montreal's South-West area – between the Lachine Canal and the Montreal Aqueduct. I didn't have much space, but I couldn't leave Tom living on the street. So, I opened my door to him until he could get back on his feet. It had been a year since then and he was still a mess: sleeping on my couch, eating my food, drinking my beer and not picking up after himself. It pissed me off, but I put up with it anyways. Tom was like a brother to me and you don't leave family in the lurch – even after all he'd done.

"Are you ready, asshole?" I yelled to him – from across the room.

"Yeah, yeah! I'm coming … I'm coming! Geez! Would you get off my back a little?!" replied Tom – shirtless, with a cigarette in his mouth.

He put on a black Dig it Up – one of the local bands we supported by buying their merchandise – t-shirt and said:

"Okay … 'Ready … Let's go" – while pouring himself a carry on mug of black coffee.

"How can you drink coffee with nothing in it?"

"Well, I like my coffee like I like my women: dark, strong and bitter."

I actually laughed at that one.

We went down the stairs that led from the second floor balcony to the sidewalk. These outdoor stairs – a symbol of Montreal's early 20th-century architecture – can be really icy and slippery come winter time. As we were heading down, we crossed my landlord – Misses Bouchard – who was a really sweet lady in her fifties.

"Hello boys," she said – with a huge French-Canadian accent – "I was coming up to get this month's rent."

"Sorry Mrs. Bouchard," I replied to her apologetically, "Can I give it to you in a couple of days? We are going to work right now and I'll get my pay next Thursday. I'm having a rough time right now. But Tom's working with me now, so we'll get your rent money soon," I added – pleading to her.

"I don't really have a choice, do I? You've been late for the last four months. Please try not to make a habit out of it," she replied – annoyed.

"No problem Misses Bouchard … 'Will do … and … thanks."

"Don't mention it!"

I spoke French fluently – having gone to French elementary and high schools – but I just loved to hear her speak English. Her accent was just so lovely.

We walked to the bus stop and, after about five minutes, got on the 37 bus which dropped us off at the Cage aux Sports on Newman Street – in the Angrignon shopping mall. The Cage is a sports-based restaurant with TV screens everywhere showing games. Player jerseys adorn every wall. The place would be empty that evening due to the NHL lockout. They were barely surviving with October baseball – the playoffs – and the NFL on Sunday and Monday evening.

"Now, behave today!" I warned Tom.

"Yeah, yeah! God! You really think that I'm this wild untameable stallion, don't you?" he asked – annoyed.

"No, but I know you. You don't like to get bossed around and you're so goddamn stubborn."

"Thanks for the vote of confidence. But tell me … How did a college man like yourself ended up in this dead-end job anyways?"

"That's what you get for trying to be an artist without ever really getting there. I never got anything published. But I'm getting there ... I think."

"Go bankrupt; write in a café... maybe you'll come up with the next Harry Potter or something."

"I am writing a novel in fact."

"You're finally doing it for real this time?" replied Tom – astonished – "You've been saying that since we were kids and here you are, still washing dishes. I knew you were up to something these past weeks. It must be that Shelly girl that's being your muse or something! I had just figured you were jerking off to porn alone in your room or I was just getting on your nerves."

"Well, indeed you are."

"Shut up! I know you love me, you queer!"

"Would you stop it you're your homophobic insults!"

"I'm not homophobe! Hell, half of the porn I watch is lesbian porn!"

"You're such a douchebag, you know that!?"

"Hahahaha! Says you! So ...Whatcha writin' about this time?"

"Well, it's an autobiographical novel of some sort."

"Like those *Lachine Canal Chronicles* you were writing as a teen and never finished? It must be really thin 'cause you haven't done jack-shit in your life dude. You're only turning twenty-four for God's sake. You should write my life story. Then you would have substance: crime, drugs and sex ... That's a best-seller right there."

I hadn't told Tom about what had happened to me during the time that he was away in the army, so I just went along, comforting the illusions he had about me.

"I know, but I got things to say. Thanks for the encouragement by the way, ass-wipe! In fact, you are in it," I told him.

"For real?!? Don't you go sayin' bad shit about me, though. I don't want ladies reading this and not wanting to fuck me anymore because of the things you wrote."

"Don't worry about that. Anyways, the women you have sex with, like your bad boy / "dangerous" persona that you keep bullshitting everyone with. Plus, I'm not using actual names. You're called Terrance."

"What?! Why? God! It's such a shitty name! Why didn't you give me a badass name like Duke, Mike, Arnold or better yet, Max Powers?"

"Because you're a dipshit and don't get to have a badass name. I found a name that started with the same letter as your real name."

"Okay and what are you called?"

"Nothing. I never mention my name in the book."

"Well, you should! I've got the best ones for you: Kitty, Pussy or Sissy."

"Go fuck yourself!"

"I always do and you know that … By the way, I want to tell you about that chocolatier I fucked yesterday…"

"No, we don't have time. The boss is about to meet you. So, no dirty talk in front of him."

"Yeah, yeah! … Since when did you become such an uptight asshole?"

"Since you're sucking out all my savings, because you can't control your sorry ass."

"Don't be so sour. I'll make it up to you someday … I promise!"

"I'll believe it when I see it."

"God! You can be so anal sometimes!"

We got to the Cage and met with the boss.

"Hi, Mr. Townsend. This is Tom," I said – presenting one to the other.

"Good morning, sir. I'm really glad that you're giving me a shot here. You won't be disappointed," said Tom – shaking Mr. Townsend's hand.

"I'm glad to hear that. Eamon will show you what to do. I will need your social security number and a specimen check for your pay."

"Of course; 'will do that, sir."

I then got Tom to the kitchen and showed him what he had to do for morning food preparation and how the dishwashing machine worked and where everything went afterwards.

As we were pealing and cutting potatoes and carrots, Tom said:

"Like I was trying to tell you, last night was awesome …"

"Not the chocolatier story again?!" I replied – exasperated.

"Well, you never gave me time to tell it to you."

"Frankly, my dear, I don't give a damn."

"Oh, shut up! You love my stories. You used to beg me to tell them to you. Plus, it could be good for your novel. It'll add more kink and raunchiness."

"Okay, go ahead. Anyways, I know you'll never shut up about it until you get it out of your system."

"You know that's true … So … Like I was saying … Yesterday, while you were in your room reading, sleeping or jerkin' off to your mom's pictures …"

"Get bent, Motherfucker! Between you and me, I bet you're the one doing that!"

"Hahahaha … You got me there! You know I've always found your mom sooooo hot!"

"God! You're sick!"

"Hahahaha! Anyways … I had been chatting with this girl I met on Tinder …"

"Since when do you own a smartphone?"

"I don't. In fact, I used yours and went on your account."

"What? No, you didn't!?! You asshole!"

"Sorry dude; I really needed to get laid. Anyways, like I was sayin', I got talking with this girl … She found you cute by the way … I told her, later on, that I wasn't you, though … To have a better chance with her … You know:

the Murphy charm ... Plus, I ain't no catfish. So, I invited her to the Skratch pool hall on Newman Street and ..."

He then went on and on, relating the events of the previous night with way too much details for my taste. He had this verbal diarrhea all the while working like a goddamn machine. I had forgotten how good Tom was in a kitchen, especially when he was hyper-excited about something

Watching Tom telling his story – while mechanically working – just brought me back to my teen years. You see, I had met Tom in a similar situation. It just made me so nostalgic to relive those years in my mind. Tom kept talking, but I didn't listen to him. I was daydreaming about the past; a time when everything was so much simpler.

II

I was born on October 18, 1988, in Côte-Saint-Paul. My dad, Henri Jovanovski was of Macedonian descent. His grandparents fled to Greece during the Nazi overtaking of Yugoslavia in 1941 – only to be caught in the war there too. When the Greek Civil War started, after World War II, they were fed up and immigrated to Canada and established themselves in Montreal's St Henri quarter. Since it was primarily a French-Canadian quarter, they made their kids go to French schools. My grandpa grew up there and married this obnoxious Saguenay woman in the late fifties. My dad was their last-born child. In the late eighties, he met my mom – a year prior to my birth – at the Dairy Queen on the corner of Jolicoeur and Laurendeau Street. My mom, Maureen Magauran, was from Irish descent. She was born in 1963 in Verdun, but was living with a friend of hers in Côte-St-Paul, on Cardinal Street between Hadley and Eadie Street. My parents hit it off immediately. Less than a year later, I was born. It was quite a shock to my dad to find out that my mom was pregnant. My mom's roommate moved out and my dad moved in with my mom. My dad worked for Via Rail at Montreal's Central Station and my mom, at the Sears in the Angrignon shopping mall.

I grew up as any – close-to-poor – kid did back then: hanging in the alleys playing with the neighborhood boys, bicycling around the quarter, getting fries at the Lafleur on Monk Street and, during winter, crazy-carpeting down Newman Hill. Ever since I was in grade first, I had befriended a kid named Frank Dilallo. We did everything together. We started to grow apart during high school though. I went to Honoré-Mercier High School, on Desmarchais Street. I was really good in English – my mom being Irish and all – and in art class, but totally sucked in Math and French.

In the summer before my grad year, my friend Frank landed me a job in a restaurant owned by his family. You see, they were the proud owners of the Dilallo Burger restaurants – which were an institution in Montreal's South-West district. The first one had opened in 1929. It was famous for its Buck Burger – which was dressed with lettuce, onions, tomatoes, mustard, relish, cheese, capicole and homemade peppers. When I was in primary school, my dad used to take me there every weekend after my soccer practice. Frank got me a job at the one located on Allard Street, on the corner of Hurteau. The manager took me in and showed me the basics and what was expected of me work-wise. I was ecstatic to start my first real job. I had delivered newspapers as a kid, but I never considered it a real job – and hadn't done it for a very long period of time.

About an hour later, another employee came in and started to prep up for work. He was about 5'10", 150 pounds, had a blue Mohawk, green eyes, stretches in his ears and I could see a half-sleeve tattoo that exceeded the length of his t-shirt. He took off his earrings, put on a hair net and a Montreal Expos baseball cap.

"Salut, j'm'appelle Eamon. Toi c'est quoi?" I asked him – holding my hand up to shake his.

"Sorry dude, my French is really awful. Do you speak English?"

"Yup! My mom's Irish."

"So's mine! Hey I'm Tom ... Tom Murphy," he said – wiping his hand on his apron and giving me a friendly handshake afterwards.

"I'm Eamon Jovanovski."

"Oh! An Irish Pollock?"

"No, my grandpa's from Macedonia actually. He fled during the war and …"

"IT DOESN'T MATTER WHERE YOUR FAMILY COMES FROM!" he loudly replied.

I instantly froze and felt really intimidated. Tom then laughed and said:

"Dude, don't take it like that! I was just imitating The Rock. You know … Wrestling! Hahahaha! Anyways … 'You from around here?'"

"Yeah, I live on Cardinal Street."

"Not too familiar with this quarter. I'm from La-Salle. I used to work at the Dilallo down there, but they needed people here ASAP, so I volunteered. 'Just been workin' here for the last month or so."

"Oh, okay. Are you still in school?"

"Yup. I go to LaSalle Community Comprehensive High School. It kinda sucks. I flunked last year so I have to do it again. Still two long years to go and then I'm off to the army."

"Why would you do that?"

You see, I'm a convinced pacifist – especially with all the stories my grandpa told me about the war; at least what he could remember because he was really young.

"Well, because it's kind of easy money when you think about it. You get paid for doing push-ups in the mud and getting screamed at. My mom screams at me for free. So why not get paid for it," he jokingly replied.

"Aren't you scared that they could send you off to war or something like that?"

"Nah! I'm pretty sure the Afghan war will be over once I finish my training."

"It's your life. I'm a convinced pacifist for my part."

"Anyways, they wouldn't accept you in the army. You look more like the artsy type, with your geeky glasses and your weakly arms."

I looked at him open-mouthed. That guy didn't know me at all and he was already insulting me. What a prick!

"Don't take it wrong, dude. You look like a real straight-up guy with great qualities. You just don't have those. I'm really good at deciphering people's personalities. From the looks of you, I can tell that you that you write or play music, you're faithful in your friendships, that you have built up rage because your parents are separating and that you're still a virgin," he said – in one rapid and long breath.

I couldn't believe my ears. Who did he think he was; making assumptions about me like that?

The problem was that he was right on everything and I was a little ashamed of him sizing me in one glance. I was dumbstruck; I just gazed at him. He patted me on the back and said:

"Hahahaha! Jackpot ... I was right on everything, weren't I? Yup, I'm that good. That's how I get all my women. I'm like a hunter who knows his prey's next move before she does it. Like yesterday, I stuffed myself this broad. God she was a feisty one. Her parents were out of town and she was in love with my "exotic" accent. French-Canadian girls love a British accent, even if it's Irish ... They're so dumb ... But that's how I "Hugh Granted" my way in her bed. She was a little older and into some kinky shit. She liked it when I insulted her and I even let her stick a finger up my ..."

He just continued on and on about his sexual prowess and conquests – all the while continuing to mechanically work – not even lowering his voice when clients came in. I had known the guy for only ten minutes and already he was babbling about his intimate life. I didn't know if he was bullshitting me or not, but the amount of details he procured was just too astonishing to have been made up. Here I was: a nerdy artsy virgin to whom girls didn't even give the time of day. But Tom already had several experiences with girls of all ages – even if he confessed to liking older women way more. The guy was a beast.

As the weeks went by, Tom and I started to become really close – to the point that I was hanging less and less with my usual friend. I started to leach off his extravagant life and vicariously lived my life through him – which was way more interesting than my own. Plus, it gave me an exit out of the hellhole my home had become. My dad was acting like drunken asshole to my mom and I. One day, I even found him passed out on the kitchen floor, reeking of vodka fumes. My mom was really fed up with his behavior and was thinking about throwing him out – even if it meant that she would have a lot of financial problems – because my dad had put a lot of money on a credit line that he never paid. My mom would be stuck paying half of the debts he owed, but she could not stand him anymore.

Since it was a living hell at my place, I started hanging at Tom's more and more often.

"Hey Mom! This is Eamon; I work with him," he said to his mom.

"Hi, Eamon!" she greeted me.

"Hi Mrs. O'Donnell! Glad to meet you!" I replied.

"Listen, Mom ... Eamon's parents are in a break-up mood and I was wondering if he could crash here for a couple of days ... at least until the tension cools down over there?" Tom asked his mom.

"Of course, Tommy-Bear! No problem! He can stay as long as he wants," she tenderly replied.

I got close to Tom's ear and tauntingly whispered:

"Tommy-Bear?!"

He half-turned his head and whispered through his teeth – in a very menacing way:

"Shut the fuck up or I'll punch your teeth in so hard that you'll have serum for breakfast tomorrow morning."

"I'll just keep that as a counter-attack if one day you diss me in front a pretty girl."

"Get bent, you piece of shit!"

"You're welcome, you prick."

III

"My mom's officially kicking my drunk-ass dad from our house!" I sadly said to Tom – but somewhat relieved at the same time.

"It's a good thing! ... I sometimes wish I had met my dad. You see, he left my mom before I was even born and we never heard from him ever again. My mom never talks about him even if I ask. It's like a taboo subject around here. Here listen ..." He then screamed: "Hey Mom?! ... Can you tell us a little about Michael Murphy? ..."

I then heard a loud voice from another room, with a huge Irish accent, screaming:

"Thomas Elliot Murphy! ... You better stop this right now if you don't want to be grounded 'till the next millennium!!!"

Tom turned to me, with a grin, and said:
"See... Told ya!"

I kept on reflecting on my family's situation and questioned Tom:

"Maybe ... But what am I going to do right now?"
"Whattaya mean?"
"Well, my mom paid for everything while my dad was drinking and snorting his paychecks away. She endured

a lot. I don't want to be a burden on her. She has suffered enough."

"Well, you could always live here."

"I think your mom has suffered enough with you! Hahahaha! … No seriously, I think that after high school, I'm gonna find myself an apartment somewhere."

"But wouldn't it be simpler to just pay her some kind of rent?"

"Have you ever tried giving money to that woman? I tell you, it's impossible! Plus, I'm her only son … She would never accept it. So, I guess moving out seems like the best option."

"Hey! I could come live with you and help you pay the rent!"

Tom had so much enthusiasm in his tone that it was hard to bring him back to reality. How could I tell him that he was not trustworthy without insulting him? Then it hit me; the perfect lie.

"Well, it's not that I don't want to live with you, but I don't want to hear you bang a different woman every night. I'll be going to college and I'll need a little peace and quiet to study and sleep."

"You're right, bro! I do know how to make the ladies scream. You see, you have to get your middle finger inside her pussy and rub that rugged spot in the northern part of it vagina while you lick…"

"God, Tom! Don't you ever stop?!"

"I'm trying to give you tips … You being a virgin and all."

"You don't know that!"

"Dude, you would have soooo bragged to me about it. You know I'm right."

"You're such an asshole!!!"

"Hahahaha! Love you too bro!" he ended – while taking my head under his armpit and giving me a knuckle rub on my scalp until it burned.

"I think I'll ask my cousin Andrew if he wants for us to move together. We get along real good," I said – thinking out loud.

"Yeah! Maybe that's a better idea than me. Plus, if I don't have a rent to pay, I'll have more money to take the ladies out and maybe have some left to buy some Jack Daniels."

"God, you're such a player!" I replied – discouraged.

"No, I'm a romantic!"

"Wanting to get laid every day by a different woman doesn't make you a romantic."

"Says you, bro ... Says you."

I spent the next months working with Tom at Dilallo's, going to class, writing songs and poetry, trying to get Noémie – my science lab partner – to notice me, all the while allowing Tom to bring me down to the "dark side". It was always like this: – the phone rings –

"Hey, Eamon! Whatcha doin'?"

"Not much ... Studying for this science exam next week."

"Forget about it. You'll never fuck that lab partner of yours with your brains. Get your ass out here. I'll show you a good time."

I would always put down my books, get to his place – where we would get high on pot – and played *GTA* or *Need for Speed* on his PS2. When we got bored of playing, we would stroll around on our bikes, prank people in the Lachine Catholic Cemetery, smoke joints in LaSalle Park or try to pick up girls along the Lachine Canal bicycle path.

Tom was, like me, a sixteen-year-old kid, but he actually looked like he was twenty-one. Confidence and a rough life made him look way much older. I didn't really mind because he could get beer from corner stores – only if I wasn't going in with him.

One Saturday afternoon, I was studying science – I really wanted to hook up with that lab partner of mine –

when the phone rang. My mom answered and said – as she continued listening on the line – waiting for me to pick up:

"Eamon! It's for you. It's that no good friend of yours: Tom! … Hun hun … God, Tom, quit it … You're getting creepy … Here sweetie, talk to him or I swear I'll go down there and smack the life out of him!"

I picked up the phone and said:

"Hey bro! What did you say to my mom?"

"What I usually say to girls … If you get my gist … I swear one day, she'll be mine. Oh yes, she'll be mine!" he replied – quoting *Wayne's Wold*.

"God! You're so obnoxious! One day you'll have to stop or I'll prevent you from calling my house!"

"I can't help it bro … Your mom is so hot … Have you seen the tits and ass on that g…"

"Tom! Would you just stop it! That's my mom you're talkin' about!"

"Yeah! Even better! I have always dreamed of having sex with one of my friends' m…"

That's when I hung up on him – boiling with rage. The phone rang immediately again. I picked up and Tom said laughing:

"Okay, dude … I'm sorry! It's just so easy to get you mad that I just can't help it … Although your mom's so …"

"If you say one more word, I swear you won't hear of me again!"

"Okay … I promise … So, watcha wanna do today?"

"Well … I got to study science because …"

"I told you to forget about that virgin nerd partner of yours. I'm sooooo bored dude. You gotta find something for us to do or I swear I'm going to do something stupid like steal a car or fuck a hooker!"

"Okay! Okay! Hold on! Let me think … Hey! My cousin Andrew's playing rugby at the Montreal Irish Rugby

Football Practice Field, on Joseph Street, in Verdun. Wanna go?"

"I don't know anything about rugby. But if you're implying football with no equipment ... Fuck yeah! ... I'm in!"

We went to go see my cousin's team – the Montreal Wanderers – play against the Montreal Rugby Club. My cousin Andrew was a little older than I. He was twenty-two years old, was about 5'7", weighed around 220 pounds – all muscle – had short black hair and a freshly cut beard – underlining his chin. He was studying 3D animation & computer generated imagery at Dawson College. He was already in his second year and he had landed an internship at Ubisoft, on St-Laurent Street – on the corner of St-Viateur – the Mecca for any gaming programmer. On top of that, he was a MMA – mixed martial arts – fighter. He had already broken four guys' arms – before having his broken a couple of months later. His arm had healed since then and he was back in training for some big competition.

We were there in the stands cheering – but not understanding any of the rules. I didn't even think my cousin Andrew understood all of them; he just liked the competition – and hurting people. They won the game 25-15. Tom and I then went on the field to congratulate him. He came to us with blood running down from his nose.

"Hey Cous'! Great game!" I said to Andrew.

"Yeah, it was a hard one. I got one of those fuckers' knee on the nose. Don't ask me how, but it just stopped bleeding a couple of minutes ago," he replied – trying to get some blood out from under his nose – with his already bloodied fingers.

"Yeah, we saw that ... Hey! By the way, I would like you to meet Tom," I replied – pointing in Tom's direction.

Tom looked pale as he was stretching his arm for a brotherly handshake. My cousin looked at him – his left eyebrow lifted – like he was thinking or something. He finally asked Tom:

"Aren't you the guy I beat the living crap out of because you slept with my girlfriend-of-the-moment about a year ago?"

"Yeah, that's me," shamefully confessed Tom – shamefully scratching the back of his head. "Dude, I'm sooooo sorry. I swear on my mother's grave I had no idea that she was seeing someone. If I had known, I would never have done such a thing!"

I got closer to Tom and whispered in his ear:

"Dude! Your mom's alive!"

He whispered back through his teeth:

"Yeah I know! Just go with it! I knew his girl was seeing someone."

They shook hands and Andrew said:

"That girl was a total skank anyways! Don't sweat it. A friend of Eamon is a friend of mine."

I thought to myself: "One day, Tom's going to get killed!", but I just went along with his lies – he was beginning to be some sort of a lab rat for me to study. I was examining his every move and learning from his mistakes, but especially from his victories. I looked up and Tom was high-fiving the entire team on the field. I was pretty sure he had slept with half of their girlfriends and I admired him for that back then – his cockiness and his "fuck the world" attitude.

Andrew started to hang out with us from then on. He and Tom were way more adventurous than I was. They were always challenging and daring each other with stuff that I wasn't able or comfortable of doing.

About a week later, I met Andrew – who lived two blocks from my place – on his way to take the subway to Dawson College. I yelled:

"Hey Andrew, wait up!"

"Hey lil Cous'! How you doin'?"

"I'm doin' great! Listen ... Ummm ... I'm graduating from high school this year and my mom's having some financial problems ... you know ... since she threw my dad out. I have a couple of hundreds saved up and was wondering if you wanted to rent an apartment with me. It could be really cool!"

"Why don't you just give some money to your mom? That would be a little cheaper for you."

"I thought about that, but I really need to leave the nest and be my own man!" I half-lied to him.

"Suit yourself ... But did you ask Tom first? You guys are like inseparable."

"No, I didn't. Tom's too much of a loose cannon for me to live with. But he knows about my plan and is fine with it. I told him I would ask you."

"Well, that's very thoughtful of you. Can you give me some time to think about it?"

"Yes, of course! It's not for a couple of months anyways."

"Okay, let me check my finances. It should be fine with the internship at Ubisoft and the MMA courses I give. I tell ya dude, there's no greater satisfaction than seeing a ten-year-old girl getting a twelve-year-old boy in an arm lock. It's friggin' epic!"

"Well, everyone has their kicks one way or another."

A couple of months later, I co-signed a lease with my cousin for this apartment on Jacques-Hertel – between d'Aragon and Hamilton Street. It was a second-floor apartment. It wasn't very spacious, but it was going to be my own place, so it was all good. I brought Tom to look at it from the outside – after work one day. His only response was:

"Dude! It's your prom soon. Have you got a date yet?"

"I'm not going to prom!"

"Bro! You totally hafta go! You'll regret it if you don't. If it's a money thing, I will pay it for you. You can't not go to your prom ... Come on!"

"To be honest, I don't really care."

"Shush! I will find you a date and a tuxedo. Just be on your best behavior and, I tell you, you will get out of there a non-virgin guaranteed. Just let me organize everything."

"Will you stop with your fixation about me losing my virginity!"

"Dude! You're seventeen! It's about time!"

"Says you!"

"Says every man in history. If not for you, do this for me. I may never graduate. So let me do this for you please!"

"Okay! If it makes you happy ... And gets you to shut up for once!"

"Yay!!! I'm gonna get my boy a classy girl for him to take to prom," said Tom happily dancing on Jacques-Hertel Street – as bystanders looked at him like he had just escaped a mental institution.

IV

Prom night was arriving way faster than I had imagined and I still had no date. I was studying for my finals that were coming up a month later, working my ass off at the restaurant and slowly packing my stuff to move on July 1st. I barely had time for anything else. Tom was always harassing me to do stuff with him. He always had these crazy and barely legal ideas on how to pass the time. But, in the end, it always ended up with us trying to meet girls and getting drunk or high.

"Dude, I met this girl last night ..." said Tom – over the phone.

"Tom I don't have time. I've got tons of homework to do," I replied.

"Shut up! Just listen."

"Okay ... But hurry up!"

"Like I was saying, I met this girl, Marla, yesterday. I'm telling you she's hot!"

"You find all girls hot ... Which makes your point irrelevant."

"But this time, I had you in mind."

"That's a little gross, don't you think?"

"Shut up and listen! ... You remember that I promised to find you a girl for prom? ... Well, I think she could be the one."

"And how do you know that? Where did you meet her?"

"I met her at the Foufs yesterday. I went to see the Sainte Catherines and she was in the crowd. We danced together through the entire show. Well, I actually danced with this French girl, Ophelia, who's studying in Montreal. Anyways, Marla was with her. After the show, we got to talk and we went out for pizza. Marla's a really cool girl and I'm pretty sure you'll like her. I know I did!"

"You mean you liked her or you "liked" her."

"Well ... Ummm ... both, I guess. She and her friend Ophelia at the same time. Dude! French girls are nasty!"

"God! You want me to take a girl you just fucked to my prom?!?"

"Well, I had to test the merchandise first, no?! I wanted my best bud to have "Grade AAA" meat."

"OH MY GOD!!! You ... are... such a misogynist!"

"Don't worry bro. I'm pretty sure she doesn't even remember me ... She was pretty wasted. That's when they are the most vulnerable and the most real at the same time, because their defenses are down. Anyways, she's not really my type; too young for my taste. I was really more into her French friend, but she came with her ... And came she did. Hahahaha!"

"I've heard enough! I'm going back to my homework."

"Ah, come on, dude! Just keep an open mind about Marla. I'm throwing a party tomorrow and she said she'd be there. I invited tons of people to my place. My mom's out of town on a seminar for her job. She hates those teacher workshops, but she likes the free hotels. She'll be in Quebec City for the next two days. So it's PARTAY time!"

"I can't ... I work tomorrow."

"No, you don't! I told the manager that you had a 104°F fever because of some contagious virus and that it would take you at least two or three days to fight it off."

"You did what?! God, Tom! You know I need the money. I'm moving out in a month and I still don't have the money to rent a tux for prom ... to which I still don't have a date."

"Would you relax and live a little. You'll have a date. You're going with Marla. I'm sure you two will hit it off."

"I don't want your sloppy seconds."

"Just get that out of your head and give her a try ... Please!"

"Yeah, yeah," I replied – just so he would shut up and let me study.

"As for the suit, I found one for you as well."

"What the fuck are you talking about?"

"Well, my godfather passed away a couple of months ago and it seems that he left me some money and the suit he wore at my christening."

"What a weird guy!"

"It doesn't fit me well, but I'm pretty sure it'll look great on you. At least try it!"

"God! All that prom crap, I feel like that you want it more than I do."

"Bro! It's a rite of passage like your first hangover and your first fuck ... sorry no disrespect; I always forget. Anyways, I may never graduate at this rate and I know you're brilliant and also I kinda live this through you."

It was really weird for him to say that. I had always lived through Tom – looking up to him – because he could do anything he wanted without fearing the consequences – without giving a damn about what other people thought. And now, the situation was reversed; Tom was living through me. Maybe he was more fragile than he was showing everyone. I had always known that behind that cocky douchebag persona was hiding a scared little boy with a heart of gold – that may actually be the reason I stuck with him from day one.

"Anyways, the party's at my place tomorrow at 8:00 pm. Don't you ditch me or I'll make your life a living hell!" he added.

"And that's not what you're already doing? Hahahaha!"

"Get bent!" he replied – hanging up afterwards.

The next day, I went straight from school to Tom's place. We got supper from Pizza 2 Pointes, on Provost Street. We ordered two large pizzas with extra bacon topping on it. In my opinion, you can put bacon on everything. It's like the perfect condiment. We ate like pigs, at least I did. Tom could always eat way more than I did, but stayed pretty slim and cut. I never understood how his metabolism worked and how his body processed food. I was more like a girl on that chapter: "Ten seconds on the lips; forever on the hips." At seventeen, I already had this small belly. Tom could eat an entire cow and not gain a pound. He knew it and he was hard on his body – and not only concerning food. He was always in excess about everything. He smoked like a chimney, ate like a Texan and drank like … well like an Irishman.

"So who's coming tonight?" I asked Tom.

"Surprise, surprise bro!" he replied – taunting me with the anticipation.

"Ah, come on! It's not like it's Christmas or an ambush intervention. It's just another one of your lame parties … Just another pretext for you to get even drunker than usual."

"Ok … I'll only tell you two words: family and pussy!"

"Usually those two don't mix! Dude, you're grossing me out right now!"

"Don't worry about a thing. Tonight is gonna be legen... wait for it... dary!!"

"What do I keep telling you?! Enough with the quotes!"

"Sorry! I can't help myself ... Sugar pie, honey bunch ... Hahahaha!"

"God, you're annoying!"

About an hour later, the doorbell rang. Tom stood up and went to buzz the person in. The front door opened and somebody yelled: "COUSIN!!!" and Tom replied: "COUSIN!!!!" He looked at me and said:

"Bro! This is my cousin Lisa. She's a half-Irish, half-French-Canadian retard!"

"Well ... We do have the same retarded blood... Just so you know!" she replied.

"Hahahaha! True ... True ... Lisa, this is Eamon; another half-Irish bastard."

Lisa greeted me with kisses on both cheeks adding:
"Nice to meet you!"

"Same here," I replied.

Lisa stood 5'2", weighed around 135 pounds, had dark hair midway down her back and glasses. She was 24 years old and was studying to be a judicial technician at Ahuntsic College. But until she finished her diploma, she was working at the Reno-Depot on Lapierre Street, on the corner of Newman.

A couple of minutes later, Andrew arrived and I yelled: "COUSIN!!!", but he just looked at me like I was a goddamn moron. He bro-hugged Tom – thanking him for the party invite. Tom said:

"Andrew, I would like you to meet my cousin Lisa."

They shook hands for a little longer than they should've normally had. They just stared in each other's eyes as they said: "Nice to meet you," to each other. I could sense an immediate connection between those two. I just dumbly smiled through the process. What can I say? I'm a hopeless romantic.

People started coming in – I mean a lot of people. At one point, I thought that Tom had advertised this as an open house party. People – well mostly girls – kept coming in as his home stereo system screamed the punk rock mixtapes – well actually CDs – that Tom had put together especially for the occasion. It was mostly local bands intertwined with your occasional NOFX, Lagwagon, Dropkick Murphys or Rancid songs coming on the stereo. That was another thing that Tom and I had in common – our tastes in music. We both liked to see local punk rock, ska and reggae bands live performances – where we would buy a lot of their merchandise in the process – ranging from CDs, to stickers and t-shirts.

Around 10:00 pm, Tom left the company of this late-thirty-something cougar he had met at Dilallo's – her name was Karen ... I think – and asked his cousin to be in charge of the guests for some time. He then took me apart and said:

"Let's get outta here for a couple of minutes."

I just found it weird that someone would leave his own party, but I followed him – as always. We walked a couple of minutes – from 5th Avenue to LaSalle Park. We both sat down with our backs to a tree trunk. Tom then asked:

"Hey bro! Did I ever tell you that I'm scared?"

"Scared of what?"

"About the army thing ... About the future ... About everything. I know I often come out as this obnoxious self-centered prick. But that's just a "façade". Deep down, I'm just this scared little kid. I have no future; nowhere to go. I'm stuck in this dead-end Lachine Canal-bound lifestyle. That's partly why I wanna join the army. I wanna live something else; I wanna live somewhere else ... Wow! Would you look at those stars?! It's oh so magnificent!"

he said – pointing Orion's Belt to me – "They seem so free; coming and going. There may be hundreds of planets around those stars. God only knows what's out there. *God only knows where I'd be without you*" – he drunkenly sang – "Did I ever tell you that I envy you?"

"No, you never told …"

"Shut up! I'm talking! … Yeah! I envy you and you're goddamn perfect life."

"My life's thousands of light years from perf…"

"Shut up I said! … I envy your intelligence and determination; your wits and life smarts. You see, I have street smarts … But you … You, my man … You've got the right smarts! … Your smarts are so much more precious. I wish I could have a future like you do. I'm doomed, if you ask me. I got nothing to look forward to. But you … You lucky bastard … You've got everything at your grasp. You just have to learn how to reach down and grab it. Me … Me, I hafta fight for everything. I have to act like a goddamn prick to have a little respect because I ain't got nothin' else … Nothin' else but misplaced attitude. You know, I coulda had class. I coulda been a contender. I coulda been someone, instead of a bum. Which is what I am …"

"Wait! … I heard this before … Brando in *On the Waterfront*, right?!"

"You caught me there … Hahahaha! I always thought it suited me well."

I was so in shock about all those revelations that I just let Tom speak out his mind. It was the first time that he actually opened up to me since … Well, since I met him. In fact, I think it was the first time that he opened up to anyone. I wanted to comfort him and tell him that he was a real swell guy and that he too had a lot to live for. But these things don't come very often, so I let him speak.

"One day, bro … One day you're goin' to be someone. You're gonna get out of this stink hole and hurl to the world: "Hey, look at me! I'm Eamon Jovanovski! The best goddamn author or musician or … you know … crap like that … in the world!" You can do anything and don't you ever forget it! You gotta be somebody for all the nobodies like me. You gotta tell our stories; you gotta sing about our lives. You gotta paint this South by South-West reality with your pen on a piece of paper, for everyone to read and understand, so they can relate and not feel alone … Even if they're in Winnipeg, Portland, Lexington, Austin or … even … and I'm about to vomit … Boston or Toronto! That's just sayin' bro! … Well, enough of this drunken psychology … Let's get back to the party and conquer some pussy!!!"

For fifteen minutes, I had had a whole different human being in front of me and it felt good. For once, I think that he was real – that he needed to be real for once – before reverting to his Neanderthal self again.

We got back to Tom's place and the first thing we saw – as we entered – was Andrew and Lisa French kissing on the sofa.

"Get a room, you goddamn perverts!" Tom and I said, in unison.

There was also Tom's cougar who was sitting on the other couch, looking a little displeased about him running off and leaving her alone with a bunch of twenty-something young adults – and a couple of underage teens. Even though Tom was back to his old self, I had a newfound respect for him.

Then – a couple of minutes later – without notice – the door swung open behind me and a girl entered the room. It felt very dramatic – but I think it was because I was really drunk. I turn around and saw this gorgeous girl. She was very short – not more than 4'11". She had long blond hair, green eyes, scarlet lipstick and charcoal eyeliner that exceeded her eyelids. She wore a black dress with lace gloves. From the bottom of her dress, I could distinguish black fishnet stockings with small suspenders – which I figured led to a garter belt. She looked around, came to me and asked:

"Hi! I'm Marla Tillman. I'm looking for Tom Murphy. Have you seen him anywhere?"

I slammed my elbow into Tom's ribs – who had his back turned to me – and said:

"Hey, Tom! Somebody's here to see you!"

"Well, everyone's here to see me!" he replied.

He turned around and said:

"Hey, Marla! You finally came! I'm so glad! I think you have met my friend Eamon. Remember, I told you about him? I think you two have so much in common. Here ... Mingle!"

He turned around yet again and left us alone – heading to the kitchen to see his cougar and mix drinks for the guests. It kinda felt like the "Have you met Ted?" routine, but I didn't care. This girl was gorgeous.

"Oh! Hey there! How're you doin'?" she asked – advancing to kiss both of my cheeks.

As she was approaching, I could smell her perfume and it was so friggin' enticing. I melted right there on the spot. As our skin touched – and I felt her breathing close to my ear – I almost came in my pants – figure of speech.

I was so nervous that I didn't say much at first. But for some odd reason, Marla kept close to me all evening – being all falsely independent, but never being more than three feet from me. At one point, Tom crossed the room with two beers in his hands and came to give me one. While putting it in my hand, he came close to my ear and said:

"I really think she likes you, bro! Loosen up a little and just go for it! Just be yourself... You got me wet the first time we met ... You can pull it off again."

He laughed and then went to talk with Karen. At first, I didn't understand why he had invited her – I fully understood later on – when the party was over and they kept me awake all night with their – well, her – wailing.

Marla and I spent the remainder of the evening and night talking. She was a conceptual artist who bartended at the Escogriffe – a bar and venue on Saint-Denis Street, near the corner of Mont-Royal Avenue. Neither one of us could stop talking. Every time one of us would start a subject, the other one would go on and on about it. It was like magic – the perfect first date – if this was actually a date in the first place. At the end of the party, when Marla was about to leave, she looked into my eyes and brought her head close to mine – slowly closing her eyes. I did the same thing until our lips touched and her tongue came out of her mouth looking for mine. My tongue met hers and they romantically caressed one another and swirled in a frenetic lustful slippery dance. We kissed for about fifteen minutes. I was in another world – although I could feel Tom looking at me like a proud new mom watching in admiration as her toddler was making its first steps. Marla left the party after having slipped her phone number – that she had written on the lid of a cigarette pack she had torn off – in my jean's back pocket. I didn't want her to leave, but like they say: all good things come to an end. Tom was all smiles – proud of his prodigal son.

    I went to sleep in Tom's room – when everyone left – and tried to fall asleep – it was hard not to take notice of the ruckus Tom was making banging the cougar in his mom's bed. What a perv! I thought that Tom was so gross at that point, but I didn't really care. I was just thinking about Marla and her long blond hair.

V

I didn't see Tom a lot that month because of all the time I was spending to study for my finals. We only saw each other at Dilallo's – and when I went to his place to try his godfather's suit. It was a particularly hot month of June and I was already sweating from just trying it on. I was dreading prom night and the rising heat. I wasn't used to wearing different layers of clothing. I must admit though, I looked good in black and white. Although classy, the suit was more in a *rudeboy* fashion with suspenders, two-tone shoes and all. The fedora made all the difference. I looked like a goddamn horn player for The Specials or The Slackers.

I had called her the next day – right after the party – and we saw each other almost every day after that. She would lie in my bed, sketching blueprints for her art, while I was studying for my exams. I felt such like a kid compared to her. We had a four-year age difference, but she didn't give a damn – although sometimes it embarrassed me that she was more advanced in life than I was.

Two weeks before prom – as she was lying on my bed, deep into her art – and I had my head deep in my Cotemporary World Studies book – I asked her:

"Hey! You wanna go to prom with me? It's okay if you don't wanna. I would understand you know, since you're elsewhere and it's probably gonna suck anyways. I'm only going because Tom made me and all. Plus, I..."

She put her sketchbook and charcoal stick aside and said:

"Would you shut up and man up! Have the balls to back up your proposition ... I would be honored to go to your prom. To tell you the truth, it's actually my first ever proposal. I didn't even go to mine because no one had asked me and, to tell you the truth, I didn't even want to go with all those preppies and daddy's girls. You know, I'm from Town Mount-Royal, with all the snobs and right-wing proud Canadians. You couldn't have paid me enough to drag my ass there. But like I said, I would be honored to be your date. In fact, I kinda find it romantic that you asked me. You're cute... You know that?"

I didn't know what to say. This was all so new to me. But as she was expressing her enthusiasm, she got on the edge of my bed – on her belly – stretched to grasp my arm and pulled me towards her. I didn't give her much resistance. She pivoted me on the bed – where I fell down – my back on the mattress. She got on top of me and we started kissing passionately.

After about fifteen minutes of intense caressing and fondling, I had an unstoppable throbbing in my pants. There was no way in hell that she couldn't feel it in her cowgirl position. She got back straight up and took off her shirt and bra – in a haste. "Holy Mother of God!!!!", I thought to myself. My hands were going up and down her naked smooth milky skin – as she bent down to kiss me some more. It got to the point where we were dry humping one another.

She then started taking off my clothes and the rest of hers. When she was down to my boxers, I embarrassingly said to her:

"Hey listen! I just thought you might like to know that … this is … like … well … Ummm … my first time."

She stopped everything, looked up to me – with a grin and wickedness in her eyes – and replied:

"Thanks for the heads up. I will take my time and have a little fun with you. I will "torture" you until you beg me to cum."

Holy shit! I had a nasty one on my hands. Well, if Tom presented her to me, she must have been … No! No! No! I was not about to think about Tom and her at this point.

I chased away those awful thoughts from my mind and just fell into the moment. She then took off my boxers – slowly – in a taunting way. She came back up – again slowly – kissing my inner thighs. She was driving me crazy. She was skimming her skin and her lips between my legs just to torture me – bringing me to the verge of insanity. She then took my penis between her lips and slowly engulfed it into her mouth. My heart just stopped as she was motioning up and down on it. I could feel her small but perky breasts going back and forth – brushing against my inner thighs – I was totally at the mercy of her fingers and lips.

"Oh God! You gotta stop! I don't know how long I can take this!" I begged to her.

"Just breathe and try to get a hold of yourself. I'm not done with you … you silly boy!" she answered – a naughty gaze in her eyes.

She reached back to her purse and took out a condom.

"I came prepared. I had hoped that you would let your guard down tonight," she added.

"What? I don't have a guard!?!"

"Shut up, silly boy! Just enjoy. You're mine tonight."

She slid me inside of her in a cowgirl fashion – as she was finishing her last sentence. I just lost it and fell into a pre-coitus coma. The only thing I remember was her smell, her moist body and her mount of Venus on top of me. I was crazy; crazy in love.

It's funny how, as a teen, you associate love with lust and sex. Well, anyways, that's what I felt at the time. I couldn't hold it in very long – although she tried her best to change the rhythm and break the beat to take me to cloud 9. What she didn't know was that I was already on cloud 23. Cumming was just the drop that made the barrel overflow. I felt like an epileptic having a stroke. I grabbed her arms, scratched her back and banged my fists on the bed as I, uncontrollably, screamed from the top of my lugs. God! I felt so ridiculous. When I opened my eyes again, Marla – maniacally staring at me with a corner smile – said:

"Well … Looks like you had fun! 'You still alive? Hehe!"

"God! That was incredible!" I replied – still not having come down from my cloud.

"Yeah! I might just keep you as a pet!" she taunted me.

"You're so bad!"

"I'm not bad, I'm just drawn that way! Hihi!"

As she was finishing her sentence, I turned her over, got her in an extreme fighting lock my cousin had taught me and tickled her to submission. She laughed so much that she was crying her eyes out.

We made love three more times that night. I was going to flunk my exam because I hadn't studied anything – but I was finally a man … So fuck it!

Marla had refused to show me her prom dress and I didn't really care or made big deal out of it. I was just glad that things were developing so nicely between us. I had never felt anything like this before. She looked like the perfect fit to complete me. She was funny, artistic, could hold a conversation and was jaw-dropingly gorgeous. I was at her mercy and she knew it!

June 27th was prom night. I was still hung over from the Saint-Jean-Baptiste – Quebec's national holiday on June 24th. Not that I gave it much importance – my mom being Irish, I was more into Saint-Patrick's day – even though my dad tried to push Macedonian Republic Day on August 2nd – but no one really gave a rat's ass ... especially me. I got dressed at Tom's place. His mom was watching us from the other room with watery eyes. Goddamn it! She wasn't even my mom and, still, she cared so much. Her and Tom were really like family to me. When I was done, Tom backed up a little – looked at me – and said:

"You look like a goddamn *rudeboy* pimp. The girls will be all over you!"

"I don't want all the girls to be all over me. I'm going with Marla and I think I'm really falling for her."

"Well, somebody got laid for the first time and didn't tell me!"

"Maybe so or maybe not! ... But that's none of your business! My sex life is personal. Anyways, I know you ... You'd make fun of it."

"Suit yourself! But don't you go putting all your eggs in one basket. You gotta keep your options open. She may be your first, but you don't want her to be your last," he replied – pushing his nonsense "wisdom" onto me.

"You don't understand ... I think I love her."

"Every guy falls in love with the first girl who's ready to give him sex. Even if, in your case, it would be pity sex. Hahahaha! But you can't stop there!"

"Ah, come on! She's perfect for me and you know it!"

"Maybe for now ... But keep your options open, dude."

"You're saying all that like you speak from experience. You fell in love with your first as well?"

"Well, it depends on whom you're talking about."

"What do you mean?"

"Well, there were two of them, my first time being a threesome and all. That girl and her cousin were nasty. It was just legen … wait for it …"

"Oh, shut the fuck up, bastard! That never happened!"

"Says you!"

"Even if it did happen, as you say it did, I don't wanna hear about it. Marla's different. She digs me."

"Every seventeen-year-old boy is willing to admit that and regrets it three years later, when his heart is left in shreds."

"Says you! Would you not compare me to you, for once, and admit that there's maybe another path possible between a man and a woman and that there are some good people out there?"

"Okay, okay! Don't be so uptight! I was just saying."

"I know you were and I appreciate your advice. But just have some confidence in me, please!"

"Okay bro! 'Will do. You're all done now … So go and get her!" said Tom – spraying some Hugo Boss perfume on me.

"God! Stop that! I don't want to go on smelling like you!" I added – making my hands fly in the air – like I was swatting flies or something.

"It'll drive the ladies wild!"

"Fuck you, douchebag!"

"You're welcome! Love you too, bro!"

I left Tom's place and walked to the Angrignon subway station. I waited about five minutes for the train to make a U-turn – Angrignon being at the end of the Green Line. I then got on the tail wagon. I felt so ridiculous and like an outcast. Everyone was looking at me funny. The more stations I passed, the more people got on the train and the more I felt ashamed. I was really not myself and it showed. I got off at Lionel-Groulx and changed subway lines – from the Green to the Orange Line – and went up to the Place-d'Armes station.

The prom committee at my school had chosen – I must admit – a cool place. They had rented a boat – the Cavalier Maxim – which held special events on the Saint-Lawrence River. I walked from Place-d'Armes to the piers – admiring the 18th century architecture and brick roads – saluting coachmen riding their carriage with French or American tourists kissing under the hot Montreal sun. I got to the Old Port and found my way to King Edward Pier – through the caricaturists and street performers. Marla was waiting for me next to the bridge to get on the boat – searching through the crowd to see if she could spot me.

God she was beautiful! She was a wearing a white pin-up dress with black polka dots, black stockings, a headband and a tiny purse. Her long blond hair was bobbed in a rockabilly fashion. She looked anxious to greet me. My heart skipped a beat. I knew, at that moment, that she was the one for me. I snuck up behind her, hugged her and kissed her neck. She jumped – startled – turned around and said:

"Finally! I've been waiting here like a freak for the last half hour!"

"Sorry! I couldn't go faster than the subway."

"You got here by train?" she asked – bewildered.

"Yes!?! How else did you think I would get here?"

"I don't know … A cab, like I did … I didn't want to mess my dress and my hair."

I laughed and held her by the waist – as we got on the ramp to get on the boat.

About an hour later, we were sailing off east on the Saint-Lawrence River. Marla and I were walking back and forth on the deck – talking. The scenery was beautiful. You had, on one side, the Montreal skyline and, on the other, the suburban south-shore towns. Two worlds only separated by bridges. Marla and I kissed intensively – as we passed under the Jacques-Cartier Bridge – with its four mini-Eiffel Towers – which led to the man-made islands built for the 1967 Universal Expo, the La Ronde amusement park and the boring Longueil town. As we got to HoMa and Boucherville, the sun was setting on the horizon. A couple of minutes later we went to eat. The meal was okay, but after it, the DJ turned the music louder for everyone to dance.

"Yuk! Black Eyed Peas… Wanna get out of here and go back outside?" I asked – disgruntled.

"Of course! I can't stand that garbage anyways. If I stay here, I'll go nuts."

"I hear ya!"

We spent the night talking about the future, her art, the scenery, Tom, her parents, my parents, Tom again. There was something about the way she talked about Tom that started to bother me. She was always defending him – being the devil's advocate on everything he did. I found it odd, but didn't give it more thought. We just watched the night coming down on the city. Montreal is just the most beautiful city at night. All the lights – from the north and south shore – and from the bridges – started to light up simultaneously. The skyscrapers illuminated the downtown area – with the rotating light of Ville-Marie Place as a focal point and the Mount-Royal cross as a silent guardian on the top of the hill.

The boat docked back to the King Edward Pier at the end of the evening. I felt like it was just a couple of wasted hours – where Marla and I could have done something else way more interesting – damn you Tom and your stupid ideas! As we walked down the ramp onto the docks, I asked Marla:

"Watcha' wanna do now? You wanna call it a night? Or …"

"Hell no!" she replied, "We heard a lot of music I can't stand tonight. You dragged me here, so now I'm gonna drag you to good music and beer."

"You know I'm only seventeen, right?!"

"Yeah, but at this time, they don't really check. Hurry up before we miss the last train!"

"Where are we going?"

"You'll see!"

We got back to Place-d'Armes station and took the subway west on the Orange Line – down to Lucien-L'Allier. We got off and walked up Crescent Street. About five minutes later, Marla stopped and said:

"Here we are!"

I looked up as we walked up the steps to this place called Brutopia. We got in and there was this band playing reggae and ska on a tiny stage. I fell in love with Marla all over again. Marla had introduced me to the pleasures of the flesh and the pleasures of the ears. That was the day that really I got into the Montreal underground scene – and I'm not talking about that Indy shit the city was famous for – I was talking about punk rock, ska, psychobilly and reggae.

Marla ordered a lady drink and, I, some nasty homebrewed IPA. I was in heaven: awesome beer, awesome music and an awesome lady.

After about an hour of being all sweaty from dancing – as the band was pouring its heart out – Marla said:

"Hey! The pub is closing soon. What do you wanna do after?"

"Well, we can always go back to my place?"

"With your mom sleeping in the next room? I don't think so, silly boy," she replied – winking – "Listen ... My parents are out of town for the next 4 days ... 'You wanna go back there?"

"And have you all to myself? Hell yeah!!!!" I replied – with way too much enthusiasm.

She smiled and – as soon as the band finished its set – we walked to Guy Street – where we took the 165 night bus – which took us to the corner Côte-Sainte-Catherine Way and Laird Boulevard. We rode this never-ending bus

– feeling so peaceful – holding her in my arms – not saying a word. We got off on Jean-Talon Street and walked to her place on Kindersley Street – between Dunkirk Road and Athlone Way. I don't think I had ever been to this part of the town. The urban landscape was way different from my South by South-West roots. Her house was actually a home – not a filthy apartment.

We got in, exhausted from the night and the bus ride. But that didn't stop us from making sweet love for the next hour or so. We eventually fell asleep naked in each other's arms – only waking the next afternoon around 1:00pm. We spent the next two days eating crepes and filet mignon – which I cooked while she did charcoal-stick drawings in her sketchbook – half-naked on her parent's couch. It was just a romantic two days of food, art and sex – that would be engraved in my memory for eternity.

But like all good things come to an end, I had to go back to work at Dilallo's. I was coming back down the social ladder – which was actually just downhill going from Sherbrooke Street to the Lachine Canal – a world separated between the uphill English Protestants and the downhill French-Canadians and Irish Catholics. A part of the city built on social inequities and racial domination. Getting back from cloud 9 to cloud 1 was hard – but that's just life. I really liked Marla, but she came from a really different world than I. She was an artist by choice and she didn't have to work that much – because her parents supported her as for I – on the contrary – was a working-class Irish boy trying to survive.

VI

A couple of days later, I moved in with Andrew in the apartment we had found on Jacques-Hertel Street. All of our closest friends came to help us out. It cost us a fortune in pizza and beer. Within a three-day span, they helped us paint the whole place, bring our furniture and boxes and unpack our stuff. The fridge and stove were included with the rent – but we had to do our laundry in a laundromat, on Jolicoeur Street. Half of the time, I would bring my dirty clothes to my mom's place and wash them there – so I wouldn't have to pay all those quarters. Marla came to visit me and slept over quite often – well at least more than I would go up to her place – and when I did go, her parents were never there – like she was ashamed of me or something – or maybe it was just a coincidence. Tom would come by a lot also and would end up sleeping on my couch half-baked or half-drunk.

It wasn't long before I received my Ministry of Education report card. I had passed every course in the curriculum – and with better grades than I had expected – all but Math, with a 61%. At least, I had passed the course and wouldn't have to repeat that bullshit once more. I had gotten accepted at Dawson College. Now it was official, I was going to study in *creative arts, literature and languages* that September.

Dawson was located on Sherbrooke, near the corner of Atwater Street, right across the old Montreal Forum – where the Montreal Canadiens used to play until the mid-90s. Over twenty-something Stanley cups were won in that building. It was also close to the Alexis-Nihon Plaza where my aunt used to work. It was an area I knew very well. I was so stoked to finally leave high school and just do what I liked – no more Science or Math classes – I had gotten accepted in a program that resembled me.

That summer, to pay the rent, I had gotten a second job. I was still doing shifts at Dilallo's – but they had cut my hours because business was a little slower than usual – so I had had to find another source of revenue. My mom had offered me a job at the Sears where she was working, but I didn't want to work with her. Working with a parent is just weird ... I think. I got myself a job washing dishes and prepping food at the Magnan Tavern on St-Patrick Street – in Pointe-Saint-Charles – facing the Lachine Canal. I really loved it there. It felt good to be working outside a fast-food joint. Sometimes, the boss would even give me beer. I was still underage – barely – but he didn't really mind. He cared about his employees and it showed. I felt like part of the family – even though I had only been working there for a short while.

The Magnan Tavern was a family-owned restaurant that was passed down from generation to generation. It had opened during the Great Depression, in 1932, serving pork and beef sandwiches to factory workers during lunchtime. It was one of the first taverns in the entire Province of Quebec to offer food. Since then, they have expanded the Tavern and it has become an institution in Montreal where people from all social and ethnic backgrounds – from minimum wage workers, to policeman, politician and hockey players – came to have a good meal. I was really glad to be working in a place so rich in history – even if I was only washing dishes.

In mid-August, Tom came to my place, got in my room and inquired:

"Watcha doin' there, dumbass?"

"Writing."

"Writing what?"

"'Don't know yet"

"Whattaya mean you don't know yet? You don't know what you're writing? You can't write about nothing ... Anyways, it's already been done ... And you ain't no Seinfeld."

"But you could be a hardcore version of Kramer."

"Oh, shut up, you jerk! ... Lemme see."

"No! It's nothing yet ... Just some ideas ... That's all."

"Oh come on! I just wanna see."

"I told you no!!"

"You asked for it!"

He then jumped into the air and elbow-dropped me on my bed and ripped my notebook from my hand – while giving me John Cenna's "You can't see me" hand gesture.

"Ouch!!! You motherfucker!!! God! You got me right in the ribs!" I said – in pain.

"Hey! I asked nicely and you wouldn't comply. You had it comin' bro!"

"Give it back now!"

"Hell no! ... So what have we here? ... *The Lachine Canal Chronicles* ... Nice title ... What's it about?"

"Not really sure yet ... You, me, this forsaken quarter, life in general ... Marla ..."

"Oh shit! Nice! You gotta make me even handsomer than I already am. I want a harem squirming around me."

"It ain't science fiction ... Just reflections on existence and choices we make in life."

"Ohhh! Mister College man now uses big philosophical principles."

"If you would pick up a book once in a while, you would maybe have a different view about life."

"I prefer to watch the movie instead of reading the book ... Anyways, I never heard of one good lesbian porn novel ... Hahahaha!"

"God, you're annoying!"

"I love you too, bro! ... So, whatcha writing about Marla? ... That you are holding hands and calling her "sweetie" and that you have been friendzoned?"

"Well, actually, I have been sexually active with her for the past two months."

"Get outta here, you dawg!!!" he replied – in astonishment – pushing me, with his two hands, down back on my bed – "Why didn't you tell me!!??!!"

"Because it was none of your goddamn business. I don't like to talk about sex and you know it. I always felt that it was something private between two human beings."

"You're such a prude ... Sooooo ... How was it?!?"

"None of your goddamn business, I told ya"

"Oh! Come on! Only one word ... Pleeeeeeeeeeease???"

"I'll even give you two if you promise to leave me alone afterwards."

"I promise ... So?"

"FUCKING AWESOME! ... Now you have your two words, so, shut up about it."

"Okay, okay! God, you're so uptight!"

He then looked at me in a *sprinter-waiting-for-the-starting-gun* motion and let out:

"Told ya she was good ... I found her awesome too!"

My face turned red in anger.

He sprang out of the apartment laughing. He knew for sure that I would beat the crap out of him for that remark – so he fled, laughing like a madman. I ran behind, trying to catch up with him. I finally was able to tackle him a couple of blocks down the road, on the grass near the municipal pool in the Ignace-Bourget Park. We both fell to the ground. He got up to sprint again, so I gave him a hard low blow. He fell down in pain and I said out of breath:

"And you know my name is the Lord when I lay my vengeance upon you!"

He maniacally laughed – still in pain – and replied:
"Good one, bro!"

I helped him up and he threw his arm around my shoulder as we walked back to the apartment. He then said:

"Dude! I was going to surprise you with this … You know, as a graduation gift. But now that you are no longer a little boy here it is … We are going on a road trip to New York City! You, me, Marla and Andrew!"

"Why?"

"I'm offering you a trip to the Big Apple and all you are saying is "why"! What is wrong with you?"

"I'm just asking what are we going to do there exactly?"

"You, my friend, have been chosen to come see the friggin' Dropkick Murphys at the friggin' CBGB's with me next Friday!"

"Holy shit!!! Bro, I love you … You're fuckin' awesome!"

"I know … Right!? I was able to get tickets online. But only two though."

"So what're Andrew and Marla coming with us for?"

"Well, they are both over twenty-one and Andrew's the only one that can stick shift your aunt's car. They're both fine with the situation. They said they'd go sightseeing during the show. After all, NYC is the city that never sleeps."

"Okay. This is all good, but you and I are underage in the US, so this is useless."

"Have no fear man of little faith ... and ... voilà!" said Tom – pulling two cards out of his pant pocket – "Fake IDs, bro!"

"No shit!" I replied in amazement – grabbing them out from his hands.

"A guy I knew owed me a favor, so I got them for way less than they are worth."

"This'll never work!" I said – in disbelief.

"Oh, come on! Of course it will. And don't worry about work. All is set up with the manager at Dilallo's and that tavern you've been working at. I've been planning this for some time now. You don't have to worry about a thing and just enjoy."

I was speechless. I took Tom in my arms and hugged him.

"Hahahaha! You're welcome dude! You deserve it," he said – while patting me on the back.

VII

On the morning of August 18th, Tom and I were waiting on my apartment's front gallery for Andrew to come pick us up – he had gone to get his mom's car. Since we would only be gone for twenty-four hours, we brought very little luggage. I double-checked if I had my passport, a letter from my mom saying it was okay if I left the country – just in case the US customs guy was to be an asshole about it.

"Do you have the fake IDs on you?" I asked Tom.

"Yes ... But I have to find a place to hide them just in case we get searched at the border."

"Why would we get searched?"

"I don't know. We are four young people trying to get to the US. That's a damn good reason for them. Border patrolmen can be real assholes since 9/11."

"Are we going to get Marla at her place?"

"No, she's on her way. I called her before coming here this morning."

"Oh, okay."

"Hey, listen Eamon ... Ummm ... I know I sometimes give you a hard time and can be a real pain in the ass ... But I just wanted you to know that I love you ... You're like a brother to me and ... like ... whatever happens in the future, I really hope everything will stay this way."

"Whattaya mean "whatever happens in the future"?"

"Well, in a year, I'll be in the army. I'll turn eighteen next February. I just want to finish my high school diploma and then I'm off."

"So you're really serious about that army shit?"

He lit a cigarette, inhaled and said:

"Yup ... Outside you and my 'ma, there's really nothing holding me back here."

"Well, if that is what you want!? ... Fine ... But I'll miss you, you motherfucker."

"I won't be gone that long. A couple of years tops ... Make good money and maybe even get some education there."

Andrew parked the car in front of the apartment, opened the window and asked:

"Where the hell is Marla?"

"She shouldn't be long. She left Mount-Royal about an hour ago," replied Tom.

Andrew got out of his mom's 1999 black Toyota Corolla, got up the stairs and sat with Tom and I and we all waited for Marla to get here.

She finally arrived about twenty minutes later and said:

"Sorry guys! ... I had to walk to Edouard-Montpetit station and had to change subway lines at Snowdon and Lionel-Groulx stations to get here. It took me like forever!"

"It's okay. 'You ready?" I asked.

"Yes, but I gotta pee really bad first," she replied – wiggling like a three-year-old who can't hold it in anymore – ah, women and their small bladders!

When she came back out of the apartment, Tom had unscrewed a part of the inside of the passenger door of the car and slid the fake IDs inside.

"No one's gonna think of looking in there," he said – re-screwing everything back in place.

We put our bags in the trunk and then got into the car and drove out of Montreal. We took the Champlain Bridge – which was really starting to fall apart – and then headed south on Highway 15. Andrew popped in a Celtic punk mixtape – from the Dropkick Murphys, to Flogging Molly, Flatfoot 56 and the Real Mackenzies – in the car stereo. We were heading to the border screaming louder than the music that was coming out of the speakers. It was a sunny and very hot day – there was this heat wave all across North America since the prior month. My aunt's car didn't have air conditioning, so we were boiling in our seats. We would be okay as long as we were on the highway, but I was dreading the New York City concrete heat.

We arrived at the Lacolle border crossing about half an hour later and waited another twenty minutes to get to the customs officer. Andrew asked us to be quiet – that he would do all the talking.

"Passports!" said the customs officer.

"Here you go," replied Andrew.

"Where are you from?"

"We're all from Montreal."

"Occupation?"

"We are all students, except for the lady ... She's a bartender."

"Where are you going?"

"New York City."

"For how long?"

"Twenty-four hours."

"What is your business there?"

"We are going to see a concert and do some sightseeing."

He then went back to his little cabin, punched in our passports in his computer and came back out a few minutes later.

"Pop the trunk open, please," he said to Andrew.

Andrew pulled the in-car trunk opener. The customs officer started searching through our bags. He came back and said:

"Take your car to the area over there, turn off the vehicle and get out of the car."

"Is there a problem officer?" asked Andrew – with sudden terror in his tone.

"Just do as I say, now!" he replied – with a very strict voice.

Andrew drove to the indicated area and stopped the car. As we were getting out, we saw about six agents coming out of the building. One of them said: "Come with us" – so we followed them. They split us up and got us all in different interrogation rooms. I was really starting to freak out. An agent got me seated. I asked:

"What seems to be the problem officer?"

"We found a hash pipe in one of the bags in the car."

"You what?!" I replied – in a state of shock.

"Now, we want to know where the drugs are," he asked – in a very menacing tone.

"What drugs? I have no idea what you're talking about. I don't even smoke pot or hashish. If someone brought something, I wasn't aware of anything," I replied – trying to save my ass.

"That's what we are trying to determine. Right now, we are searching the car with sniffing dogs. You better confess right now and it will really be easier on all of you."

"But I have nothing to confess. I know nothing about what you are implying."

At that point, I was almost shitting in my pants. The investigation lasted for about another three hours as the agent tried to bully a confession out of me. But since I was clean, there was nothing to confess.

The agent was going in and out of the room – I guess to talk with the other agents and see if they had anything on Andrew, Tom or Marla. After four very long hours, the officer came back in the room and said:

"Okay, you're free to go. Your stories check out and we found nothing. But we will be confiscating the hash pipe."

I got out of the room as the others were leaving too. We started walking towards the car – which was a total mess. Marla said:

"Guys … Ummm … I'm really sorry!"

Tom replied:

"Marla! You fucking cunt! Why the hell did you bring a goddamn hash pipe in your luggage?!"

"I didn't bring it. It must have been in my bag from way back. I guess I forgot to empty the front pocket before putting more stuff in," she replied – with a pitiful voice and watery eyes.

"God, Marla! Thanks for nothing!" said Tom – exasperated.

"I said I … was… sorry!" wept Marla.

Tom didn't speak to her for the next five hours.

We got back to the car and drove south on I-87. Tom said to me:

"Well at least they didn't find the fake IDs!"

"That's a relief!" I answered back.

There was some tension in the car, but it didn't last very long – our enthusiasm for the Big Apple was back and very alive. We started singing again. When we hit Albany, Andrew got off of I-87. I asked him:

"Why are you going off the interstate?"

"You think I'm gonna pay those goddamn tolls. I found another way … a free one," he answered with pride.

"Kudos to you, Cousin!" I replied – as we crossed the Hudson River and headed south on the Taconic State Parkway.

As we got to Yonkers, we hit a little traffic – nothing too bad, though. Crossing New York City was another story. In the end, I didn't really care because it gave me more time to see the city and take tons of pictures. We finally got off the FDR Drive and plunged in the heart of the East Village. We circled around a little and finally hit a parking place on East 2nd Street – which had just become available right before our eyes – almost right on the corner of Bowery Street. We couldn't have found a better spot. We had a little time to spare, so we went to get a room at this hotel in Soho which was not too expensive. After, Tom invited us to this Italian restaurant in Little Italy. It felt good because we hadn't really eaten since we had left Montreal that morning.

After supper, we walked towards the CBGB's. I asked Marla and Andrew:

"So, what are you guys going to do tonight?"

Marla answered:

"I don't know. Maybe do some shopping in Soho or take the subway and go strolling in Time Square or ... I don't know we'll see. It's too late to go to the MET or the MOMA but promise me we are going tomorrow!"

"It's a date, pretty lady!" I replied – harboring a huge smile.

She blushed and they went their separate way.

We walked to the car to get our fake ID's, got back on Bowery Street and waited in line to get into the venue. When it was finally our turn, well ... we just got in. We tried to get as close to the stage as possible. Tom then said:

"Dude, I did all this for nothing. We didn't even need our IDs!"

"Don't sweat it bro. They may come in handy another time," I replied – trying to cheer him up.

We ordered some beers at the bar and waited for the band to come on stage. When the first bagpipe notes of *Cadence to Arms* were blown, Tom and I just lost it.

We spent the night dancing in the middle of the moshpit – in that small but legendary venue. Up to *Kiss Me I'm Shitfaced*, we actually were getting pretty hammered – Tom had been ordering beer after beer. We sang our hearts out to that song as they made every lady in the audience come on stage to sing and dance to it – like they do at every one of their shows. By *Skinhead on the MBTA*, we were totally exhausted. They ended their set with a Minor Threat cover – Tom was barely standing on his feet.

"Can't wait to be your age, grandpa," I screamed in his ear.

"Fuck you, douchebag," he replied – half-falling down.

I helped him to get back up. He laid his forearms on my shoulders and screamed in my ear:

"Happy graduation, bro! I wanted to … to make a big deal out of this because I love you. You deserve it and you'll be going places. You have genuine talent. You're ugly as a donkey's butt, but you got talent. I guess that's what Marla sees in you … all that artsy mumbo-jumbo … anyways, I gotta pee … see ya!"

He went off, staggering, to the bathroom.

Tom came back a while later. He was walking a little straighter. He said to me:

"Dude, I puked and it felt good … Ideas are a little clearer now."

"That'll teach you! Hahahaha!"

"Let's get outta here and head back to the hotel. I'm exhausted."

We got out of the CBGB's and walked back to Soho. We got to our hotel – up to our room – and collapsed in each of our beds. Andrew and Marla weren't there yet. I fell fast asleep.

Later, Marla crawled up in bed, snuggled in my arms and kissed me. I held her tight as I heard Tom – half passed out – warn Andrew:

"You better not spoon me, man … I know I have soft silky skin and a tight butt, but get a hold of yourself!"

"Get bent, Murphy!" replied Andrew.

I fell back asleep right after that "poetic" exchange.

The next morning, I was woken up by Marla taking off my boxers and sliding on top of me.

"What are you doing?" I whispered to her.

"Shut up! Just don't wake 'em," she whispered back to me – as she started making slow back and forth movements – while breathing heavily in my ear.

We both came very quickly. She then got up, got dressed and screamed:

"Wake up fuckers! You promised to go to the MET and the MoMa with me … So up, up, up, you douchebags!"

"Shut up wench! Ah, my head!" plaintively mumbled Tom.

"Nothing a good coffee won't fix. Now let's go!" replied Marla – trying to motivate him.

"Hold your horses, I'm up, I'm up… God!" he replied – holding his forehead.

We checked out and went for breakfast in this little bakery on Bleecker Street. As we were eating, I told Tom:

"For an Irishman, your tolerance to alcohol is low, bro!"

Tom didn't even reply to that. For the first time, I was able to give him a verbal uppercut. Okay, he was hungover, but I still took it as a personal victory. I turned to Marla and said:

"Since it's kind of late, morning-wise, it means that we can't do both museums. I'm sorry babe!"

"You better make this up to me, you turd!" she replied with naughty eyes.

She always had a way to make me melt – even while insulting me.

When we all finished eating, Marla said:

"I gotta go to the bathroom before we leave."

"Yeah, me too ... Goddamn coffee!" added Andrew.

While they were gone, Tom turned to me and said:
"Nice show this morning, bro!"
"What are you talking about?"
"You and Marla... Hehe!"
"You saw us?!" I shamefully asked.
"Yup! A thing of beauty. Free live porn ... Loved it!"
"God Tom! You know you just sound like Quagmire!"
"Giggity! Hahahaha! Seriously, don't be ashamed, dude! It's the most natural thing on earth. Like Lennon said: We see, every day, people getting killed on TV but we are scandalized to see two people making love ... okay those weren't his exact words, but you get the point. So chill out, bro!"
"I'll give you that point ... But don't make a habit out of it. I don't want some creepy peeping Tom, Tom!"
"Don't worry, you're not that pretty ... Hahahaha!"

When Marla and Andrew came back from the bathroom, we got out of the bakery and started to head for the subway station.

"Between the two, I prefer modern art, so I choose the MoMa. You guys are up to that?" Marla asked.

Andrew said:

"Well I'm not a big art fan. And I don't think Tom is either. Why don't you guys go to the museum while we stroll down the streets of Midtown?"

"Okay. Let's set a rendezvous point ... Back at the car around 1:00 pm?" I suggested.

"Great," Andrew replied.

We walked down to the corner of Broadway and Prince Street, got in the subway and took the N train up to 49th Street. Tom knew our entire itinerary and guided us all through it. If you've never been to New York, the subway system is a real maze compared to the Montreal one. But Tom seamed to understand all of it.

"Dude! How do you know how to get around New York?" I asked him.

"Well, I studied maps before leaving. I have a very photographic memory. I'm like a walking GPS," he replied – a little full of himself.

"Wow! We finally found something you're good at!" Andrew said.

He thought that he had just owned his ass.

"No! I'm also good at making forty-something cougars squirt. You see the trick is ..." replied Tom – rotating his hand and folding his thumb and pinkie leaving the other three fingers standing.

Marla interrupted him and screamed:

"God, Tom! You don't need to be so graphic!"

Tom replied – in a very cocky way:

"Well, they don't teach you that in school and I'm pretty sure these boys would benefit from ..."

"No we wouldn't, Tom," I said – a little disgusted.

Tom and Andrew got out at 42nd Street.

"Meet you back at the car at 1:00pm ... Don't forget, you two have to get out at 49th Street. See ya later ... be careful," said Tom.

"Will do, bro," I replied.

The doors closed and we got off at the next stop. We got out of the station and walked up 7th Avenue until we made a right on 53rd Street. The temperature was already really hot – even if it was early morning. Marla and I were strolling on the sidewalk, hand in hand – like young lovers do – our heads turning side to side admiring Midtown's beauty. We got into the MoMa, paid and started our visit. I was not a big fan of contemporary art, but it was worth it just to see Marla's illuminated eyes when she stared way too long for my taste to art I just didn't understand – although

Van Gogh's *Starry Night* was breathtaking – and I had that Don Mclean song in my head for hours after that. All in all, it was still a very nice time. Around noon, I told Marla that we should be getting back to the subway so we wouldn't be late.

"Already!?! Geez!" she said – a little annoyed.

"Well, we have been here for a little more than two hours," I replied – trying to bring some sense back into her.

"Okay then. Thanks for "volunteering" to come here with me. I know this isn't your bag. I promise, if we ever get to Salinas, I'll go to the Steinbeck museum with you, even if I dislike his writing."

"Blasphemy woman! God ... can you tell me what are we doing together?! Hahahaha!"

"I guess you like it when I slide up and down your cock and my perky tits ..."

"Shhhh! We're in a goddamn museum, for God's sake."

"You don't know anyone here. Plus ... Who cares if people think I'm a skank. I fully assume my "slutitude" ... Hehe."

She grabbed my hand as we got out of the museum and went back the way we came – all the way to Price Street station.

As we were heading up Mercer Street, we crossed Tom and Andrew who were coming out of the Washington Square Village sort of little park.

"Hey guys! What were you doing there?" I asked.
Tom replied:

"Well, we came back early and just took our time. We then spotted some guys smoking joints in the distance. We met up with them, got talking and they offered some to us ... So we shared reefers with them."

"God, Tom! ... And Andrew?! I expected more of you. You know that you are driving us outta here like now and you are stoned," I replied – with a nagging parent-like tone.

"Well, not really ... I just took one small puff. Tommy boy here did most of the smoking," Andrew replied – putting the blame on Tom.

"Figures... Well, let's go ..." I ordered.

We made our way to the car while Tom was singing very loudly: "*'Cause we find ourselves in the same old mess, singing drunken lullabies!*" As we got to the car, he screamed:

"SHOTGUN!!!"

"I don't care bro; I get to cuddle my girlfriend in the back seat," I replied.

"Yes, but I control the stereo ... Mouhahahaha," he replied – ending his sentence with a Dr. Evil impression.

So, as we were driving up on FDR Drive, we must have heard *Drunken Lullabies* about ten times on repeat. We rode the same way back as we did the previous day.

We stopped to have supper in the state's capital. Andrew took the first exit to downtown Albany from I-787 and made a left on North Pearl Street. Two or three blocks later, he said: "Well that looks good." So, he found a parking space, we all got out of the car and entered The Pearl Street Pub. We ordered some burgers and some beers. The waiter asked us for our IDs. We all gave him our cards. When he left, I said to Tom:

"Told 'ya it wasn't a waste ... Hehe!"

As you would have it, American size burgers are not metric size so we ate way too much. Stomachs full, we headed north on I-87 once again, direction home.

After a three-and-a-half-hour drive – with no trouble at customs this time – we were finally home. Andrew dropped off Marla and I to my place, got Tom to his mom's and drove the car back to his aunt's. He didn't come home, though. He had planned to spend the night – at least, what was left – at Lisa's. Marla and I had the entire place to ourselves and we made the most of it – although we were both tired. It was a good thing we were only scheduled to work the next evening. We fell asleep around 4:00am with no more strength in our body. I was really starting to fall deeply in love with this short crazy blond girl.

VIII

Fall semester was about to start – my first year of college. I was not going to be able to manage two jobs as well as being in school full time. The choice was hard, but I decided to stay at Magnan Tavern. The Dilallo family had given me my first job – I had been working there for over a year – but I needed a change. I found that Magnan – although farther from home – was somewhat more gratifying.

So, when I came back from New York, I gave in my two weeks' notice to the manager at Dilallo's. I hadn't discussed this with Tom, but he overheard me. That evening, at work, he didn't talk to me about other things than restaurant orders. He felt betrayed, but I was not about to blame myself for how he felt. He was going off to the army less than a year later – who the hell did he think he was for giving me the cold shoulder? But it didn't end there and the tension worsened. Tom didn't speak to me for the next three weeks. He was being so childish about the whole thing.

In the meantime, I had started college. Outside of English, French and Humanities – which were the basic common courses for all the programs – I took *Introduction to Arts and Culture, Classical Music History, Creativity (Theories and Techniques)* and *Biography, Autobiography and Blogs*. I was really hyped about college. I thought that it would help me drive my creativity – and, in fact, it did. I had never written so much, even though, I had less and less time to do so.

On Wednesday, September 13th, I was leaving my French class – and had no other class until 3:30 pm – so I had decided to eat some Kebab on Atwater Street – just down the hill, passed the Highway 720 overpass. My class ended around 12:30 pm and I was leaving the College – through the de Maisonneuve entrance – when I heard a loud commotion, some screaming and gunshots. I saw people running out of the same door I had just gone out through a couple of seconds before. There were screams and cries. I heard a girl hysterically saying:

"There's a shooter inside … He's offing people … Get away from here fast."

My heart stopped. I was petrified – I couldn't move a muscle.

"What if I had to pee and had stayed just ten more minutes inside … I may not have even been alive to talk about it," I thought to myself – and that thought freaked me out.

About eighty police cars and twenty ambulances started arriving. They evacuated the perimeter of the college that wasn't already in lockdown – even parts of the subway were shut down for several hours. About an hour later, around 1:30pm, the shooter's body was dragged out of Dawson – he had killed himself in the process. I let out a sigh of relief, but I was still overwhelmed with fear and anguish.

Since the subway was closed, I walked home. It took me about an hour to get there. When I opened to front door, Andrew and Tom were on the couch, watching the news. As I stepped in, Tom got up, came to me and said:

"Glad you're here and okay, bro. Let's hug it out, bitch!"

After that incident, Tom and I were talking like nothing had happened between us. It's funny – in a sad way – that it sometimes takes a tragedy to make us realize the chance we have of being surrounded by loved ones.

IX

Because of the shooting, courses were suspended until the 18th. So, I took a couple of more shifts at Magnan during those days and spent some time with Tom during evenings – since Marla was working. One evening, as Tom was at my place, he said:

"Hey, bro! Your birthday's coming up in a month. You're finally turning eighteen, dude! We gotta throw you a huge party!"

"I'm really not sure about that Tom," I replied – a little anguished by Tom's suggestion.

"What the fuck are you talkin' about?"

"Well, you know that you sometimes take things to an insane level and I'm not really comfortable with that."

"I promise I won't crank it to eleven … It may be a little crazy, but not insane. Come on, dude … We gotta celebrate this. You only turn eighteen once!"

"Okay, but keep it simple … Just a couple of friends and that's it!"

"Okay, okay … I promise. Geez! Way to take all the fun out of it! So, lemme see here … Your b-day is on a Wednesday. We're gonna do this on Friday the 20th, because we are both working early on the 22nd, so we can't do it on the Saturday. You don't hafta do anything ... I'm in charge of everything ... You just have to show up."

"Don't forget ... You promised!"

"Yeah! Yeah! Yeah! Damn ... You're such a mood killer!"

I spent the next month working, going to school, going to see Marla at the Escogriffe while she was working – it was in fact the only "couple's" time we had because her shifts ended at 3:30am and I had to get up 7:00am to prep for school – so I went over there for two or three hours after my own shifts at Magnan. God, I was tired. But at least I got to see some really cool shows and discovered awesome bands.

On the first week of October, Tom called me:

"Dude! I just registered on Facebook."

"What the fuck is Facebook?"

"It's kinda like Myspace, but only better. It used to be reserved for universities, but they just opened it to everyone over thirteen. You gotta register!"

"Why? I don't even have the internet."

"Well ... your school has it, no? We could stay in touch and immortalize special moments and events. And since I'm leaving for the army soon ..."

"Wait! What?!" I replied – startled by the news.

"You knew I was going to the army. I told you several times. Don't you ever listen?!"

"You told me you were going in the future ... at least after graduation."

"I don't wanna finish school ... I suck at school. This year, the only class I'm not failing is English."

"Come on, dude! You only had one month of school; you can always pick it up until the end of the year."

"No, it's hopeless. In fact, I already enlisted. I'm supposed to pass a written test soon and some physicals, which should be a sure thing."

"Think of your future, bro! What about after the army? What if you don't make a career out of it? What if you get injured? ... What happens after that?"

"One day at a time. The only thing I know is that I gotta leave."

"Doesn't your mom have to accept this and sign some papers? You know she'll never do that."

"That's why I'm only doing the exams until I turn eighteen in February."

"Looks like you got it all planned out. I don't approve, but I'll support your choice."

"I love you man," he said – hugging me.

"I'll miss your sorry ass!"

On October 18th, it was my birthday. That evening, I was doing some homework. Suddenly someone put a pillow case over my head and two sets of arms yanked me off my chair.

"You're coming with us, you turd!" one of the kidnappers said – with a menacing tone.

"Andrew?!" I asked – with astonishment and incomprehension.

"Shut the fuck up and don't fight this or I'll fuckin' break your arm. You know I can do it!" he replied.

I didn't say a thing because – even though I was pretty sure he was bullshitting me – I had always been scared of my cousin when it came down to physical confrontation. They put a tie wrap around my wrists, behind my back, and dragged me out of the apartment. I almost fell down the stairs, missing a step, but somebody helped me up. My head was held down and I was pushed in a car. I heard doors open and close and felt two people sitting on both of my sides. The motor started and the car pulled away.

"Where are you taking me?" I asked – frightened.

"Shut up you piece of shit!" said another voice.

"Tom?!" I asked.

"No ... I'm Batman! ... Anyways, I said shut up or Andrew's gonna break your fuckin' nose!"

I didn't add anything after that. I had no idea where they were taking me and I was kind of scared. I felt slow-downs, red light stops and the car speeding on a highway. I knew we passed through a tunnel because the radio went out for a short time.

About twenty minutes later, the car came to a stop and Andrew said:

"Okay, take him out. I'll try to find parking."

Somebody took me out of the car. My wrists and shoulders were starting ache. After a couple of steps, I heard someone say:

"Hey Marla! Is this the guy?"

"Yes LeSean, it's him," she replied.

"Okay, come on in. Annie set the whole thing up."

They pushed me up a flight of stairs. I was hearing really loud dance music. I was left there standing – not knowing what the hell was going on. After the song ended, I heard a man with a very low voice say – as I was taken a little further, up more steps:

"Now a special treat for his eighteenth birthday from Club Super Sex. Give it up for Eamon!"

I heard clapping as I was sat on a chair – my hands still tied behind my back. The pillowcase was taken off my head – seeing Tom's ugly grin in the process – as the house announcer went on with:

"And now give a warm welcome to the stage for the beautiful Vanessa and the lusty Krystal!"

The crowd was clapping and cheering. Two strippers got up on stage as a new song started. They walked up to me and started kissing and undressing one another. They then turned and lap-danced the hell out of me – grinding their butts on my crotch and boob-sandwiching my face. I was hearing Marla, Andrew and Tom cheering, screaming and cry-laughing all through this, kind of traumatizing, experience. Tom got up on stage with a pair of pliers and cut the tie wrap from my wrists. One of the strippers sat on me while the other took my hands to rub her "friend's" body. I looked at Marla with a look that seemed to plea: "Help me here baby!" She just pointed at me and screamed:

"Take it like a man, Baby! Wouuuuu!"

After the song ended, the two ladies escorted me off the stage while the announcer said:

"Give it up for Eamon and the lovely Vanessa and Krystal!" – as the crowd clapped.

I got to Marla and she said:

"Happy b-day honey!"

"Thanks babe!" I replied – kissing her.

I then turned to Andrew and Tom and said:

"You guys are fuckin' assholes!"

They laughed and high-fived each other. Marla then took us to the second-floor bar and said:

"Hey guys! This is my best friend Annie," – pointing at the barmaid who was pouring Coca-Cola in a glass – "Annie ... Tequila shots for everyone!"

Annie poured five shooters and we, including Annie, downed them. Marla said:

"Annie and I met in high school. Now she's studying to be a nurse."

Annie completed:

"Bartending here just helps to pay the bills."

Tom then asked:

"Do you ever dance, yourself?"

"No, I just bartend."

"Too bad!"

She turned to me and said:

"Eamon! ... Your friend's gross!"

"I know!" I replied – sporting a grin.

We downed a couple of beers at the bar, as creepy dudes were coming up with strippers to have ten dollar lap dances in private booths. At one point I said:

"I'm gonna go outside ... I gotta smoke a cigarette."

Annie replied:

"Well, you can always go to the back room over there. Be discreet, because my boss is gonna have a fit if he finds out."

"Thanks Annie!" Marla said.

We went in the backroom and lit up cigarettes while Tom lit up a joint.

"You're really gonna smoke a joint in here?" I asked – annoyed.

"Yeah, why not? It already smelled as we got in, so I'm not the first one to do it. By the way, I have my written test for the army in a month."

"You're leaving for the army?" asked Marla – in sadness and disbelief.

"Yeah ... I got no future here."

Andrew took Tom's head under his arm, knuckle-headed him and said:

"You don't have a future anywhere, maggot! Hope the drill sergeant will make you do push-ups in your own filth until you cry like a little bitch!"

"Andrew! Lemme go! You're choking me!"

"You sissy! Hahahaha!"

We got out of the backroom and got back to our barstools. Annie poured us some more beers and tequilas. My head was starting to spin a little and my inhibitions started to go out the window. Marla and I were now rating the stripers who were coming up with clients. We sort of agreed on a couple, but our taste in women differed. That night I learned that Marla was also into girls. I found it very enticing, but a little disturbing at the same time. It's not that I didn't like the idea in general; I just disliked the idea of her with someone other than me. We had never really talked about it. I had always figured that since we were going out, we'd be exclusive. But we never actually had a conversation about the subject. She was older than me and I knew she was way more experienced, but I dreaded asking her – afraid of what her answer would be.

At the end of the night, we walked back to the car – it was parked about a block farther, on Union Avenue. Andrew – who was the designated driver – dropped us off at our place. Marla and Tom slept over – Marla in my room and Tom on the sofa. I closed the door to my room and prepared to go to bed. When I turned around, Marla was already naked and said:

"Hey, birthday boy! I didn't give you MY present yet!"

"Andrew and Tom are just on the other side of the door."

"So?! You'll just have to be really quiet then."

She stripped me out of my clothes and started to have sex with me in a cowgirl position. After about two minutes, she got off and said:

"Oh God! I think I'm going to be sick!" – running out the door, completely nude.

I heard Tom saying from a distance:

"Lookin' good, Marla!"

"Shut up, Tom!" I screamed to him – as we were hearing Marla vomiting loudly.

Marla came back to bed about twenty minutes later saying:

"Oh God! I'm going to die!"

I held her in my arms, caressing her long blond hair as she finally fell asleep. I couldn't believe I was due to wake up four hours later to go to school.

X

Three days later, it was my official birthday party. I knew Tom had planned something and I was kind of scared of what he could do – after the "abduction" that happened a couple of days earlier. I arrived at my place and Tom was already there.

"How the hell did you get in?" I asked him.

"Andrew gave me a key a while ago."

"But … Why?!"

"Unlike you, I guess he likes me … Hehe! … So ready for tonight?"

"Yeah! But to be honest, I'm a little scared."

"Well, don't be. It won't really get out of hand because, dude, you don't have that many friends."

I couldn't say anything back to him – I knew he was right. With my job, school and my girlfriend, I didn't have much time for an additional social life.

People began to arrive a while later. Tom – on top of Andrew who actually lived there – had invited Marla, his cousin Lisa – who spent the night giving mouth-to-mouth to Andrew – and some people from Magnan and from Dilallo. All in all, there must have been about thirty people in my small apartment – most of them were merely acquaintances. To my relief, the night was going, bizarrely, smoothly – even though Tom had organized the whole thing.

As time passed, it was getting late and I was getting pretty drunk. I was catching up with some old coworkers from Dilallo's when I saw – from the corner of my eye – Marla freaking out – as she was talking to Tom. I then heard her scream:

"REALLY TOM?! REALLY?! MY FUCKIN' FIFTEEN-YEAR-OLD SISTER!? You're such an asshole! You really gotta … like … grow up, you misogynist pig! Would you stop treating women like friggin' objects!

"Get a hold of yourself Marla! I'm only seventeen if you have forgotten it. You're the one who fucked a minor, a couple months ago … Well, actually no … Two minors: Eamon and I. You're the friggin' hoe!"

She then slapped Tom in the face so hard that he almost fell on the floor. I'm not sure if it was the force of the impact or the movement he made trying to avoid Marla's hand that made him lose his balance. I could see the anger in each of their set of eyes. The party fell dead silent. Marla looked around and stormed out the front door. I pointed at Tom and screamed:

"You better apologize to her!" – as I sprinted out to catch up to Marla.

Tom ran out behind me screaming:

"Dude! Your bitch slapped me! Why should I apologize?"

I got outside and Marla was heading down the stairs crying. I pleaded:

"Babe! Come back, please!"

"I'm not going back in there with that fuckin' …"

But as she was trying to finish her sentence she slipped because of the freezing rain that was pouring down on Montreal that evening.

She went tumbling down the stairs – her legs flying in the air and her body hitting the ramp railing from left to right. She finally ended up head first on the concrete sidewalk as the rest of her body just crumbled – lifeless – like a rag doll. Tom and I were petrified. I got a hold of myself and yelled to Tom:

"Call 911 ... Now!"

I then rushed down the stairs – holding onto the ramp – and got to Marla in seconds. I checked if she was still alive – thank God she was. I got close to her – crying – trying to warm her up without moving her in case her spine was damaged. The ambulance arrived less than five minutes later. They got a neck brace on Marla and put her in the ambulance. I got in with her and yelled to Tom – before they closed the door:

"They are taking her to LaSalle Hospital ... Call her parents ... or something!"

Less than ten minutes later, we entered the emergency room at the LaSalle Hospital. They took her away and questioned me on what happened. I told them everything and they sent me to the waiting room – it felt like an eternity waiting for information. They finally got me in a room and told me that she was going to be okay – that she had two broken ribs, a sprained ankle and a concussion. I was authorized to see her.

She was asleep and they kept her for observation for twenty-four hours. Tom – accompanied by Andrew – arrived about an hour later.

"Where is she? Is she okay?" he asked – panicked and concerned.

"Yes, she's safe," I replied – trying to reassure him.

"I feel so bad! I'm so sorry, dude! I didn't want this to happen. It's all my fault!"

"It's not your fault, bro! She had too much to drink and it was raining like hell outside."

"I know! But if I hadn't fucked her sister and she hadn't sent a picture of it to Marla, none of this would've happened."

"Wait?! What!?!"

"Dude it's a long story and ... you really don't wanna know! If I can do anything, just ask."

"You're right ... I don't wanna know! ... You could always take care of her after school while I'm working."

"Well, I kinda dropped outta school this morning."

"You can't just drop outta school like that?"

"As a matter of fact, I just did and there's no way I'm going back. You do your thing and I'll take care of Marla 24/7."

"Okay! Thanks!"

Marla got out of the hospital twenty-four hours later. It was the last week before mid-semester break and I had a couple of exams and a paper to give in. So, I fell off the earth during those couple of days. At least, I could count on Tom to help with Marla. Her parents hated him – of course they didn't know that he did some hot nookie with their younger daughter – which would have made things even worst. Marla was just glad to have her very own private male nurse. Tom felt so guilty that he tended to her every need.

My midterm exams having been done, I was off for a week. I was planning to work on some school papers, but I helped Tom to care for Marla. I got to Marla's place, went up to her room and she greeted me with a: "Hey sweetie!" She sounded really high. I asked Tom:

"Dude, what the hell is she on?"

"Well she has to take morphine every four hours. I'm just following doctor's orders."

"Guys! I'm hungry ... I wanna have some MacD's ... Please! Hey, that rhymes ... Hahahaha!" said Marla.

"Dude! She's totally wasted," I whispered to Tom.

"I know, bro!" Tom whispered back.

"When are we going to MacD's? I'm hungry!!!" asked Marla.

Tom, Marla and I went for a walk to get to the MacDonald's on Rockland Way. Marla was saying incomprehensible things – staggering along the sidewalk, laughing.

"Tom? How much morphine are you giving her?" I asked him – concerned.

"Only what the pharmacist told me ... Every four hours," replied Tom – puzzled.

"She looks like a friggin' meth head."

"I kind of like her better this way ... she's less nagging."

"Get bent, Tom! This is all your fault!"

"That's not what you said the other day. Anyways, she's the one who overreacted!"

"You shouldn't have slept with her sister, dude. It was a goddamn stupid move, man!"

"Yeah, maybe ... But she was the one who jumped on me. It was hard to say no once she was naked!"

I chest-slapped Tom – Rick Flair style.

"Ouch! That hurts!" said Tom – in pain.

"Stop talking about her sister, you know, in case she remembers some conversations when she sobers up," I warned him.

We got to the MacDonald's, went inside and waited in line to order. Marla spotted this cute baby in some Afro-American guy's arms.

"Ohhhh! The cute baby! Hey mister, your baby's so cute! Do you mind if I hold him?" she asked.

The man looked startled, but agreed to let her hold him. He turned around – it was his turn to order. We, ourselves, went up to another cashier to order our meal – only having enough money to order a couple of burgers from the value menu. I turned to Marla and asked:

"Hey sweetie, what do you feel like eating? ... Marla?!"

Marla had disappeared and so did the baby. The baby's father totally flipped. He stormed outside and ran towards Marla – who was walking up Rockland way. Tom and I ran behind him – fearing that the man would go berserk on her. Some lady called 911 on Marla accusing her of abduction.

The man finally caught up to her and so did we. He was screaming at her – plying the baby away from her arms. Marla was crying and the guy was now yelling at us. We tried to explain that she was on morphine, but he just wouldn't buy the story.

The police arrived soon later and treated us like criminals. We explained the whole ordeal to him, he didn't seem to believe us either. I told him:

"Listen officer … Ummm … We could call the pharmacy so they can corroborate our story … Tom? Do you have the number on you somewhere?"

"Yeah! I got her medicine in my pocket and …" replied Tom – searching in his pocket – as the policeman freaked – going for his gun.

"Keep your hands where I can see 'em," screamed the officer.

"Stay calm officer. I'm just reaching for the medicine bottle. I'll take it out slowly," replied Tom – getting his hands half up in the air.

"Don't do anything stupid," the policeman added – his hand still on his holster. Tom got the bottle out of his pocket and gave it to the officer.

He called the number that was on it and asked to talk to the pharmacist. After a couple of minutes, he came back to us and said:

"The pharmacist corroborated your story. But he said that she should take them every four hours ONLY IF NECESSARY!"

"Tom, you asshole! You've been drugging her for over a week now!" I yelled at him.

"Well, sorry! That's not what I understood when I went to get her medicine."

"We are truly sorry, again, officer. We'll get her home until she's feeling better!" I added to the police officer – taking Marla back home – as we started to get her off opiates for the next few days.

XI

On a Sunday, in early December, I was going to my weekly supper with my dad. Ever since he went into the A.A. program, we had started to talk again and had gotten close – once more. We had been meeting up for supper every week for the last two months. Since my mom threw him out, he had been living in an apartment – on the last floor of the building that also housed the Green Stop Restaurant – on the corner of Monk Boulevard and Jolicoeur Street. I checked the parking lot next to it to see if his car was there. Seeing his '99 Tercel, I decided to go up the staircase to his apartment. I knocked on his door, but there was no answer. I waited for him for about half an hour – thinking that he may have gone to the corner store or something like that. As the never ending wait took its toll, I began to get worried. I went down to look for the janitor's apartment. I knocked on his door and – when he answered – I said to him:

"Hi there ... Listen ... Ummm ... My father lives on the last floor and we were supposed to meet for supper ... That was about an hour ago. I see his car in the parking lot, but he doesn't answer his door nor his phone. It's really not like him to be late or not give any news. So I was wondering if you could open his door, just to see if everything's fine."

He agreed and came up with me to unlock the door. There was a stench of rottenness escaping from his apartment. I slowly walked in and started looking in every room, yelling: "Dad?! ... 'You there?!" I finally got to the living room and my fears had become a reality. I found my dad's lifeless body on the floor – near the sofa – decomposing in its own urine and feces. My heart stopped. I turned to the janitor and asked him to call 911.

I walked out of there backwards – in shock. I had never seen a dead body before. I was about to vomit. I was so overwhelmed with the situation – I just didn't really realize that it was, in fact, my dad lying there. I waited by the door for the police and ambulance to arrive.

When they got there, a policeman asked me the usual questions while the paramedics took care of the body. When they took him out of the apartment on a stretcher – in a body bag – I just lost it. I broke out in tears into the policeman's arms and couldn't stop crying. The officer tried to comfort me, but I just kept on uncontrollably weeping.

They took his body to the morgue. I still had to go identify him, though and the exercise was very troubling. Marla was trying to comfort me, but didn't achieve much success in the process.

After a couple of days, my mom called:

"Hey sweetie. How are you holding up?"

"I'm okay. It's hard ... but life goes on ... I guess."

"Hey, listen ... Some notary called and he gave me a number ... He was looking for you."

"What did he want?"

"You're the sole beneficiary of your father's will. I guess he took me out of it when we divorced. Anyways, give him a call."

When I hung up with my mom, I called the notary. He wanted me to come by his office for the reading of the will. I found out that he had left me two hundred thousand dollars. I also found out that my mom was managing all the burial mumbo-jumbo.

The ceremony was held in Saint-Henri at the Saint-Zotique Church, on West Notre-Dame Street – in front of the Sir-George-Étienne-Cartier Square. It was a real moving ceremony. Andrew, Lisa, Marla and Tom were there. My mom was weeping waterfalls. Even though my dad had been a total jerk to her in the end, they had been happy for years before that – I suspected my mom of still loving the man. After the ceremony, we followed the funeral procession up to the Notre-Dame-des-Neiges cemetery – on top of Mount-Royal.

December of 2006 had been one of the hottest Decembers in a couple of decades – they were still doing burials because the ground hadn't frozen yet and there wasn't any snow – people were still golfing, for Christ's sake. My heart was filled with sadness when they lowered the coffin underground. A page in my life was turning. Marla held my hand – silently – out of love and respect.

In January, I started a new semester at Dawson. On top of basic courses – Gym, French and English – I registered in *Feature Writing*, *Literature into Films*, *Script Writing* and a bullshit complementary course that was not in my domain – I chose *Chemistry of Wine Making*. I sucked big time at chemistry but excelled in alcohol drinking – this was really a no-brainer.

One night, at the end of January – as I was doing some homework – Tom came over. At first, I didn't hear him coming – being really focused on my paper – listening to *Wolves in Wolves Clothing* – NOFX's 2006 release – on my stereo. Tom snuck up silently behind me and violently kicked the back of my chair screaming:

"THIS ... IS ... SPARTA!!!"

"You goddamn motherfucker! You scared the shit outta me!" I replied – while he was almost crying on the floor, laughing. "So ... What are you doing here, bro?"

"Well, three things. First ... My birthday's next week so you, moron, better have something special planned out for me ... Second, I need to borrow a hundred bucks ... and ... Third, I got accepted in the army. I'm leaving for the Saint-Jean-sur-Richelieu base in early March."

"Holy shit! So soon? I thought it would at least take until summer before you get accepted. Are you sure you really sure you wanna go through with this

"Yes! Plus, it's too late now. I signed a contract ... So, what about that hundred bucks?"

"What do you need it for?"

"You don't wanna know ... I'll pay you back before I leave, I promise! So ... What have you planned for my party?"

I felt really bad – I had totally forgotten about Tom's birthday. God! The guy was turning eighteen and it had fallen out of my radar. What kind friend was I? I decided to be totally honest:

"Sorry, bro! I haven't got anything planned. I totally forgot. I have so much on my mind right now."

"God! You're such an ass! I threw you an awesome birthday party and this is how you repay me?! What is wrong with you?" he angrily asked.

"I told you I was sorry. I feel bad as it is!" I shamefully replied.

He then laughed.

"What's so funny?" I asked – quizzical.

"I totally knew you'd forget, so I already planned the whole thing last month. I just wanted you to feel bad!"

"You're such a dick! You know that?!"

"Hahahaha! I know, I know! So what about those hundred bucks?"

"Yeah, yeah! Wait here! ... God, you're such a pushover!"

I took five twenty-dollar bills that I had stashed away in my room, in case of emergencies. I gave it to him and he thanked me. He then got up and walked out of my room, saying:

"So, the party is on Saturday, February 3rd, my place. My mom's going to be at my aunt's place in Pointe-Saint-Charles, so it's gonna epic bro ... Be there!!!"

"Yeah, yeah, yeah! I will, bro! Take care!"

"You too, Mofo!" he replied – heading out the door.

A week later, Marla called me and asked:

"Hey baby! So, when are you coming to Tom's party?"

"I don't think I'm going to make it, sweetie. I'm sick as hell. I think I have gastro ... I'm emptying myself from both ends. I know this may crush some magic between us, but I think I'm going to die!" I plaintively replied.

"Oh! You poor baby! I'm so sorry for you! Do you want me to come down there to take care of you?" she asked – in a motherly fashion.

"No ... I may be contagious. Just enjoy yourself, honey. Have a great evening. I'm going back to bed and I just hope to sleep 'till tomorrow morning. Tell Tom I'm really sorry I couldn't be there."

"Will do, baby! 'Love you! Take care of yourself."

"'Love you too, sweetie."

I then went back to bed, hoping not to empty my stomach and bowels – yet again.

XII

Three days later, I had gotten back on my feet. Tom came over one evening. He got in my apartment as I was typing some ideas for my short stories.

"Hey Mofo! Whatcha doin'?" he asked.

"I'm trying to write some stuff. I'm kinda stuck. I keep rereading my short stories and find them quite horrible. It pisses me off. My writing has really evolved in the pass months. College has been a real eye opener for me ... I'm learning so much. I'm thinking of maybe going to university after that."

"Wow! Cool for you, dude! But I'm pretty sure what you wrote isn't that bad. Artists are always their own whinny worst critic. You can always leave them aside for a while and come back to them some time later and rework them."

"You're probably right. Anyways ... so .... What's up with you? What are you up to?"

"Well ... I came to give you your hundred bucks back. I got my last paycheck yesterday, with my four percent leave. I'm leaving in two weeks and I needed time to get my shit together."

"Where are you going?"

"To the army, you stupid fuck! You never pay attention to what I'm saying."

"Yes I do. But you're always evasive on the exact day of your departure."

"Well, I'm heading out to St Jean in thirteen days. So I got some packing to do and some goodbyes to say to a couple of people. Plus, my mom wants to see as much of me as possible. She says I'm breaking her heart. But I really gotta do this. By the way here's your money."

He got up, took out his wallet and gave me two fifty-dollar bills.

"What did you need the money for?" I asked.

"Since I'm leaving, I treated myself to an escort."

"Wait! What?! Since when do you need to pay to get laid? What the fuck is wrong with you?"

"Hey, calm down, dude! I'm going to the army and I don't know when I'm going to get laid again in the next few weeks ... or even worse: months. Plus, you know I'm into older women."

"Yes, I do, you sick puppy!"

"Ah, come on. They're the best. They're experienced and know how to please and be pleased."

"Ok ... But why a hooker?"

"First of all, she was no street hooker; she was a classy independent escort. Second, what forty-year-old woman would fuck an eighteen-year-old boy on such short notice? So, I figured that was the only option I had."

"You're twisted!"

"Oh, stop it! You and your holier than thou act. You don't fool me. You're as sick as me. You just don't let your inner beast out ... ever."

"Where did you find her? How was it?"

"Ah! Now you wanna know?! Hahahaha! ... 'Found her in the classified ads on the internet. I met her at her place in HoMa. It was just awesome. She wore black stockings and garter belt and had these big natural breasts which were surprisingly really firm for a forty-year-old woman. She was a nasty one; she ate me up alive. I even had trouble containing myself. Anyways, I just had a blast."

"I'm pretty sure you did."

"Anyways, I just came to pay my dues so there wouldn't be any debts between us before I leave. I have a lot to do for the next two weeks, so I'm off for tonight. I'll catch you later, bro."

"Okay … Well … See ya! I'll get back to my writing if I ever want something published before I'm thirty."

"Sure you will! You're a natural, bro!"

He got up and left. I didn't know it then, but that would be the last time I would see Tom for the next few years.

That night, I went to see Marla at her new job. She had quit the Escogriffe and went to work in a new co-op bar and venue called the Katacombes – which had opened a couple of months prior – on the corner of Saint-Laurent Boulevard and Ontario Street. It was a really cool place – way bigger than the Escogriffe. It had two stories, the decor was really glaucous and the toilets were disgusting – all in all a fine place. There was a show that night. I can't remember what band was playing and I didn't really give a shit. Marla – although working – was distant. People were ordering drinks one after another, but there was something off with her. I know it was a busy night, but still!

I didn't stay very long, because everything felt odd. My best friend was leaving and my girlfriend was almost ignoring me. I needed to open up to someone, but had no one to talk to. I decided to walk back home. It was friggin' -15°C outside, but I didn't care. I put on my gloves and tuque and walked under the clear star-lit February night sky – heading west on Sainte-Catherine and Notre-Dame Street – finally crossing the Lachine Canal, where my home and heart were. By then, my fingertips were freezing and my nose was running. I just didn't care – I was in a trance within my thoughts and admiring the beauty Montreal had to offer through its street-lit snow-patched scenery.

I finally got home around 2:00 am – warming up myself – and saw that Andrew was home. I silently walked to his room. He was sound asleep – spooning with Lisa. I tiptoed to his bed, poked him in the back and whispered:

"Andrew ... Wake up."

He turned around – half-confused – and whispered back:

"Eamon?! What the hell do you want? What time is it?"

"I need to talk to someone ... and it's 2:00 am."

"God! I'm working tomorrow morning."

"Please Cous'!?"

"Is this a life or death situation?"

"No ... but ..."

"Then leave me alone. We'll talk tomorrow. Goodnight."

"But..."

"Goodnight Eamon!"

I left his room disappointed – got to the pantry – took out a bottle of Jack Daniels, a paper pad and a pen. I sat down on the couch, took a shot of Jack directly from the bottle and started writing. I wrote and wrote until ... nothing – a total blackout.

I was woken up by a ruckus in close proximity. I was disoriented, my head ached and there was an empty bottle of liquor at my side. Andrew was in the kitchen making himself breakfast.

"Rise and shine, asshole!" he said to me.

"God, Andrew! Can you keep it down please?" I begged him.

"Serves yourself for waking me in the middle of the night. It took me more than half an hour to get back to sleep."

"What time is it now?"

"It's 7:00 am ... Don't you have school this morning?"

"I'm not going. I feel like shit. Tom's leaving in twelve days and Marla's kind of ignoring me lately ... Well, since Tom's party actually. Did something happen there?"

"Not that I know of. They were picking at each other all night like grade school kids ... as always."

"Oh, okay. I saw her at her job yesterday and something was off."

"Maybe she's just preoccupied with her new job and her exposition coming up."

"What expo?"

"She didn't tell you? She's doing an art expo with friends of hers in a gallery somewhere ... I don't remember where exactly."

"It's the first I hear about it. You see what I'm telling you? She's just ..."

I stopped my sentence short, ran to the bathroom and vomited all the booze I had chugged last night, as Andrew yelled:

"Way to ruin my appetite! You know I'm not holding your hair. Anyways, I gotta go ... 'gonna be late. Are you gonna be okay?"

"Yeah, yeah! Just g..." I replied – vomiting some more before I got to finish my sentence.

I spent most of the day lying half-alive and half-naked on the cold bathroom tiles, trying to vomit from an empty stomach. I felt like I had been hit by a bus. I fell asleep there in my own saliva. I woke up freezing, a couple of hours later, feeling a little better. I went to the kitchen and looked for something to eat. There were some leftovers. So, I packed them between two slices of bread, added cheese and made myself a panini. As it was cooking, I went to the bathroom and started to fill up the tub. When I came back to check on my meal, I saw the pad that was lying on the sofa – a little rippled up. I took my panini and my pad in the bathroom, got in the bathtub and warmed myself up – eating my meal and reading what I had written the previous night. I was kind of amazed at myself. That stuff was good – it was actually novel material. It was the blueprints of a story about family, friends lost, coming of age and all. "I guess I write better half-drunk," I thought to myself. So, I decided to write this thing. I didn't know how long it would take me, but it was my objective. As for Marla, I was going to wait for her to call me. I thought that if she had really cared for me, she would have at least given me a buzz.

Two weeks later, the phone rang:

"Hey bro!" said Tom.

"Hey Tom! Haven't heard from you in a while. Since you're leaving in two days, you wanna do something before?"

"Sorry dude, I was just calling to say goodbye. I'm leaving earlier. I'm going to spend two days at my uncle's home in St Jean. My mom's gonna drive me there. She's not available on the actual day of my entry into the army."

"Oh! That sucks. We won't see each other until you leave."

"Don't worry. I'll come to see you after my training."

"You better!"

"Of course I will … Don't worry."

"Okay … well … Take care of yourself and don't do anything stupid!"

"You know I will, so I'm not promising anything! You know me!"

"Unfortunately I do … Hahahaha … Just be careful okay?"

"Yes Mother … Hahahaha … Well … I guess this is goodbye?"

"Yeah. See ya, bro!"

We hung up and my heart filled with sadness. It wasn't just that Tom was leaving; I hadn't had any news from Marla either. I was on the impression that this was the end.

A week later – as I was writing yet another paper for school – someone knocked on my door. I went to open it and Marla was there – looking like a sad lost puppy.

"Oh! There you are!" I said to her, "I thought you had forgotten all about me."

"I was passing by … I didn't know if you'd be home. I took a chance."

Marla looked like she had been crying – a lot. There was this emptiness from behind her eyes – like the lights were open, but there was no one home.

"You don't look so good. What's wrong?" I asked.

"Can I come in? I'm freezing," she pleaded.

"Sure! Come on in. You want something to drink? I got beer, wine, rum …"

"No thanks. I shouldn't be drinking anyways. If you have tea, that would be nice."

I went and made her tea. She didn't say a word – nor did I. I brought the tea and sat next to her on the sofa. I broke the awkward silence that was killing me:

"So, what's up? How come I haven't had any news from you for the past three weeks? Do you know how I feel right now?"

"Sorry, but … I needed time to think."

"Think about what?"

"About all this … About us … About my future."

"What are you saying? Whattaya mean? Have you gotten tired of me already? Have you met someone else?"

I began to panic at that point – seeing my love life crumble before my eyes.

"It's nothing like that. You know sometimes you gotta live with the flow … You have a path that you intend to follow … The problem is that life sometimes takes you on another path."

"I don't understand. What are you trying to say?"

"Well … Eamon … I'm kinda … pregnant."

"Holy shit! I understand why you needed to think about this. Ouff! You're right. This is big!"

"Well … That's not the problem … Yes, of course, it's a big thing and all … but the problem is … well … Ummm … I don't actually know who the father is …"

The Lost River

I

"WHAT?! What the fuck are you saying? You cheated on me? You go around sleeping with everybody now? You're such a whore!" I told Marla – with so much hatred and pain in my tone.

"Eamon! Calm down, please! It's not like that. It only happened once. I didn't plan it ... It just kinda happened. You gotta believe me. I was sorta drunk and it happened. I'm not too proud of myself. I love you, you know. I never meant to hurt you. I know that's what I'm doing right now, but believe me I love you. I wanna be with you. It's just this. I know it's hard to swallow and for what it's worth ... I'm really and deeply sorry."

"A penis just happened to enter your pussy, just like that?! You gotta be kidding me! ... But that's not the whole point. You're fucking pregnant and on top of that it may not be mine. Weren't you on the pill?"

"Yes, but I forgot it a couple of times this month."

"And you didn't think of telling me that. I could have put on a friggin' condom. And what about that other guy? You didn't protect yourself either?! That's such a stupid thing to do!"

"Like I said ... We were kinda drunk and it just happened so fast ... I didn't think."

"Who was it?"

"It doesn't matter who it was."

"Well, it does to me. You at least owe me that."

"Okay ... But you gotta promise ... like ... not to get mad..."

"Why? It's someone I know?"

"Just don't be mad at him okay ... It's not his fault ... It's mostly mine and ..."

"OH GOD! IT'S TOM?!"

"Well ... yes ... I'm sorry!"

"I'M GONNA FUCKING KILL THAT MOTHERFUCKER!!! GOD! HOW COULD HE DO THIS TO ME?"

"Calm down, Eamon ... please!"

"Calm down!? How can I calm down when my girlfriend and my best friend, whom I considered as a brother, backstab me like this?"

"It was a mistake ... Don't take it out on Tom. He was sad to be leaving everyone behind and nervous about the army ... We had too much the drink and I tried to reassure him and ..."

"To reassure him by putting his dirty cock in your slutty cunt."

"Stop it, Eamon. Now you're just being mean."

"No, I'm being honest and pissed ... You want mean? Get the fuck outta my house! I never want to see you again."

"What about the baby? You can't just leave me like this..."

"The hell I can ... Just watch me ... As for this pregnancy thing, I just hope you do the right thing and get an abortion. Tom never knew his father and look how mind fucked he turned out to be. I don't want anything to do with you or remotely anything coming close to you ... EVER!!! Now get the hell outta my home and outta my life."

Marla stormed out of the apartment in heavy tears. My heart was pumping fast. I started to cry from rage. I had been so in love with Marla that I just couldn't believe that she had done such a horrible thing. And Tom – oh my God, Tom! – I was so dumbstruck. I got to the kitchen, took the last bottle of Jack – that was lying there half-empty – and drank shots out of it – walking in circles in the living room – mumbling to myself. After half an hour, I grabbed my coat – still holding on to the whiskey bottle – and stormed out of the apartment. It was cold outside, but I didn't feel it since I was boiling inside – and because of the whiskey. I hadn't even bothered to lock the door. I was walking down Jacques-Hertel Street when I crossed Andrew. He said:

"Hey Cous'! Where 'you going?"

I continued walking without even acknowledging his presence. He yelled out:

"Eamon!?"

This time I heard him, but I didn't turn around – continuing my fast pace down the street.

About ten minutes later, I got to my destination. I went up the stairs and rang the doorbell, while knocking at the same time. Since there was no answer, I rang and knocked a second time. The door opened – with the chain lock on – and a voice said:

"Who is it?"

"Mom, it's me! Open up please!" I replied – my eyes full of tears.

My mom rapidly unchained the door – seeing my distress.

"What's wrong laddie?" she asked – pulling me into her arms – almost smothering me in her frieze bathrobe.

She closed the door behind me and took me to the kitchen.

"Here, sit down and tell me what's wrong. Do you want anything to drink?" she asked.

"No it's okay … I have this," I replied – lifting the bottle of Jack Daniels.

"You know I don't like to see you drinking. Do you wanna end up a drunk like your father?"

"Come on, Mom! ... No lecture tonight! Just listen ... Please! I have no one to talk to and I'm not doing so well right now."

"Okay, I'll let this one pass ... So, tell me what's bothering you. Are you in trouble?"

"No, Mom, I'm not in trouble ... Well, not that kind of trouble, at least."

I took a pause and explained the whole situation to her while crying like a little kid who just fell off his bicycle for the first time.

"I just don't know what do to ... Where to go ... I just have no purpose anymore."

"Don't say that, Baby Boy. Don't let those two ruin the bright future that lies ahead of you."

"What future, Mom? I'm washing dishes in a tavern and studying to be a writer ... which will inevitably get me to wash dishes all my life."

"Don't say that, Son. You're brilliant and wise. You'll figure it out and you'll be somebody someday. Momma knows."

"Well, I won't be "someone" in this deadbeat neighborhood, that's for sure."

"Watch your mouth, young man. I've been living in this neighborhood almost all my life. I don't think I'm a nobody ... Do you understand!?"

"Yes, Mom ... But you got me wrong. I meant that I can't write a really good novel by staying here, between the Lachine Canal and the Aqueduct. I gotta live a little. I gotta see more than just Montreal."

"What are you saying?"

"Mom ... I'm leaving."

"To go where?"

"I don't know yet ... I'll figure it out soon."

"How are you gonna live?"

"Well, I still have the 200k Dad left me and I have some savings from Magnan as well."

"If this is what you want, I can't really stop you. You're eighteen now ... You gotta figure things out by yourself. But know that I'll always be here and that you better call your mother often ... Do you understand!?"

I smiled and said:

"Promise, Mom!"

I spent the night there – in my old room – half-drunk and weeping. The next morning, I woke up and I was alone – my mom had left for work. She had made me fresh coffee and had left a note on the table saying: "Please, think this over. But no matter the decision, I will support you. I love you. Have a good day. Mom xxx". I was glad that there was at least one person in this world who wasn't going to backstab me.

I grabbed my coat and got back to my place – Andrew was still there.

"Hey Cous'! What's the matter?" he asked, "I crossed your path and yelled out your name yesterday, but you didn't even turn around."

"Marla came over to tell me that she had cheated on me with Tom and that she was pregnant and didn't know who the father was."

"Holy shit!!! I'm sorry to hear that. What now? What are you going to do?"

"I told her she could go fuck herself ... I think I'm gonna leave this place and disappear from the face of the earth ... You know ... Live a little ... See something else than *Browntown* here ... Meet new people ... Different cultures ... Different landscapes."

"How are you gonna manage that?"

"Well, I have some money to leech off of for two to four years without working. I think I'll just go somewhere secluded and write ... Maybe travel a little, if I get the blank page syndrome."

"Okay ... When are you leaving? Where are you going?"

"I wanna leave ASAP .... And as to where? ... I don't know yet."

"So, you're sticking me with the full rent ... Geez! ... Thanks!" he sarcastically replied.

"Well, I thought of that and I'm really sorry. Maybe your girlfriend could come live with you. You're always together anyways. You won't have your stupid cousin banging on the wall when your girlfriend's climaxing and he's trying to do a school paper."

"Hahahaha! True ... True ... I guess that could be feasible. Well ... Good luck Cous'."

He then gave me a "buddy-handshake" and bro-hugged me.

I went into my room to figure out where to go and what to do – looking at the North-American map that was pinned on the wall – deep into my thoughts. I didn't want to go too far at first – so the West Coast was cut out of the process. The problem was that I didn't know much about the world outside of Montreal. The only logical destination – due to my Irish origins – was Boston. It was also the only city that came to mind that kind of looked like Montreal.

From then on, I started planning on where to stay, what to bring and all. I had decided to leave in April because I didn't want to start my new life in the cold. So, I dropped out of college, gave my final two weeks' notice at Magnan Tavern and packed some easy to carry luggage – consisting of three days of clothing and my laptop. Since I was leaving in spring, I didn't need winter clothes nor boots. I told Andrew that I was leaving on April 27th.

"Dude! Why don't you ride to Sherbrooke with me and then take the Greyhound to Boston afterwards," he suggested.

"Why in the world are you going to Sherbrooke?"

"I have to go get my sister who's studying at Bishop University in Environmental Science. Her semester ends that week and she wants to come home for the summer. My mom misses her a lot, so she asked me to go get her."

"But why do you want me to come with you?"

"Well, you know I hate driving long distances alone. Plus, you could get to see my sister whom you haven't seen in a while. She often asks about you."

"Oh! Okay ... Why not!? I have never seen Sherbrooke, anyways. Plus, it's not like it's a long detour."

"That's the spirit!"

During those weeks, Marla tried to call me a couple of times, but I hung up on her upon hearing her voice – to the point that I let Andrew pick up or simply send it directly to voicemail. She left me tons of messages, saying how sorry she was, that she was keeping the baby – hoping I could forgive her someday. I didn't buy her crap. It just drove me, even more, to get the hell out of the country.

I spent the last remaining days at my mom's, at her request, because she wanted to spend as much time with me as possible. I took this moment to take most of my stuff – my clothes, my CDs, my unfinished manuscripts of The Lachine Canal Chronicles, etc. – out of my soon-to-be ex-apartment. Andrew's girlfriend had already moved in – so me being at my mom's gave them a little more privacy.

On the 27th, Andrew came to get me. I put my backpack in the car and my mom endlessly hugged and kissed me on the cheeks. She couldn't stop crying.

"Don't worry Mom. I'm a big boy now. I can manage on my own," I assured her.

"I know you can ... But a mother always worries."

We then left, got on the Champlain Bridge – where I took one last look at the Montreal skyline – before heading east on Highway 10. I had a little melancholy in my heart, but I was anxious to start over again.

We rode east, under cloudy and rainy skies. Andrew was rambling on and on about his MMA training, his rugby season – that was about to start – and the games he was working on at Ubisoft:

"Dude! *Assassin's Creed* is gonna kick-ass. I think it's gonna be our most successful game since *Prince of Persia: the Sands of Time*. I'm pretty sure they'll still be talking about this one in the next ten to fifteen years."

"Well ... That's a little presumptuous ... Don't you think?"

"That's because you haven't seen it. The company has been working on it since 2004 ... I tell ya, it rocks big time!"

"Okay! Okay! I believe you."

The hour and a half trip went really fast. Andrew's continuous blabber distracted me from the journey that laid before me.

We got off Highway 10 and got on the 410 that led to Lennoxville. We got in the back of the Bishop University campus – where the Abbott Residence was located. We got out of the car, got to the building and went up two flights of stairs to where my cousin's room was. Andrew knocked on the door – which opened in haste – and a girl came jumping out of the room into Andrew's arms:

"Bro! I missed you so much!"

"Missed you too, Sis'!" replied Andrew – sporting a huge smile on his face.

She turned to me, smiling, and said:

"Hey lil' cousin! How's it hangin'?"

"Hey Julie! I'm doing good, considering the circumstances," I replied.

"Whattaya mean?"

"Ah! Long story ... I don't really wanna talk about it."

"Suit yourself ... Come on in!"

I looked at Julie and God I found her hot. I don't know if it was the fact that I was newly single or that I hadn't had sex in almost three months, but she aroused me. If she hadn't been my cousin, I would have totally hit on her. I tried to chase those thoughts from my mind, but it was hard since she was only wearing a camisole and panties. Her hair was wet, so I figured she had just got out of the shower. She said to Andrew:

"I didn't expect you so soon. My things are packed and I just need to get dressed."

As she was putting some clothes on, she asked me:

"You didn't tell me what you are doing here. Not that I'm not glad to see you, but I'm just wondering."

"Well, your brother, here, doesn't like to take the road alone. 'Must be the fact that he can't shut up for two seconds and needs to piss someone off with his incessant stories," I replied.

Andrew punched me on the upper arm. Julie laughed and said:

"Hahahaha! Thanks for the heads up!"

"Ouch, Andrew! That friggin' hurts!" I said to him – in pain.

"Oh, tough it up, you sissy! You're going to go to Boston, for God's sake. You need to get a little tougher than that or they'll eat you alive down there."

Julie replied:

"Oh, you're going to Boston?!"

"Yup! I'm gonna be living there for a while. I'm planning to take a Greyhound from here," I said to her.

"You do know that there are no direct busses from Sherbrooke to major cities in the US? You have to pass through Central Station in Montreal."

"What?!? Oh, God! I have to make it way back west before heading out south-east again? That sucks!"

Andrew, a little ashamed, said:

"Oups! Sorry Cous' ... My bad!"

Julie fell silent – thinking – and then said:

"Wait a minute! There's a bulletin board on campus for people who want to car pool outta here and split the gas money. Maybe you'll find someone. You better hurry up because this is the last day of school."

Julie got dressed and she took us to the board. I was in luck. There were actually two ads for people looking for carpoolers heading for Boston. Julie lent me her cell phone and I called the first ad. The person on the other end told me that he had already left and had forgotten to take the ad off the board. I called the other number and, this time, luck struck. The person was actually leaving that evening. I was kind of glad it was a female voice. Who knows?

She told me to meet her in the parking lot next to the John H. Price Sports Center around 6:00pm.

"How would I recognize you?" I asked.

"Look for the black Mazda hatchback with a W.E.S.C. logo sticker on the rear windshield."

"Oh, okay! See you then! And thanks!"

"My pleasure!"

The only problem was that Andrew and Julie were leaving around noon, so I had six hours to kill. Before heading back to Montreal, they both hugged me and wished me good luck. But now, I was alone in a place I didn't know.

I walked around the campus which was filled with red bricked wings, built in a New England style – the kind you see in American teen movies. After having strolled around the entire campus on foot, I entered a building and found the University bookstore. I spent about half an hour looking at the various books. I stumbled upon a nice copy of Kerouac's *Big Sur* and bought it – to pass the time until I had to get to my rendezvous point.

After having read about seventy-five pages of the book – my back to a tree – I got hungry, so I went into the cafeteria to get myself a snack. I sat down at a table and ate while continuing to read. About fifteen minutes before 6:00pm, I went out and walked towards the parking lot where I would meet my driver. I found her car and waited for her while smoking a cigarette – book in hand.

A voice startled me out of *Big Sur*:

"Hi! I'm Shelly ... Shelly Sullivan."

"Hey! I'm Eamon Jovanovski," I replied – all smiles.

"So you're going to Boston? Got family there too?"

"No … I'm just in a process of reorganizing my life and want a new start."

"But why Boston?"

"I'm half-Irish."

"Figures … Hahahaha. Got any luggage?"

"Just this backpack and my laptop."

"You're planning to do a lot of laundry?"

"Yup! Hahahaha!"

"Well, hop in … We got a long ride ahead of us."

We then got into her car. She drove out of Lennoxville and hopped on Route 143 South to the border. Shelly was a really gorgeous red-headed girl. She was about twenty-four years old, wore glasses with brownish-green eyes behind them. Her hair fell a little below her shoulders. She was not skinny but not chubby either – just the right killer curves that would make any man drool. She had a smile that would ignite a thousand fires. I couldn't stop looking at her, but I did it discreetly – I didn't want her to think I was some sort of creepy guy.

"So …" I asked her, "Are you from Sherbrooke?"

"No, I'm from Quebec City, actually. My mom works for the health department. My parents got divorced a couple of years ago and my dad moved back to Boston … He was born there … So, every summer I go to my dad's and every Christmas vacation, I go to my mom's."

"What does your dad do for a living?"

"He works for the Boston Bruins, in the communications department."

"So … You're telling me we CANNOT be friends!"

"Montreal Canadians fan, hein? Hahaha!"

"Yup! Since 1909! What are you studying in?"

"Well, I'm kind of wanting to follow in my dad's footsteps, so, sports media communications."

"Oh! Cool! It's not often that we see a woman who likes sports."

"Yeah, I know! I just love it. I even beat all my male friends at sports trivia. It just pisses them off ... Hehe! ... What about you?"

"Well, I was studying in arts ... Mostly literature ... I wanna be a writer. My mom works at Sears and my dad was a welder. He died a couple of months ago."

"I'm sorry to hear that!"

"No, it's okay ... We weren't very close. It was a shock at first, but I'm over it now."

"So ... What do you write about?"

"Nothing much yet. I have written a couple of short stories, but I'm not too happy with them. So, I'm letting them sit a little. Having not really been outta Montreal, I find that I have to live a little to have stuff to write about ... So that's why I'm fleeing."

"Well, what you are doing is kind of exciting. For my part, I could never do something like that. I need a plan, a path to follow. It takes courage to do what you're doing."

"Not really ... It's more desperation, on my part."

"What do you mean?"

"It's kind of a long story. I don't really want to get into it. Sorry!"

"That's okay. We barely know each other. I am not the one to unleash my whole life story on a stranger either," she replied – winking.

We got to the border and waited about fifteen minutes in line. I was dreading the moment – remembering what had happened the last time I tried to cross to the US. When our turn came, the border patrolman asked us for our passports and said:

"Where are you both from?"

"Sherbrooke," Shelly replied.

"What do you do for a living?"

"Student"
"What about him?"
"Him too."
"Where are you heading and for what purpose?"
"We are going to see my dad in Boston. We are spending the summer there before returning for the fall semester."
"What's your relation with this man?"
"He's my boyfriend."
I was dumbstruck by her answer, but kept shut.
"How long have you been together?" he asked.
"Just a couple of months. In fact, we met at school."
"Anything to declare? Fruits, vegetables, meat, alcohol, tobacco?"
"Well, he has his personal cigarettes but nothing more, sir."
"Okay, well, you're all set ... Have a good summer."
"Thank you, sir ... Have a great day," she said – smiling at him and driving off down I-91.
I turned to her and said:
"That was just a big bag of bullshit you just fed to him."
"Well, it was half-true anyways. American customs are always a little stiff. You have to give them the easiest explanations possible. If I had said that I was carpooling with a complete stranger, they could have ripped my car apart and hold us off for questioning and all. It was an innocent lie. You seem like a good guy. You don't have that Unabomber vibe to you."
"Gee ... Are you coming on to me? Hahahaha! It's actually the nicest thing a girl said to me in months."
"So, you're not a nice guy?"
"Oh, yes I am. I just have bad karma when it comes to relationships. I got backstabbed recently and I am still trying to recover from it."

"You mean that literally or …?"

"No … I just mean I got screwed. 'Hurts as much though."

"You poor thing! … Hey! Do you mind if I put on some music?"

"No, of course not! It's your car, anyways."

She reached for a CD that was lying around and put it in the car stereo. She turned the volume up and some country-pop music screamed out of the speakers. I asked:

"Who's that?"

"Oh! It's Carrie Underwood. I just love her. Do you like country music?"

That was a tough one because I hated country music – well outside of Johnny Cash and some classic-rock bands that experimented with it like the Grateful Dead or the Byrds. But I kinda dug this redheaded fox. So, like all men do when they want to please, I twisted the truth and said:

"Well, it's not my first choice, but, yeah, I like it."

"Cool!" she said – turning up the volume – to my demise.

In St Johnsbury, Shelly got off I-91 to hop on I-93 South. We drove for another forty minutes with incessant country music coming out of the speakers and Shelly singing her heart out – to the point it was starting to drive me mad. But she was cute in her passionate rendition, so it put a balm on the pain inflicted to my ears. Suddenly, the road narrowed and gigantic mountains arose out of nowhere – like the silent guardians of the now two-lane I-93.

"What the hell are those?!" I asked Shelly.

"Those are the White Mountains. We are entering the Franconia Notch State Park."

"My God! It's beautiful!" I said – awestruck.

"Yeah, I know!"

The hills were filled with springtime trees being reborn and pine trees at their summit. I fell dead silent at the view of this incredible scenery. After about ten minutes of curve after curve through the valley, I turned to Shelly and said:

"Fuck Boston! You gotta drop me off here!"

"Wha ... What?! Are you crazy? This is a State Park."

"Well ... Drop me off at the nearest town down the road."

"Okay! ... But why?"

"I don't know why. I just have a gut feeling. These mountains are calling to me. Please! I'll pay you the gas money for the rest of the trip. You don't have to worry!"

"Well ... The closest towns are North-Woodstock and Lincoln ... A couple of minutes ahead."

"Perfect!"

"Suit yourself," she replied – disappointed.

She got off at the first exit she saw and got on the Daniel Webster Highway. I told her:

"Just drop me off at the first low-budget motel you find and I'll manage from there."

"Okay! As you wish" she replied – with an almost imperceptible sigh.

After about three miles, I spotted a quaint little place called the Autumn Breeze Motor Lodge.

"Stop there!" I said – pointing at it.

She pulled over in the parking lot and stopped the car.

"Well, this is where I get off," I said.

"It's a shame, I think. Boston is really a nice city," she replied – trying to get me to change my mind.

I really didn't notice, at that time, that she was in fact hitting on me. I only figured it out a couple of days later, but it was too late.

I got out of the car and so did she. I took my backpack out of the trunk, turned to her and said:

"Well ... I guess this is goodbye. Here is eighty bucks for the trip."

"That's way too much!"

"I don't care. You were nice enough to drop me off in the middle of nowhere and lie at the border for me. It's the least I can do for you."

"Gee thanks! ... Can I ask you something?"

"Yeah, sure!"

"I would like to have some news from you sometimes ... Well ... Only if you'd like to ... Anyways here's my phone number and my email address if you ever want to talk."

"I don't have a phone, but I'll email you sometime. Do you have Facebook?"

"No ... Not yet."

"Well, you should. It would be easier to stay in touch."

"Okay ... I'll look into it. It may give me a chance to see your cute smile."

"There you go!" I replied – too stupid to see it again – no wonder I had been a virgin until I turned seventeen.

We kissed each other goodbye on the cheeks – God she smelled good! She got back in her car and drove off southbound – getting back to I-93.

I got into the motel and the clerk greeted me:

"Hello sir! How may I help you?"

"I was wondering if you had a room I could rent for a couple of weeks ... with a fridge, a microwave and all."

"Of course ... Hold on ... Lemme check one second ... Yes, we do ... For how long will you need that room?"

"I really don't know yet. I want to settle around here, but have no clue on how or where to start."

"Okay, well, I could leave the reservation open. I will need a credit card and identification."

"Well, that's sorta my problem, I don't have a credit card. But I could pay you cash right now. How's three months in advance sound to you?"

"Hum! ... That could be okay ... But I don't want any trouble ... And I will need to see some identification first."

I was going to give him my passport, but since this was going to be a clean slate stage of my life, I had an illumination. I reached in my wallet and took out my fake ID – the one Tom had gotten me almost a year prior – and gave it to the clerk. He wrote the information in his registry – while I was counting and giving him a couple of Ulysses S. Grants in advance.

"Well, everything seems in order. Welcome to the Autumn Breeze Motor Lodge Mister Thompson!"

II

Tom was such a jerk. He had given me the name Skipper Edward Thompson on my fake ID. I guess he thought that would be hilarious. Now I was stuck with that identity, goddamn it! I decided to shorten it to Kip Thompson – which sounded so W.A.S.P. to me. The Irish Catholic in me wanted to puke. But I wanted a clean start and I got it.

I took the key from the clerk and went to my room – which was kind of a shitty – but for the price it was perfect – although there was a smell that I just couldn't put my finger on. It had a double sized bed, a microwave and a fridge – the simple basics before getting back on my feet. I spent the night in my room, thinking and writing. I got a couple of ideas down, but nothing really relevant.

The next few days, I walked around the area and sat on the bank of the Pemigewasset River – smoking cigarettes – trying to find out what the hell I was to do with my life. I knew no one, had no idea where I was exactly and had no plan whatsoever about the future. But I was free. I had no obligations and no one to check in with. Plus, I had this new identity. I could be whoever I wanted and undo the wrongs of my past.

As I was strolling down Main Street, I noticed a red wooden building called Truants Tavern. Instantly, I was drawn to it. As I entered, I saw a sign on the door saying: *assistant cook needed / part-time*. I sat down and a waitress came and gave me a menu.

"Would you like something to drink before your order?" she asked.

"Sure! I'll have a pint of your best IPA on tap, please."

"I will need to see some identification."

"Well, of course," I replied – giving her my fake ID.

She gave it back to me and went to get my beer – as I looked at the offerings on the menu. I was so hungry that everything looked delicious. The waitress came back with my IPA and took my order. My choice ended on a panini – I just love paninis.

When she came back with my sandwich, I hastily devoured it. It was actually my first real meal in a while. As I was eating, I looked around me and I thought to myself: "Hey! This place is very nice!" The interior was made of wood and bricks. There were tables all around and a bar which seemed to have a lot of different beers of tap. Looking out the back, I noticed that the tavern also had a terrace – which is always nice on summer days. I could feel that this place and I would be real good friends for the time being.

The waitress came back and asked me if I needed anything else. I told her that, in fact, I did and enquired about the part-time job they had to offer.

"Well, I don't know much. Wait here ... I'll get my boss," she replied.

"Perfect! Take your time. I'll just finish savoring my beer."

She went to the bar and talked to a guy – pointing in my direction. The man left the bar and came in my direction. He was kind of imposing. He was about 6'2" and a little over 250 pounds. He had brown eyes and graying brown hair. He looked like he was in his mid-forties. He came up to me with his hand held out and said:

"Hi! I'm Gerry Sadler and I run this fine watering hole. Sofia tells me that you're looking for work. What's your name, Son?"

"My name's Ea ... Kip ... Kip Thompson, sir!" I replied – shaking his hand – almost forgetting my new identity.

"Haven't seen you around here before."

"No ... I'm a newcomer in the area."

"What brings you here?"

"Well ... I was actually on my way to Boston with a friend, but, I don't know why, I just fell in love with the surroundings. She dropped me off a couple of days ago and continued her way down south."

"Okay ... But ... Where do you live?"

"I rent a room at the Autumn Breeze Motor Lodge until I find a place of my own. That's where you come in sir!" I replied – smiling.

"Well ... Don't get ahead of yourself ... Do you have any experience in a kitchen?"

"I worked for two years in a fast food restaurant and three in a tavern ... So yes, I know my way really well around a kitchen."

That was only a half-truth – having only worked a couple of months at Magnan Tavern washing dishes where the chef had showed me a couple of his tricks.

"Oh! Good! But ... How old are you, Old Sport?" he asked.

I almost laughed when he called me that. I was picturing an older, fatter and poorer version of Gatsby, but I restrained myself and just answered:

"I'm twenty-one, sir."

"Okay ... I'm willing to give you a try. When could you start?"

"Whenever you need me ... But there's only just a slight problem ... I'm from Canada ... and ... I kinda don't have a Green Card."

"I see ... well ... I don't really care. I won't put you officially on the pay roll. You'll receive your pays in cash and will make a little less than the minimum wage. But, on the other hand, you won't have to pay income tax, so it evens out. But all this is theoretical ... 'All depends if you do an okay job."

"Oh, you won't be disappointed, sir!"

"I sure hope not. So how does Friday morning sound? We're not open, but I'll get John to come in a little earlier to show you what to do."

"That's perfect. I can't wait!"

"You look like an okay kid. See you Friday ... and by the way ... meal's on the house, Old Sport ... Now you owe me!" he said – walking back to the bar.

I was ecstatic. I had been there for less than a week and already had a job in a cool place.

I left the tavern, after my meal, with lightness in my heart and a feeling that karma hadn't abandoned me after all. I walked around, under the hot early Mai sun, got to the Pemigewasset River and started skipping stones. It reminded me of the times when Tom and I used to skip stones on the Aqueduct – half-drunk or half-baked – as he was telling me his stories of decadence and debauchery. Even though I could never forgive him for what he had done, I still missed the poor bloke – and that truly pissed me off – I really didn't want to miss him – being too busy hating his guts. I fell in a trance watching the ripples that the rocks made, as they ricocheted on the water.

"Hey, you!!!" said a loud lady's voice from afar.

I turned around wondering if the person was, in fact, talking to me.

"Yeah, you! This is a private property!" said a twenty-something girl from a second story window.

"I am truly sorry, Milady!" I replied bowing.

"And it's not the first time that I see you trespassing these last few days!" she added – fairly mad.

"I truly am sorry. I didn't know this patch of trees was part of your domain. I'll be on my way Principessa. Have a beautiful day!"

"Don't try to sweet talk your way out of it … and don't come back."

"No problema, Principessa," I finished – walking out of her yard and blowing kisses at her.

God I was arrogant, but I was having such a nice day that I just didn't care.

The next Friday, I woke up early and got ready for my first day of work. I walked down to the Tavern, knocked on the door but there was no answer. I leaned against the building, lit up a cigarette and waited for the chef. About fifteen minutes later, a Greek-looking guy came to the door and unlocked it. He turned to me and asked:

"'You the new guy?"

"Yeah! Hi! I'm Kip," I replied – shaking his hand.

"I'm Ioannis. But you can call me John … Everyone does!"

"Pleased to meet you."

John was around 5'10", about 210 pounds, had long black grayling hair with a thick beard – also turning gray. Minus his older-looking hair and beard, he looked like he was in his mid-thirties. He was wearing a Guns n' Roses t-shirt with blue-washed jeans and old Adidas shoes. He really had that 80s glam metal feel to him – minus the mullet or the puffy hair.

We entered the restaurant and he started to explain how everything worked, what was on the menu, how to prepare it, etc. It was a lot of information to assimilate at once, but I was a fast learner. Plus, I was working rapidly. When you've worked in a fast food joint or washed dishes, you're used to the fast pace and the pressure. The restaurant was about to open and the waitress came in.

"Hey John! How you doin' today?" she asked.

"Doing great! Thanks!"

"And you ... You're the customer from the other day, right? So, Gerry gave you a shot, hein?! Sorry, I haven't properly introduced myself. I'm Sofia," she said to me – handing me her hand to shake.

"Hi! I'm Kip!" I replied – shaking hers.

Sofia was a short slim blond girl. She kind of reminded me of Marla. Maybe that's why, even though she was a really nice and attractive girl, I never hit on her.

A couple of minutes later, Sofia screamed: "Okay, it's show time boys!" as she unlocked the front door and changed the sign from "CLOSED" to "OPEN". Clients were starting to come in for their lunch breaks. The orders were pilling up, but John and I handled the situation quite well. Even though it was my first day, it felt like I had done this for years. Gerry came in about an hour after opening time. John said:

"The boss always comes in late. He's a heavy sleeper and you don't want to see him in the morning ... The horror... The horror! Lesson number one: no matter what, you don't wake him up in the morning or you'll get yelled at like if you were a trainee in *Full Metal Jacket*."

"Thanks for the tip," I replied.

John was really a talker while he was working – kind of like Tom was. I almost knew all his life story, just from that first day. He was a nice and sweet guy. He lived in a cottage house across the river, in Lincoln, was married to an Italian girl, had a four-year-old son – his wife was expecting another child. His in-laws had a pastry shop in Franconia and he would do some shifts there too. He was a really busy guy. On top of that, he was heavily into sports. He was a huge Bruins and Red Sox fan. So from the beginning, we started ranting on each other – the old Canadiens vs. Bruins rivalry. He was in all these hockey and baseball fantasy leagues and even asked me to join them. He was also a huge music fan. We had similar tastes concerning 90s music, but he disliked punk rock and I disliked hair metal. As the weeks went on, our talks became even more passionate. In a very short time, he had become a true friend, even though we were almost had a twenty-year difference. He had this big brother attitude towards me – looking over my shoulder and giving me advice and all. He was always inviting me to barbecues at his place – never actually doing any of them.

One day, I came in and there was something bothering me. Since I had been working there, I had noticed a guitar case lying around in the kitchen – always at the same spot. I asked John:

"Hey, bro! Whose guitar is this?"

"It's Gerry's. He bought it in a pawn shop about six months ago, because he wanted to learn how to play … You know a midlife crisis thing … But never really got around to it. It's been lying there ever since, accumulating dust and grease."

"Oh, okay! Do you play music yourself?"

"I used to play drums. But due to lack of time and having a kid, I haven't touched my kit in years."

"That sucks!"

"It's called growing up, Bro."

"Can't wait to be your age … Hehe!"

"Get bent, Kip!"

"Love you too, Malaka!"

When Gerry came in that day, I went to him and asked:

"Hey, Boss! John tells me that it's your guitar that's been lying in the kitchen for the last six months."

"Yes, it is … What's your point?"

"Well, are you planning to use it?"

"I don't know! … Why?"

"Well … To tell you the truth … I've been looking into buying one and I don't know any guitar shops around here and I don't have a car. So, I was thinking that since you're not using it, that maybe I could buy it from you."

"Ummm … Why not?!"

"Cool! How much do you want for it?"

"I don't know? ... It's not a really good guitar."

"I don't care. I just wanna play."

"Let's say ... Ummm ... A hundred bucks. Does that sound okay to you?"

"It's perfect ... Can you take it out of my salary?"

"Ummm ... Yeah! Why not?"

I had the money – it was just easier that way. I still hadn't touched the 200k my father had left me, so the job was just for cash flow. I finally had a pastime outside of watching TV and walking around town. My novel was kind of going nowhere – the damn white page syndrome.

I finally decided to call my mom. I had to use collect call – it would have cost me an arm and a leg calling long distance from my hotel room.

"It's about time you called! I was worried sick! I was picturing you dead in a ditch somewhere!" answered my mom – in a very worried and motherly way.

"I'm sorry, Mom! Don't worry, I'm doing great! I'm living in a hotel room and I'm looking for a permanent place to stay. I got a job, made some friends and all," I reassured her.

"How's your novel going?"

"Slow ... I have no inspiration."

"I'm sorry to hear that. So, I guess, Boston's not that inspirational."

"I never actually made it to Boston."

"What?! ... How come? Where are you?"

"I'm in New Hampshire ... I fell in love with the White Mountains along the way and decided to stay there instead."

"Good for you! I'm glad to hear everything's okay. You better call me more often, young man, or I swear you'll be the death of me."

"I promise, Mom. Well, 'gotta go. I love you!"

"Love you too, Laddie."

III

A few weeks had passed and I had been looking through the classified of the North Country News – the local bi-weekly newspaper – for places to stay. But there was never anything in my price range. To pass the time, I started composing songs and learning a couple of covers. My room didn't have Wi-Fi, so I had to go to the Cascade Coffeehouse and Café – on the corner of Main and Center Street – a block north of my workplace. Shelly had befriended me on Facebook and we were chatting frequently. She was about to come back North to Sherbrooke – for the fall semester. I invited her to make a pit stop on her way up I-93 and spend some time with me. She gladly agreed.

She left Boston on the morning of August 27th and arrived in the valley about two hours later. She met me at the exact same place where she had dropped me four months earlier. I was sitting on a chair outside my room trying to write song lyrics on a piece of paper. She got out of her car and said:

"Hey, you! How's it hangin'?"

"Hey, Shelly. I'm doing great! How about you?"

"Great as well! I'm not too keen on going back to school, but you gotta do what you gotta do!"

"I hear ya! ... So watcha wanna do?"

"Well, it's up to you really. I don't know much about this place."

"We're lucky because it has been raining for the last week down here. It feels good to see the sun once more. I haven't gotten around much either, not owning a car and all. I hear Flume Gorge is beautiful. It's about ten to fifteen minutes north on this exact same street."

"Oh, okay ... Sure! Having been in the city all summer long, a little nature would be welcomed."

We got into her car and drove northbound on Daniel Webster Highway until we got to the Flume. We got into the entrance's main building, I paid for both of our entries and we were on our way. We walked through the ever-elevating path through the woods and talked along the way.

"So, have you met anyone recently?" Shelly asked.

"Not really. Outside of the people from work and the waitresses at the Cascade Coffeehouse, I don't really talk to anyone. So how's your dad?"

"He's great. He's been seeing a new girl recently. She seems nice, but I haven't really got to know her."

"Tell me that next season's Bruins' roster sucks!"

"Nope! You're gonna get your asses handed to you ... Biatch! Savard and Chara are going to ravage your team. Kessel and Krejci are progressing nicely. Plus, we got this new guy coming in called Milan Lucic. He's a 6'3" pest. He's going to destroy your puny players!"

"You'll see ... Kovalev, Plekanec and Streit are going to kick your sorry asses. Plus, we drafted a new goalie, two years ago, called Carey Price. He's supposed to be the next big thing. He may make the team this year. I think Huet's years in Montreal are done."

"Well, we'll just see about that. Care to make a little wager? Fifty bucks says that Boston finishes the regular season with more points."

"You're on!"

We continued the three-mile loop that circled the gorge. It was just magnificent. Suddenly, Shelly did something I didn't expect. She took my hand in hers. I was in shock. I had figured out by then that she had hit on me last April – but I didn't think she would try anything. Having been *friendzoned* so many times, it had always amazed me when a girl made a pass at me. She looked at me and said:

"You're cute when you blush."

"Th ... Thanks," I stuttered back.

We finished our tour and got back in the car.

"I'm starting to be hungry, you wanna go eat somewhere?" she asked.

"Wanna grab a bite at the tavern where I work?"

"Sure! I would love to!"

We got to her car and drove back to North Woodstock. She stopped in the parking lot that was located behind the tavern – next to the Pemigewasset River. We got out and went to sit on the back terrace. Sofia came out and said:

"Hey, Kip!"

Shelly looked at me with a quizzical glare – raising one eyebrow in the process –like The Rock. I uncomfortably said:

"Sofia, this is my friend Shelly!"

"Pleased to meet you!" Sofia said to Shelly, "So can I get you two something to drink?"

"I'll have my usual IPA," I replied.

"And what about you Shelly?" Sofia asked.

"I'm not really a drinker ... Just a glass of water would be fine."

"Coming right up!" said Sofia – as she left to get our orders out to Gerry.

Shelly then turned to me – bowing her head in my direction – and loudly whispered:

"KIP?! What's up with that?"

"Not so loud! … It's a long story. You see, I'm only eighteen, well almost nineteen, and everything here is twenty-one. So, I used a fake ID that one of my old friends had gotten for me. I think he found it funny to put Skipper Edward Thompson instead of my real name. So now, I'm stuck with that name. I use Kip as a diminutive. I wanted a clean slate, well I've got one."

"So, what's your backstory?"

"I haven't gotten around to that yet."

"What have you been telling people about your life?"

"Nothing really … Except that I'm Canadian. I couldn't drop that because my fake ID is a Quebec driver's license."

"Oh, I see! Well, you should really get a backstory. You're a writer, it should come easy."

"Yeah! I guess so."

After our meal, we got back into her car and then to my room.

"Well, I should get back on the road soon. I still have two hours to go and unpack and all," said Shelly.

"Oh okay! I'll let you go on your way."

"I said soon, not now. Mind if I come in? I haven't had a chance to see how you were settled in."

"It's not much. I keep looking in the local paper for a better place."

I unlocked the door and went in. She followed me and closed the door behind her. I turned around and she "jumped" on me – frantically kissing me. She looked me in the eyes and asked:

"Hope you don't mind?"

"Of course not!" I replied – kissing her back.

Our hands were all over each other's bodies. She started undressing me. I couldn't believe it – God! It had been so long! I started undressing her as well. When I was down to my boxers, she pushed me on the bed. She swung around, slightly turned her head towards me – looking at me with her naughty green eyes. She slowly unstrapped her bra and gently pulled down her panties. She turned again in my direction revealing her naked body – damn she was beautiful! – her fiery red hair covering her perfect voluptuous breasts. She walked towards me in a taunting way, took off my boxers and came back up – slithering her nude white silky skin against mine. She *cowgirled* her way on top of me and slid my penis inside of her.

"Don't worry ... I'm on the pill," she said – slowly grinding her hips on me.

I didn't have enough blood making its way to my brain to even think about STDs. It had been so long and I was so excited that it didn't last very long – fortunately long enough for her to cum – in fact, that's what made me explode. She fell next to me – sweaty and out of breath – and said:

"Well that was fun!"

"Oh God, yes! You're amazing! ... Can I confess something?"

"Yes, of course."

"You're actually only my second."

"Well ... You'll always remember me then ... Hehe!"

"Of course! But ... Ummm ... What now?"

"What do you mean by "what now"?"

"Where do we stand?"

"The same way we did twenty-four hours ago: we're good friends. You have your life here and I have mine elsewhere. I don't do long distance relationships. But I would gladly start all over if we ever meet again."

I was a little astonished about what she was saying. I had never met a girl so open, down to earth and pragmatic like that. After the Marla debacle, I wasn't ready for a steady relationship, so it was all good. We then cuddled for another half an hour – talking and caressing each other's skin.

"Now I really gotta go, Eamon … Or should I say: Skipper … Hahahaha!"

"Very funny!" I sarcastically replied.

We both got dressed, she passionately kissed me goodbye and drove back up to Bishop University. I fell back down on the bed thinking that good karma was finally coming back to me.

IV

One Tuesday – mid-September 2007 – I was at the Cascade Coffeehouse, checking my emails, when I noticed a poster on the wall that said: open mic every Wednesday. I thought to myself that it would be nice to finally play in front of other people.

I finished my Earl Grey tea and headed off to my room to practice and figure out a list of songs I could play. I practiced so much that my fingers started to hurt – especially when I was playing on the three smaller strings.

I took a small break and went to the tavern – with my guitar in a backpack-style case – for a couple of beers. I just didn't play really well without having at least two or three beers inside me – I never actually understood why – maybe I felt just more relaxed when alcohol unleashed my inner muse. I tried to get my coworkers to come see me, but they were all working that night. I downed two IPAs and one stout – but wasn't able to get any food in my belly – nervousness and stage fright was getting the best of me. I never played in front of strangers and – especially – no one had ever heard any songs I wrote. I didn't know if people would actually like them.

Around 7:00pm, I left the tavern and headed to the Cascade Coffeehouse. I was a nervous wreck – my breath was short and my heart was racing. I got into the place, talked a little with the owners on how the open mic thing worked out. The lady who was in charge told me that they would take out some tables and chairs near the window and they would install a stool and a microphone there. I was actually the only one that had manifested interest in performing that evening.

About half an hour later, the "stage" was all set up and the lady told me that I could start whenever I wanted. I exhaled a long nervous breath, walked up to the stool, unpacked, tuned and plugged in my guitar, arranged the height of the mic stand and said into it:

"Hi. I'm Kip Thompson and I'll be entertaining you tonight with a mix of original and cover songs. Hope you enjoy."

I then played my "a little over an hour" set. My originals were mostly breakup songs about disappointment and treachery. I was telling my story in them and it showed. Nobody knew me, so they didn't understand. The songs were titled: *Dusk in the Arctic*, *Urban Tales of Cheat and Deceit*, *Lovers in Arm*, *Half-Ment Words* and *Clouds Over the Lachine Canal*. Even the songs I covered reflected how I felt – I played Lagwagon's *Losing Everyone*, Graham Nash's *Better Days*, U2's *Love is Blindness*, Rancid's *Poison*, the Police's *So Lonely*, the Door's *Your Lost Little Girl*, Bruce Springsteen's *My Best was Never Good Enough* and John Lennon's *The Luck of the Irish*. I laid my guts out on that stage singing and playing my acoustic guitar with all the intensity I had built up inside of me.

The people in the coffee shop – which was half-full – were half-listening. Most of them were talking amongst themselves and some were un-vigorously clapping in between songs. There was only one person – a girl – who seemed to give me her undivided attention. She was sitting on a couch in the middle of the place – a coffee mug in her hand. She seemed to pay even more attention to the lyrics of the songs I had written myself.

After my set, I packed my guitar in its case – the audience talking in utter indifference. No encore was asked of me, but I didn't give a crap. Since it was my first live experience, I was just glad to have been able to play. As I was ready to leave, "my only fan" from that evening – the girl from the sofa – stood up and came up to me.

"Hi! I really dig what you're doing. Your lyrics are really deep and personal … A real difference from all that pop crap that's playing on the airwaves," she said – in a somewhat groupie way.

"Thanks! It means a lot to me. I like to reach out to people, even if it's one person at a time."

"But I have a feeling that I have seen you somewhere," she said – quizzical.

I had totally recognized her – but hoped she hadn't.

"I don't see where we could have met. I'm kind of new around here," I lied.

She had that frown that girls have when they are thinking in a suspicious way. I was feeling a little nervous. She had that look that seemed to peer into my soul. That frown then turned into enlightenment. Damn, she had figured it out!

"Yeah, I remember you!" she said – pointing at me – "You're that arrogant bastard that was skipping stones on the Pemigewasset!"

I didn't know what to say – feeling cornered. I said the first thing that came into my head:

"Buongiorno Principessa!"

"Sorry, I don't speak Italian!" she replied.

"It's just a quote from the movie …"

"I know … It's from *Life is Beautiful*, you dimwit! I'm just messing with you!" she replied – winking.

I smiled and asked:

"Hey, listen ... You wanna grab a beer somewhere?"

"Sure!" she replied – with much enthusiasm.

"We could go to the Truants Tavern, I ..."

"Well, to tell you the truth, I prefer the Woodstock Inn Station & Brewery."

"Oh! It's just that I work there and have a discount."

"All the more reason not to go there; you won't have home-field advantage!"

"Fair enough! If it's okay with you, I'll just bring my guitar back to my room at the Autumn Breeze first. Get us a table and I'll meet you there in about fifteen minutes?"

"Sure! I just hope it's not a devious plan to get rid of me."

"Of course not! Who do you take me for? Who does that?"

"Well, you'd be surprised. Some guys are pricks and don't have the guts to say that they're just not interested. Once, a guy came over to my place and, while I was in the bathroom, left by the window, taking my laptop with him!"

"You're kidding me, right?!"

"No! I'm dead serious!"

"Holy shit! What a dickhead! I promise I'll be there in fifteen minutes top!"

"Okay! See you there."

I got my guitar to my room and walked back to the Woodstock Inn feeling ambiguous. This girl seemed to be interested in me – but I was never the one to be good at deciphering those early signs. I walked into the Inn and tried to spot her. She was sitting at a high square table surrounded by stool-like wooden chairs. I walked up to the table and sat in front of her.

"Hello again!" I said.

"Hey!" she replied.

I hadn't really noticed at the café – maybe because of my nervousness – but this girl was gorgeous. She had half-length, semi-curvy black hair, brown eyes, rectangle glasses, scarlet lipstick – uplifting her pearly white teeth – a wonderful smile and enticing curves.

"By the way," I asked, "What's your name?"

"Miranda Wright."

"You've got the right to remain silent!" I added – already regretting the words as they were leaving my lips.

Her smile gave way to annoyance.

"Like I've never heard that one before!" she replied.

"I'm really sorry. I say stupid things when I'm nervous," I shyly said.

"You're nervous?"

"Yeah! A little."

"Don't be … My parents thought it would be funny and original. But I get the same stupid joke every time I present myself and it's starting to piss me off."

"Must be. I'm Kip Thompson by the way."

"I know. You introduced yourself before your set earlier."

"Oh, yeah! That's true … So, tell me about yourself."

"Whattaya wanna know?"

"Well … the basic stuff … like … How old are you? … What do you do for a living? … What do you like? … You know …"

"Well … I'm twenty-four years old … I'm a teacher. I teach tenth grade Social Science at Lin-Wood Public School, in Lincoln … And you already know where I live … You stone skipper, you!"

"Yeah, true!" I replied – a little ashamed.

"I actually live with my dad. I recently got divorced and it took a toll on me. We were crazy in love, but married way too young and it fell apart really fast. We were trying to have a kid, but I have this syndrome that's affecting my ovaries and I had to take these hormones that almost killed me because I had this huge reaction to them. Anyways, the pressure drove us apart and I went back living with my dad and this crazy Cuban refugee he married in Miami a couple of years ago because he impregnated her. She was only eighteen back then ... We only have two years' difference. She's a crazy bitch, I can tell you that. Even my dad is fed up with her, but he hasn't got the guts to leave her. She has him by the balls. He talks to me, sometimes, about disappearing to Panama, but he never does it."

I barely knew the girl and she was unleashing all her life on me. I found that to be a real vote of confidence.

"What about your mom?" I asked.

"Well, my mom passed away. She and my sister committed suicide a couple of years ago. I used to live with them in France, but I decided one day to come to live with my dad because they were becoming heavy on my moral. Looking back, a part of me wished I hadn't left. Maybe I could have done something. I miss them so much. Anyways, that's me: a train wreck trying to get her life back on track and it's not always easy. Other than that, I dated a couple of jerks in the past months, which did nothing to help my self-esteem. As for what I like ... Well, I'm a musician myself. I play acoustic guitar. I also take a ton of photographs. I'm planning to make a side career out of it someday ... You know ... Taking pictures of pregnant ladies or their newborn babies ... Give them the best souvenirs as possible. Other than that ... Mostly reading, listening to music, movies ... The basic stuff that everyone likes."

She paused and asked:

"What about you?"

"Well ..."

I was screwed. I hadn't come up with a back-up story for my false identity. I had to improvise – use my writing skill to come up with something ... and fast. I took a sip of my IPA – which I had ordered while she was telling her story. I began with what I had already come up with:

"... I'm 22 years old. I arrived in the area, from Canada, last April. I work at Truants' Tavern ... Well, you already know that ... I'm trying to find a place to stay other than the motel room I rent for now."

I took another sip of beer trying to come up with something plausible, but I was lost. I then had an illumination.

"My parents both died in a car crash a while back. My mom was working for the health department in Quebec City and my dad was a public relations guy for the Boston Bruins. I had been living with my aunt on my mother's side, in Sherbrooke, since then. Last April, I decided to visit my family on my dad's side in Boston and, while passing through here on I-93, I fell in love with the area and decided to take a footing in the valley. The only problem is that I don't have any papers, being born in Canada and all. My dad was American, but since he passed away, it's almost impossible to have American citizenship papers."

I silently thanked Shelly for half of that origin story.

"I'm sorry to hear that! But the Bruins! Nice!!! Hope they have an incredible season this year," she enthusiastically said.

"Me too!" I half-angrily replied through my shut jaw – ashamed at the blasphemy I had just let out – "Anyways, here I am, trying to restart my life again on new foundations."

"Well, I'm glad you fell in love with the area or else we would've never met."

Her eyes pierced right to my heart and it skipped a beat. My cheeks reddened and I nervously stuttered:

"Yes ... I'm ... I'm really glad."

"So what do you do in your spare time?"

"Outside of playing music ... I wanna write a novel. It's the main reason I set foot here. It felt like a good place to write. I haven't had much luck and inspiration yet though. 'Got a couple of ideas down, but nothing definitive. Next spring, I wanna hop on the Appalachian Train and lose myself in the woods to write. I hear it's not far from here; a couple of miles down Lost River Road."

"Yes! It's so beautiful! We could both go there, next summer ... You know ... Together. I've been up there a lot when I was younger."

After that last part, I was in shock – this girl was implying that we would still be seeing each other next summer. "Well, that's an encouraging sign!" I thought to myself.

We spent the remainder of the evening talking about nothing and everything – like we had known each other for years. After a couple of beers, I walked her back to her place – a split-level off Profile Drive – on the bank of the Pemigewasset. When we got there, she kissed me on the cheeks and wished me goodnight. Her perfume was intoxicating and my heart skipped another beat as her lips touched my skin. She smiled, turned around and got inside her house as I walked backwards out of her driveway – to witness every second of her passing into my life. I then turned around and walked back, light-hearted, to my hotel room.

V

For the next month and a half, Miranda and I saw each other more and more often. We didn't have that much time though, since she was working weekdays at her school and me mostly evenings from Wednesday to Sunday. Our schedules didn't really fit, but we made the most of it – non-stop kissing and having wild passionate sex.

On October 18th, I went to work. Gerry looked pissed off.

"What's the matter boss?" I asked.

"My mom! God she can be annoying!" he replied – discouraged.

"How come?"

"Well, she's pressuring me into meeting and marrying a nice Jewish girl."

"You're Jewish?!"

"You haven't noticed from the kosher burgers we've been serving?"

"Well, no! Sorry!"

"Don't be, because they're not. I'm a goddamn atheist, but I haven't come out of the closet and tell my mom yet. She would just try to cure me or something. Anyways, who would want a forty-six-year-old fat guy who wakes up at noon and manages a pub in the middle of nowhere and who spends his spare times playing PS2 and watching sports on TV."

"I would totally do you, Gerry. I've been secretly in love with you all this time. But I'm not Jewish so your mom won't like me!" I replied – with sultry eyes.

"Shut up Kip!" he replied – unwilling to have a laugh.

"Hahahaha … Love you too, Boss."

"Just get back to work, you dimwit!"

"Yes, Gunnery Sergeant Hartman!"

"Get bent, Thompson! Why are you so cheerful today?"

"Well, it's my b-day!"

"Didn't we celebrate your birthday, like, four months ago, in June?"

Shit! I had forgotten that Tom hadn't put my real birthday on my ID. He had made it June 24th, Saint John the Baptist Day in Quebec; easy to remember, but not close at all to my actual birthday. I didn't know how to lie my way out of that one. I was cornered and had to improvise … yet again. I stuttered:

"Well … Ummm … It's just that today … Is the day … that I…"

"That you what?" replied Gerry – without letting me finish, because I was taking way too much time – he looked really annoyed and quizzical.

I then lied my ass off and hoped he would buy it:

"Well … that I lost my virginity … that I became a man. I celebrate it each year. I call it my second birthday."

"Well, kudos to you. I will never understand you Canadians … Now get back to work!"

"Yes Boss!"

I really came close to being screwed with my own lies, but, yet again, I slithered my way out of there with my inventive skills.

My writing binges, around that period, became really intense. I guess that my meeting with Miranda gave me a boost of creativity – she had become somewhat my muse – if I had really believed that sort of bullshit. Every minute of spare time I had, I was putting down line after line of a future novel. My relationship with her and my environment was finally inspiring me. One morning, Miranda came to pick me up and we headed west on Lost River Road. She parked her car at the Beaver Head Trailhead parking lot and we walked up the Appalachian Train – strolling on for three miles and two thousand feet of elevation – until we reached Gordon Pond. I was so exhausted – trying to catch my breath as we took a pause. Miranda didn't seem affected by the physical and cardio effort.

"How come you're not tired?!" I asked – panting.

"Because I've been running up and down the Appalachian Trail all my life. I'm not a puny city kid like you are! Hahahaha!"

I didn't comment on her rant and just admired the scenery. It was simply so beautiful. The pond was surrounded by mountain tops and spinets – with the occasional broad-leaved trees turning orange and red – reflecting on the mirror-like water. I held Miranda in my arms as we watched the landscape in utter silence – only broken by the sound of birds flying away – maybe heading south for the winter – and squirrels climbing the trees; jumping from one branch to another. We both sat down on the leaf-covered bank of the pond. I took out a pad of paper and a pen from my backpack and scribbled down some ideas – my string of thoughts was rapidly flowing. Soon, I had filled three pages of place descriptions, character backgrounds, glimpses of discussions and a timetable that held everything in place. I was right, back in April, the area had a strange vibe that pushed some button inside of me.

"Hey sweetie, we should start heading back down; night will eventually start to fall," suggested Miranda.

I got out of my thoughts, a little lost, and felt like I had been in trance for a long period of time – like I had just come out of a cavern and was blinded by the sunlight.

"Yeah, you're right. Okay! Let's go!" I replied.

I held her hand and we got back on the Appalachian Trail – the way down was really less tiring than the other way around. An hour and a half later, we were back in her car and she said:

"I'm starving! You wanna go eat somewhere?"

"Yeah sure! You wanna go to Truants'?" I suggested.

"Aren't you a little tired of eating the same food every day?"

"Not really. Pub food and beer could feed me 'till the rapture."

"I never heard you talk religion before. What religion are you exactly?"

That was another thing that I had forgotten. I was raised Irish Catholic, but Kip was a real W.A.S.P. and I didn't know shit about Protestant churches. I knew it was something important in the US – contrary to Canada – and especially Quebec – so I gave her the first one I could think of.

"I'm a Presbyterian ... But I am not a fervent follower. I don't really go to church. I try to keep the link between God and I really personal," I replied – which was a load of crap because I had, in fact, become an atheist around the age of ten – but definitely couldn't say that to her – remembering that Americans are a little too crazy when it came down to the question of religion – "What about you?" I asked – diverting the attention from my lack of knowledge about the Presbyterian Church.

"Well, my dad and I are Episcopalian and his wife is Catholic from the Cuban Church," she replied – the last part being filled with disgust.

She never referred to her as her step-mother, but, instead, as her father's wife or crazy bitch – depending on the situation.

"I don't really go to mass often either ... Maybe once or twice a month," added Miranda.

"So ... Where do you want to eat?" I asked her – to change the subject once and for all.

"Well, I'm more into a traditional American restaurant; a little home style. Do you feel like it?"

"Yeah, sure!"

"OK! I'll take you to this 50s-style dinner on Highway 3. You'll love it! They don't have beer though ... I know you like your beer while eating."

"I don't mind at all. I'm always up for trying new places ... And just to be with you, I would do anything."

"Ah! You're sweet!"

We drove up Daniel Webster Highway – passed my hotel room by less than a mile – and got to the Sunny Day Diner. It was everything that I had expected from a diner – gray metal exterior, red leathered benches and rotating stools – all in a really retro décor. This was awesome – just like in the movies. We sat down and I ordered a filet of meatloaf and mashed potatoes with a Coke.

Miranda was right; it did feel good to eat a home cooked-like meal – it kind of reminded me of my mom's cooking. For the first time since I emigrated, I felt nostalgic – even a little homesick. Miranda pulled me out of my daydream and asked:

"So ... Have you found a place yet?"

"No ... Not really," I replied – discouraged.

"Well, my dad has been renovating this small house, for the last couple of months, which he bought for really cheap because it needed a lot of work to be done on it. He's almost done and he's planning to lease it. If I make my Puss In Boots eyes to him, I'm pretty sure that I could get you a good deal on the rent."

"That would be so awesome! Where is it located?"

"It's about halfway between here and the Lost River Boulder Caves ... Close to the Lost River Road."

"Wow! That would be great!"

"We could go see my dad tomorrow. It's his day off from work, so he'll be at the house renovating it."

"Sure! Thanks ... Really ... You're a life savior!"

"No problem, sexy!"

She bent over the table and I joined her halfway for a kiss.

After dinner, we hopped back into her car and Miranda drove me back to my hotel.

"You wanna spend the night with me?" I asked.

"Sorry Sweetie, I can't. I have to babysit my sisters tonight."

"Oh okay!" I replied – disappointed.

"Don't be sad, Baby! We'll see each other tomorrow morning!" she said – in a motherly reassuring tone – before kissing me goodnight.

The next morning, she came to get me and we drove up to the house she had mentioned the day before. It was located on Russell Farm Road, about two and a half miles from my hotel room. It was a small trailer-park-like beige house with a greyish-blue roof and a small extension in the front of it. We drove up the dirt and gravel driveway and got out of the car. I looked around the entire site. The front yard was huge. The house had been built at a forty-five degree angle from the street – giving it more privacy. It had a patio in the back – which is always practical for summer bar-b-cues, reading or just writing with a nice cold beer in hand. The entire lot was surrounded by trees. It was a real step-up from my second-story apartment in Ville-Émard. After having circled the house, Miranda and I got to the front door and entered my soon to be place.

"Hey Dad! We're here!" she said – as I closed the door behind me.

"Hey sweetie! I'll be right up! 'Just need to screw this thing back together," answered a deep voice coming from a different room.

We took off our coats, sat on the sofa in the living room and waited for him. He finished what he was doing about five minutes later – it had given me time to snoop around while sitting and waiting. The house had an open-air kitchen, dining area and living room – giving it much more space. Everything looked kind of new inside – except for the appliances and furniture – but I didn't really care. Her dad finally came out. Although not very tall, he had that severe and imposing stature that kind of spooked me – having that menacing vibe to him for someone who didn't know him.

"Dad … This is Kip … Kip, this is my dad," she said to both of us.

I held my hand up to shake his.

"Nice to meet you, sir!" I said to Miranda's dad.

"Nice to meet you Kip! You can call me Lloyd."

"Can I call you Frank?" I instantly replied – regretting my wisecracking personality.

"What?" he asked perplexed – stopping shaking my hand but still holding it in a firm grip.

"Well … you … you know … Frank Lloyd Wright?" I answered – ashamed and stuttering.

He turned to Miranda and said:

"So you got yourself a wise guy, eh?!"

I almost peed my pants at that moment. He turned back to me with angry eyes – stared deep into mine – which were filled with terror. He then started to laugh loudly and said:

"You should have seen your face! It was priceless!" – tapping me on the shoulder as Miranda was laughing as loud as him – she knew her dad very well and just went along with the subterfuge to see my reaction – "Don't worry, Son; it's not like it's the first time I heard that one!" he said to reassure me, "I hear you take good care of my baby, that you are a real gentleman, so in my book you're alright to me. Come on; I'll show you around."

We strolled around the place – which came with all the furniture, appliances, electricity, cable, telephone and internet connection. He was charging me eight hundred dollars a month, which was directly in my price range. I was making about 1k a month at Truants and since I hadn't still really touched my inheritance, it suited me well. At first, he wasn't too keen on renting to a paperless guy because I couldn't really sign a lease. But Miranda vouched for me and I offered to give him three months of rent in advance. He accepted the arrangement and we shook on it. I could move in two weeks after that so I had a lot of shopping to do – not having anything outside of a few clothes that were really worn out due to the constant washing. Miranda helped me do my shopping because I didn't own a car – I couldn't even buy one, even if I had the money, because I had no papers. I couldn't find anything directly in the area, so we had to drive to Plymouth's Walmart – a little less than half an hour south of North Woodstock. I had to start from scratch; buying the basics: plates, utensils, kitchenware, food, towels, soap, linen, winter clothes, boots, a shovel, etc. It cost me a fortune. On top of that, we had to make three trips back and forth because all of the stuff didn't fit into her car. I offered Miranda to pay for her gas, but she declined … as I had thought.

A month later, I was all settled in. Winter was slowly creeping in and snow started to cover the surrounding grounds. I was really happy about my new place. It was peaceful, quiet and oh so inspiring. I was writing like hell – erasing half of it in the process because I was never satisfied with it – the God awful artistic angst! Since I had the internet now, I was writing to my mom more often. I was sending her some drafts of my work. She said she really liked it, but what's a mother going to say to her child: "Your work really sucks, Son!"?

I was also chatting with Shelly about once a week. She was really glad that I had found someone that was so good to me and a place of my own. I invited her to come to see me by the end of April – when she was going to go back to Boston – to have a drink, see my new place and maybe meet my girlfriend. "It's a date!" she wrote back.

The only downside to where my home was located was that I had to walk forty-five minutes to get to work and another forty-five to come back – and that was when it was not snowing like hell – sometimes, I would get so cold that my fingers burned like hell when they thawed in Truant's kitchen. Once a month, I would bring my guitar because I would go play a set at the Cascade Coffeehouse – during my hour-long break at the Tavern.

In late January 2008, Miranda, who was almost always at my place, woke up one morning, came to living room – where I was writing another snip of my novel and asked me:

"Do you ski?"

"I'm not sure. As a matter of fact, I've never tried it."

"Do you wanna try today? It's mildly snowing outside and the cover is just perfect."

She kind of caught me off guard and I surprised myself saying: "Yes". I regretted my answer the second it left my mouth. I was kind of a chicken-shit when it came to those kinds of things – needing to be in control of my movements at all times. So skiing, car racing, snowmobiling and all those things where I don't feel a 100% in control were always out of the question. But men always want to please women and try to prove they are tougher than they really are. So I went skiing that day. I dressed up for the part and we left in her car.

"I'm taking you to Loon Mountain. It's going to be so much fun! I haven't skied in years. I used to do it frequently. I even won medals when I was young," said Miranda.

That did nothing to help me appreciate the situation more; it just made it worst. Here I was, a newbie, scared as shit, going to go down a mountain for the first time just to impress his medal-winning girlfriend. Way to go Eamon!

We got to Loon Mountain – on the other side of I-93 – on the bank of the East Branch of the Pemigewasset River. Miranda insisted on paying for my chairlift ticket and rental equipment. We geared up and she gave me the beginner's tips on flatland, as we were heading to the chairlift. It didn't look so hard – a simple question of balance – moving my body weight from one side to the other while maintaining my skis in a pizza slice position.

All seemed well, until the chairlift hit the back of my knees – making me sit and dragging us upwards to the mountain top. There was no turning back now. That's when fright got to me. I started to breathe heavily. I looked at the skiers under me almost *downhilling* their way to the bottom – it looked so easy. We got to the top – the tricky part. As my feet landed on the snow, I had to get up and slide out of the chair. I kind of managed that part. I wasn't too strong on my skis though – like a toddler learning to walk or a three-year-old learning to skate.

I managed to slowly slide my way to the south part of the mountain – trying to follow Miranda who looked so gracious – even though she was wearing a snowsuit. We didn't get very far. She stopped at the entrance of the Bear Claw trail – the easiest one of the mountains.

"Are you ready?" she asked.

"I'm not so sure anymore!" I replied – watching five-year-olds gaining speed to take the hill head on.

That "really helped" with my self-esteem. I looked out at the horizon. The view was breathtaking – mountaintop after mountaintops of pure magic. All around me, it was hill country at its best.

"It's now or never honey ... Follow my lead!" joyfully screamed Miranda – as she pushed herself down the slope.

I loudly inhaled a glacial breath of air through my scarf and followed her. I was sloming my way down the hill – making huge "S" style maneuvers – always ending a little uphill to slow me down before heading in the other direction. After two turns, I knew that I definitely hated skiing. Miranda was nice enough to wait for me all the way down.

"Don't look behind you. The other skiers will avoid you. Don't worry!" she said.

Well, if they were as good as me, no they would not. Every time I went at it again, I thought to myself: "I'm fucking gonna to die!!!" I tried not to show too much that I was scared as hell – I didn't want Miranda thinking I was afraid. When I was almost at the bottom of the hill, I started to go at it with more ease. If I were to fall, the tumble wouldn't go too far – I was more confident. It was not the speed nor the height that scared me, but the fact that I could hurt myself. When we finally came to a stop – at the bottom of the hill – Miranda said:

"Let's go again!!!"

"No way!!!" I thought to myself, but I lied and replied: "Sure! Maybe I'll be better the second time. I think I'm starting to get the hang of it. But this time, go on a harder slope and have fun; don't wait up for me. I'll manage on my own."

"Oh! Okay, Sweetie!"

We got back on the chairlift, up the mountain – I was going to slide down to the same trail I had previously skied on. Miranda kissed me good luck and went further south – taking the Tote-Road Quad lift to the expert slopes. I took a deep breath and went at it again. Through my teeth I was mumbling: "Fuck! ... Goddamn it! ... Why did I agree to this shit! ... I fucking hate skiing! ... Never again! ... I wanna die!" all the way down the hill. It took me like forever to finally end my suffering. At the bottom of the hill, I took off my skis and Robocop-like walked my way back to the rental shop and almost threw the gear at the clerk. I put my boots back on and it felt really weird walking with comfortable and less robot-like footwear. Miranda arrived about twenty minutes later.

"God! That felt so good! I went down three different trails," she joyfully said.

"I only went down the same one and only once."

"It's okay; you'll get the hang of it next time."

I finally had the courage to say:

"Sorry, honey. There won't be a next time for me. I really hate skiing. I'm not cut for this. I did it to please you, but I'll be damned if I ever put on skis again. I love cross-country though, if you want to do that sometime. Yeah! Your boyfriend's a city guy!"

"Hahahaha! Don't sweat it! It's okay. You're not less of a man because you don't like skiing."

"It's not just skiing, but motor speeding and more adventurous stuff as well."

"It's okay. I knew you were the artsy type when I met you ... You city boy you! And you call yourself Canadian! ... Pfff! ... Hahahaha!"

"Hey! Give me skates, a hockey stick and a puck and we'll see who has the last laugh! ... Hehe!"

"Okay! Okay! You got me there. I still don't know how to break."

"There you go!"

"But I don't cry when I skate, though! Hahahaha!"

"You're such a little bitch!"

"I love you too, Sweetie!"

We got back to the car and that was the end of my first and last experience at downhill skiing.

VI

I spent the remainder of that winter indoors, writing, cuddling with Miranda, chatting with my mom and Shelly on Facebook, playing sets at the Cascade and working my ass off – winter was a busy season because of all the people coming in to ski. When we were in a hard rush at work, I would be inside a bubble, focused on the task before me, humming Bruce Springsteen, Simon & Garfunkel and CSNY songs.

      Ever since I had been down there, I was a little less into punk rock and more into folk music – rooted in Americana. It really started to show in my music and some excerpts of my novel. I was drawing inspiration out of the roots of these mountains and their snow-covered tree tops; by the interstate system that brings life from the heart of the continent to all the limbs like arteries; by the people who would listen to what their hearts would say and those hearts were all filled with love and friendship. John would bitch about his wife, but he loved her deeply and would do anything for her. Gerry would complain and scream at us when it became hectic at work, but hugged us at the end of the night, tapping out free beers for us while he bitched about his pressuring mom. I really loved my life there. I was starting to be less Eamon and becoming more Kip. I was always afraid that someone would uncover my lie, but I had covered my tracks so damn well – forging myself a real concrete-like back story.

At the end of April, Shelly wrote to me that she was riding down to Boston and said that she wanted to hop by my new place and check it out for herself. I cleaned the house to make it a little more presentable. In general, I'm not the really clean type – well outside of dishes that is – Miranda was always saying that it was at the point of OCD. My place could be a pig sty, but there were never any dishes lying around on the table or in the sink.

Shelly arrived two days later and knocked at my door early on a Tuesday morning. I got up and answered the door. She looked at me with angry and disappointed eyes and said:

"Here's your fifty dollars, you motherfucker!"

"You're such a sorry ass looser! Hahahaha!"

I had won my bet. The Montreal Canadians would have, that year, their best season since they had won the Stanley Cup in 1992-1993 – their first over a 100-point season in fifteen years.

"That's what you get when you root for losers who haven't won the cup since 1972," I replied – in a very nagging tone.

"You'll see, it's just a matter of time," she replied – annoyed.

"Yeah, right! Like that's gonna happen sometime soon!" I sarcastically said.

After she paid her due, I showed her around my new place.

"Your girlfriend's not there?" she asked.

"No, she's working. You'll meet her another time."

"Yeah, I can't wait! You talk about her so much that I feel like I already know her … I wanna see the woman who made you lose your mind for her," she continued – while exploring each room of the house.

"Yeah, next time!"

But I wished there wasn't a next time – well at least not a next time that she would be there. God! That was a mistake! I had forgotten how Shelly was so awesome and beautiful. I acted all friendly – even brotherly – around her, partly because I knew that she and I were an impossible thing – she just didn't see me that way. Sure, we had sex less than a year prior, but she made it clear that it was just a booty call. But still, I couldn't help myself but think: "What if?" I rapidly brushed that idea from my mind. She was just a friend. I deeply loved Miranda, but still, I had Shelly under my skin. I found her so darn beautiful and interesting. I drank from every word she said and fed through every anecdote. I suddenly understood unfaithful people – not that I would ever do such a thing. It was against all I stood for, but, for the first time, I understood. It was just an animal, irrational craving that was eating me from the inside. But then I thought of all I'd gone through with Marla and I could never make someone live what I had.

We sat down on the couch and we caught up with our respective lives. There was only so much we could write about on the internet. Nothing beats a good old-fashioned face-to-face conversation. She was ranting about school and about the guys she had met on dating sites. She seemed to really have a bad karma when it came to romance – attracting douchebags who only wanted to jump her bones or guys who were not single. She even dated this guy who told her after three weeks that he was leaving a couple of days later for the army. Of course I liked Shelly, but I liked her to the point that I just wanted her to be happy with whomever she was with. I was overseeing her like a brother – caring and protecting her. The situation felt really weird, but I didn't care. Like I said, I just wanted her to be safe and happy. I was giving her advice with the little experience I had. Words just flew out of each other. What could you expect? A writer with a girl in public relations – it was just a marathon of verbal diarrhea. About three hours later, I got up to get myself a beer and asked:

"Do you want anything? I have beer, wine or I could make you a girly drink or something."

"No thanks! I'll take a glass of water though. I never drink anything when I know I'm about to drive."

"That's very noble of you. I, however, am on foot. So I'll drink this one to your health."

"Hahahaha! I wouldn't have it any other way."

We continued to talk for a part of the afternoon, when Shelly said:

"Well, I gotta go if I want to get to Boston before supper."

"Of course! I'm really glad you stopped by."

"Yeah! Me too! You really have a nice place. I'm glad you're all settled in."

"You come back any time you want!"

"I sure will."

"Have a safe trip back and take care of yourself."

"Thanks! 'Will do! Say hello to your girlfriend for me. Hope I'll see her next time. You really seem well and I'm so happy for you!"

"Thanks!"

I leaned towards her to kiss both of her cheeks and she did the same. But as I was getting closer to her, her perfume overwhelmed my senses and it drove me mad. I stayed stoic though. I walked her back to her car and she drove off to hop back on I-93 South. I didn't know it back then, but it would be the last time I would see Shelly in New Hampshire. The next time we would see each other, it would be in a whole different situation.

That summer, I spent all my spare time on the Appalachian and other trails leading up to Cannon, Lafayette, Liberty, Kinsman, Flume and Moosilauke Mountains – with or without Miranda. I brought my laptop with me in my backpack everywhere I went and wrote anywhere the landscape inspired me. I still had nothing definitive, but my novel kept progressing. I kept sending snippets of what I had written to my mom – being the only one to actually read any of my writings. I didn't want anyone else to get a glimpse of it. I read some parts to Miranda, Shelly and even John, but nothing in its final form. I wanted it to be perfect before I made anyone read the whole thing.

End of August came again, but this time, Shelly didn't come back to my place because I was working double shifts – John being sick as hell. He would always get these never ending colds two or three times a year. I was kind of pissed that I had missed Shelly going back to Sherbrooke, but I had obligations, so I missed my chance.

Fall and winter fell in the valley and – before I knew it – Christmas was back again. The weird thing that year was that Miranda had invited me to her dad's place. Of course I had already been there – in their backyard skipping stones on the Pemigewasset – but never before was I invited to come in. I never understood why Miranda had never wanted me there. Of course, I had seen her dad a couple of times – when he came over to repair some things around the house – but I had never actually met her dad's wife nor her sisters. I would get my answer why a couple of hours later.

For one of the rare times in my life, I actually dressed well – which meant that I combed my hair and put on a tie. Miranda and I left for the traditional Christmas Eve supper at her family's place. Her uncle and cousins were there too. They came all the way from Lincoln – not the one less than a mile from there, but the one in Nebraska.

We arrived kind of late that day, because it took forever for Miranda to get ready. She asked me, all afternoon:

"How do I look?"

I would answer every time with a different accent – from Southern to British:

"You look goddamn amazing, Baby! Gawd! You're one fine sexy momma!"

She would say, afterwards:

"No, I don't like how I look! Maybe I should put this on and do this type of make-up instead."

I was starting to be annoyed. I had been ready for the last three hours and was waiting for this insecure princess. Miranda just wanted everything to be perfect. I told her:

"Everything is already perfect. We have each other."

She smiled and kissed me.

We drove to her place, rang the doorbell and waited for someone to answer. The door opened and her dad greeted us with a smile. He shook my hand, kissed his daughter and welcomed us into the home. Miranda introduced me to her cousins and to her two little sisters – who were six and four years old. They looked like two South-American angels with their great big smile. Finally, I met "the" stepmom. Her name was Rosita. She was about 5'3" and weighed about 120 pounds, tops. She had black hair to her shoulders and bangs down to her eyebrows. I shook her hand a wished her merry Christmas. She did the same. There was something about her that I couldn't put my finger on. She was tiny, but had this bitchy craziness vibe that emanated from her entire being. I didn't know if that's what she put out or that I had heard Miranda criticize her too much. After some chitchat, we all settled down to eat the Christmas dinner – a mix of real American and traditional Cuban food. I helped myself to some turkey, stuffing, black beans, rice and fried plantain. It was just amazing. Miranda's dad kept pouring wine into my glass. Being a little drunk, I tried to stop him at one point, but he winked at me and said:

"Come on, Son ... You have a designated driver. Rosita doesn't let me drink this much usually. But if you drink with me, it won't show as much."

I had no choice but to let him pour some more.

After supper – before it was time for dessert – Miranda gave me the grand tour of the house. It was really nice typical American home – resembling at my idea of what a typical American house was supposed to look like. We got to the second floor and she showed me her room. It still had that teeny girly look to it.

"I know it's kinda tacky, but I'm almost never here. I didn't want to invest in redecorating the room," she explained.

I stared out of her window and the view was just breathtaking. You could see the rusted train bridge overlooking the Pemigewasset with I-93 in its back. It was dark, so I couldn't see the tree filled snowy mountains in the distance, but I'm pretty sure it was beautiful. Miranda then said:

"Yes, that's the one! The window where I screamed at you for the first time, you arrogant stone skipper you. Can you believe that it's been already a year and a half ago! Time flies, don't you think?!"

"It sure does, Love ... It sure does."

She held me from behind as we continued to admire the scenery through her window.

"Well, we'd better get down for dessert," said Miranda.

"I'll be right down. I just gotta pee first," I replied.

"It's the second door on your left."

I kissed her and she went down the stairs as I went to the bathroom. I closed the door, pulled down my zipper and started to empty my bladder. I suddenly heard in the distance – with a rough Spanish accent:

"Don't you tell me how I should or should not behave in my own house!"

And then I heard loud screams and things breaking.

I stormed out the bathroom and rushed down the stairs. Miranda was on her back weeping and Rosita was on top of her hitting her like a goddamn hurricane. Lloyd tried to crab his wife, but she held on and continued to hit poor Miranda. I totally froze. I didn't know what to say or how to act. I had a real disdain for violence – to the point that I was unable to do anything when something like that happened. Lloyd was finally able to rip his wife off from on top of my girlfriend. Rosita was still in total hysteria – throwing punches in the air like she was shadow boxing – well more like shadow bitch-slapping. I ran to help Miranda get back on her feet. She was shaking and crying – so were her little sisters. I got our coats and we left the house in a hurry. Before we passed the door, I waved to Lloyd without even looking back.

I got Miranda to the car. She was absent-minded and totally out of it. I couldn't let her drive, so I made her sit in the passenger seat. I sat behind the wheel, started the car and backed out of the driveway. I never passed my driver's permit, but Andrew had made me practice a while back. I was a little hammered, but I stayed focused. So many things could have gone wrong at that moment, but all went smoothly during the two and a half miles to get to my place. Stick shift gave me a hard time. But after two street corners, I got the hang of it.

"What happened sweetie?" I asked Miranda.

She answered in a low and shaky voice:

"My dad was drinking himself silly and Rosita was starting to give him a hard time about it. I only said to her that it was Christmas and that she could lay off him just for one night. After that, she totally lost it and went ape-shit on me. You saw the rest."

"I'm so sorry, baby!"

"Can I stay at your place?"

"Of course! That's really a no-brainer."
"But I mean indefinitely?"
"Same answer … It's a no-brainer."
"Thanks, Love!" she said turning her head towards me. As we passed a streetlight, I noticed something.
"Honey … Don't freak out … But you got a black eye!"
"For real?! Goddamn it!"
She opened the roof light and pulled down the passenger sun blocker. She looked at herself in the mirror, noticed the black eye and said:
"That fucking bitch! I'm gonna beat the living crap outta her!"
"Don't do anything stupid. You could really get in trouble. It could cost you your job. You can't work in a school with a criminal record."
"Yeah! I know … But it would feel so good!"
"I hear you!"
We finally arrived at my place – I could now start breathing again. Miranda asked me – as she got out of the car:
"By the way … Since when do you drive?"
"Since … like … now … I guess," I replied – ashamed.
"It just hit me. It could have been dangerous!"
"Don't worry about that. You were in no shape to get behind the wheel, so I did the only logical thing I could think of."
"We could've walked! It's really warm this year for December 25th."
"Yeah! I didn't think of that … Sorry!"
"It doesn't matter now, does it? Let's just go to sleep. I'm exhausted."
"Sure! But you should put something on your eye to reduce the swelling."
We got inside the house, took off our clothes and Miranda went to the freezer and got a small bag of frozen

peas. She applied the bag on her eye and fell asleep really fast. For my part, it always took me about one to two hours to fall asleep – always having way too many thoughts running through my head. The only time that I fell asleep quite rapidly was when I was drunk. Alcohol saved me from a lot of nights of insomnia.

VII

Miranda had officially settled in with me. She had gotten her stuff from her dad's place when her crazy stepmom wasn't there. She had "girlyed" up my home a little, but I didn't mind – it actually looked nicer. Being a history teacher, she liked vintage stuff from the 50s. She also revamped old furniture – as a hobby – that she bought in garage sales or flea markets. We had our little couple's routine life and it secured me. We were still on different schedules, but made the most of it when we were actually together – watching movies or TV series, playing board games, jamming out songs or hiking along the Appalachian Trail.

During that summer, Gerry gave me a week off – from July 11th to the 18th – so Miranda and I rented a chalet on the bank of Lake Winnipesaukee. It was just a magical week. The first day, it rained a lot, but the rest of the week was almost fully sunny. I had brought my guitar and my laptop and I was letting my creativity run its course, while Miranda went swimming or read a book. We drank ourselves silly as well during the entire week. At 10:00am, beer bottle caps were already popping and – at night – we would be on wine or mojitos. I had never been so drunk over that long a period of time in my entire life. I had never written nor had sex as much as I did either in the course of that week. Like I said, it was just magical – that was until the last night.

I was sitting on the beach – beneath the stars – holding Miranda in my arms as she was sitting between my legs. She then asked:

"How would you feel about having a kid? I'm not saying now, but in a not so distant future."

"FUCK!!!" I thought to myself. I was ambushed, I had no idea what to say. I hadn't thought about Marla in over a year and it all came back in flash. I didn't want to piss off Miranda or offend her in any way, but I didn't want kids ... ever. I never had that paternal instinct to procreate. So I slithered my way through this landmine filled conversation and tried to stutter my way out of it:

"Well ... Uhmmm ... You catch me by surprise here ... I had never really thought about it ... Not that I don't want kids ... It's just ... that ... it didn't cross my mind yet ... But I'm not closed to the idea ... It could be swell ... You would make an extraordinary mom."

"You really think so? You're sweet! But with my ovary syndrome, we may have to consider adoption as a possibility. Are you open to that option?"

"Let's take this a day at a time. We'll see when we get there. But I really mean it baby. You're the most incredible person I have ever met and you have great values. Any child would be lucky to have you as his mom."

"Oh! Stop it! You're making me blush!"

"Don't be shy and accept your awesomeness. I love you, Sweetie!"

I was starting to get out of it by shifting the focus on her. It's then that she finished me:

"I love you too. Like ... I don't want a baby right now ... It wouldn't be right."

"Of course."

As I was ready to sigh in relief, she added:

"We should get married first ... You know ... To make things right."

"FUCK! FUCK! FUCK! FUCK!" was all that was running through my head. As a left-wing atheist, marriage was really not in my values – I just didn't believe in it. I was dumbstruck. My mouth was open, but no words came out.

"So ... Whattaya think?" she asked.

"Well ... Ummm ... Sh ... Shu ... Sure," I stuttered back to her.

I couldn't believe the words coming out of my spineless mouth. I didn't want to get married. In fact, I couldn't even get married. I wasn't Skipper Edward Thomson, a twenty-three-year-old assistant chef and writer from North Woodstock. I was Joseph Eamon Colin Jovanovski, a twenty-year-old Irish-Canadian sonavabitch who had been running away from his problems for the past two years. I had a feeling that my lies would come back to haunt me someday. Damn you, karma!

So here I was: engaged without having gotten on one knee and a soon-to-be father. I was so screwed that I was even starting to think of putting birth control in her food without her knowing it. But I wouldn't sink so low – my mind just wandered a little sometimes.

At the end of that week, we got back home and our lives went back to their "normal" place and routine. The only thing that concretely changed was that I had lost all my inspiration. The idea of marriage and fatherhood artistically emasculated me. I had the blank page syndrome again.

The only person that knew what had happened was Shelly. She was always a big help and a good listener. We thought alike and it did me some good – even though I was heading straight into a brick wall. Still, I played along with the game.

Miranda started telling everyone about the wedding and tried to find a date and a place for the reception. At first, it was supposed to be a really intimate thing – just the two of us with a witness at city hall – or something like that. But – like it is with most women – the wedding blew out of proportion. After a couple of weeks, it was an over a hundred people ceremony – where only three would be from my side – in her church and all. I was discouraged as hell. What had started as a simple non-pretentious thing was turning into some kind of monster. I was trying to slow her down, without any luck. I had myself a progressive girl with fairy-tale principles. I cursed the ghost of Walt Disney at that point – I was no Prince Charming and she was no damsel in distress. We didn't need all this, but I didn't know what to say to her or how to say it. I was kind of stuck. I couldn't walk up to her and say: "Listen honey ... Well, I've been lying to you since day one, but don't leave me, please! I don't want to start over yet again!" Plus, I loved the girl and breaking her heart was way down on my bucketlist. I knew it would have to happen someday – but not like that.

She had scheduled the wedding for the anniversary of our first meeting – not the skipping stone incident – but the Cascade Coffeehouse meeting which was on September 19th. The date was set for September 18th of 2010 and it was coming way faster than I had expected. Miranda was pressuring me into doing stuff that I was always pushing back for later. I didn't want any of this, but I was too afraid to say anything. Money was flowing out of me like a fireman plugging his hose into a fire hydrant. On the other hand, Shelly was pressuring me to tell Miranda – she did deserve the truth – I just couldn't get myself to do it. I was so screwed!

June 19, 2010 was a really hot cloudy day. I had broken a real sweat working that day. After my shift, I took my usual walk back home. When I got on Russell Farm Road, all the lights were off. A power shortage was pitching the neighborhood into darkness. I got in the house and Miranda – who was usually sleeping at this hour – was sitting on the sofa. Candles from the coffee table were illuminating her face from aside. She was looking gloom. I walked a little closer and could tell that she had cried ... a lot. I stopped dead in my tracks and – with insouciance – asked her:

"What's wrong, Sweetie? You look sad."

"Oh, you think! I was doing some cleaning and stumbled on this book."

She took out Steinbeck's *East of Eden* from her side and held it up. My face turned to white and my heart stopped. She continued:

"I had never read it. So after I had done ALL the cleaning ALONE, as usual, I decided to read a little. Then, when I opened the book, oops, something fell out. Can you explain this to me, you lying sonavabitch?!" she screamed – holding up a Canadian passport.

More "FUCKS!" were repeating over and over again in my head. She was looking straight into my *little-kid-who-just-got-caught-doing-something-really-bad* eyes with her disappointed, melancholic and deceived gaze. A discomforting silence filled the entire house – which lasted for what felt like an eternity.

"So ... Who the fuck are you really?" she angrily asked – breaking off the silence and throwing my passport right in my face.

I picked it up and put in my jeans pocket.

"And don't you lie to me now. You at least owe me that, even if it's a little too late," she added.

I deeply inhaled and confessed:

"My name is Eamon Jovanovski and I'm a twenty-one-year-old kid from Montreal, Canada."

"Why are you here?"

"A girl broke my heart and my best friend backstabbed me. I was on my way to Boston and I just fell in love with the place on the way. Then ... I fell in love with you. I was a minor when I arrived with no papers that could get me anywhere except this fake ID that my backstabbing friend had gotten for me. So, I just went along and created this persona."

"So, all this time, you were playing a game. Which part of you is real and which one isn't. And don't you lie to me again!"

"My mom works at Sears and still lives in Montreal's South-West. My dad passed away a couple of years ago from a heart attack. I have never set foot in Boston. I was studying in Montreal to be a writer ... So, that part is true. What I said, what we shared ... That was all true ... All me ... The real me! ... I never meant to hurt you. I forged this identity before I met you ... But by the time we did meet, it was already too late. I'm terribly sorry."

"How can I trust you now? You've broken everything we stood for. This is too big, goddamn it! You're leaving me no choice ... It's over! I never want to see or talk to you again. I called my dad earlier. I'm moving back there. I'm really hoping you rot in hell! Leave and never come back. I loved you so much Kip ... Or whatever your real name is ..."

"It's Eamon ..."

"It doesn't matter what your name is! ... You are dead to me ... 'You understand? ... Dead!"

Even though the situation was so tense, I almost laughed at the involuntary The Rock reference Miranda had just screamed at me. I continued:

"I'm terribly sorry! I love you so much and ..."

"Oh! Cut the crap, please!"

"I do love you! Don't leave me, Baby!"

"Don't "Baby" me!!! You brought this upon yourself! I came this close to calling the authorities. But out of respect for what we had, I didn't. But now, you gotta go and leave me alone."

"I can't go back there … I was dying … Well, you … you brought me back to life. I love you so much!"

"You should have thought of that before you based our entire relationship on a lie. God! I hate you so much right now!"

Tears started coming down my cheeks.

"I'm really sorry!"

"Don't be! You made your choice and …."

"That's what you don't understand; it wasn't by choice, but by necessity that I did what I did."

"It doesn't matter in the end; all you are is a goddamn liar. I'm leaving … Don't try to follow me or try to stop me. It's over … Eamon … Or whatever you call yourself. If you reap what you sow, you'll get yours soon you little motherfucker. I'm outta here!"

She got off the sofa and stormed out of the house going back to her parent's place. I blew it! I totally did.

My heart was beating a hundred miles an hour and I had trouble breathing. I went to the pantry and took out a brand new 40 oz of Jack Daniels. I opened it and started to drink heavily. My throat and stomach were burning from the passage of the hard liquor. I let myself fall on the sofa, took my guitar, put my feet on the coffee table – being careful not to knock the candles down. I played and banged on my guitar, singing my heart out while tears were falling down my cheeks. I continued to engulf as much alcohol as I could.

After about an hour, I had drunk around 20oz and was starting to be pretty shitfaced. My eyes were closing uncontrollably – tiredness and drunkenness were catching up to me. I got up to pour myself a glass of water, tripped on the coffee table and fell flat on my face. My guitar went flying in the air. I was too tired and drunk to get up and fell asleep on the spot. Last thing I remembered was vomiting on the floor – being too wasted to get out of my own filth. Afterwards, everything went black.

VIII

I was woken up by a strident high-pitched sound resonating through my aching head. It took some time for me to get my thoughts in order. I was sweating like a pig. I painfully opened my eyes – trying to focus. Behind me, the sofa, the drapes and the walls were on fire. The sound I was hearing was the smoke detector. It must have been screaming for way longer than the time I was actually aware of it. The adrenaline picked up and I ran out of there – reeling – as fast I could. I stood in shock in the middle of the front lawn and watched, in panic, fire starting to engulf the entire house. First of all, I could have died – if I hadn't woken up in time. Second of all, I had lost everything – the only thing I had left were my clothes, my wallet and my passport that I had put in my pocket earlier that night. It was the middle of the night – everybody was asleep – so no one had noticed the fire yet.

Panic then morphed into terror. What was going to happen now? I did the only thing I could think of at that time: I ran the fuck out of there. I sprinted down the street and made a turn on Lost River Road, heading west

– as far from North Woodstock as possible. I ran until my legs couldn't stand the strain anymore. I stopped to catch my breath and then continued to walk.

I must have walked another three miles when suddenly headlights broke the dead of night. I stopped, turned around and lifted my thumb to signal to the driver that I wanted to catch a ride. He passed me, but slowed down and pulled over on the side of the road. I ran to his car. He pulled down his window and asked:

"Where are you going?"

"As far west as you can take me."

"Oh, okay ... Hop in!"

I opened the door, sat down in this Nissan Versa, buckled up and he got back on the road.

"Hi! I'm James. What's your name?" he asked.

"I'm Eamon. Thanks for the ride by the way."

"No problem. I hate driving alone anyways. When I was your age, I used to hitchhike all the time. Now, every time I see someone hitchin' a ride, I try to pick him or her up."

"I wish more people could be like you. When you need gas, tell me. It's gonna be my treat."

"Gee ... Thanks!"

"Well, you're kind enough to have picked me up."

"So, where are you heading exactly?"

"I'm trying to get back home to Canada ... Montreal to be precise."

"Okay. I can only take you as far as Williston, in Vermont. I'm heading back to my house. I was at my best high school bud's wedding, in Conway, but I didn't want to pay no goddamn hotel. So I sobered up and left the place."

"What time is it exactly? I kinda lost track."

"It's 2:00am ... So ... What about you? What are you doing out here, in the middle of nowhere at this hour?"

I could have lied, but I told a half-truth:

"I pissed off my girlfriend because I lied to her and she threw me out. Having nowhere to go, I thought of going back home, on foot, hoping someone would pick me up."

"Poor bastard! What did you do? Cheat on her?"

"No, nothing like that ... It was a simple issue of trust .... It was always something important to her."

"I hear ya. 'Happened to me once to. I said to a girl, I was getting serious with, that I was going bowling with my buddies, but we ended up at a strip club instead. When I came back, she smelled the cheap perfume and saw glitters on my face and threw me out. Never lie to a woman, that's all I gotta say. They always find out in the end. 'Better be honest from the start, so you'll always have a clean conscience and she will never say that you bullshitted her. What you see is what you get. So ... How old are you, Son?"

"I'm 21."

"I'm 37. Whattaya do for a living?"

"Well, I was working in the kitchen of a pub, but now I have no clue what I'm gonna do."

"For myself, I'm a history teacher. 'Been teaching American history for the last 13 years."

"God! Another goddamn history teacher!" I thought to myself.

We talked all through the almost two hours separating North Woodstock from Williston. When we were close to our destination, he asked me:

"So, what now, Kid? What are you gonna do?"

"I don't know. Maybe try to find a place to sleep a little and try my luck again tomorrow morning."

"Listen ... You really seem like a good kid. You can always crash on my couch for a couple of hours and be on your way after that."

I was a little hesitant to accept an invitation like that from a complete stranger. For all I knew, he could be a serial rapist and be bullshitting me for the last two hours.

But I was so beat and desperate that I accepted his offer. We stopped for gas at a Shell on Williston Road. I paid for it and got myself a bottle of water and some Advil. I was still a little hungover and needed to kill the headache I had. We got back to the car and drove out. He turned on Essex Road and went north for about a mile and turned into his driveway.

James lived in a small mobile-like home, quite similar to the one I had just burned down. We got into his place and he said:

"Well this is my home. You can sleep on the couch. I'll bring you a blanket and a pillow."

When he came back, he added:

"Here you go. Sleep well."

"Thanks! You are a real life savior."

"Don't sweat it. It's a pleasure."

I laid on the sofa and fell asleep – but a light sleep – I still wasn't a 100% safe about sleeping there.

I woke up to the sound of something cooking. I opened one eye and saw James in front of the stove. My movement alerted him and he turned around and said:

"Hey there! I'm making eggs. You want some?"

"Sure, that would be nice. I'm starving!"

I got up and he cooked me some eggs and toast which I ended up devouring. I looked at the time on his microwave. It was already noon. I had slept heavier than I had thought. After my meal, I shyly asked James if I could take a shower.

"Sure go ahead! The towels and washcloths are in the closet next to the shower," he replied.

I went and washed myself. It felt good to get rid of the smell of smoke and the dry vomit I still had on my chin. When I got out of the bathroom, James said:

"Listen Kid, I need to go to Burlington for some errands. Maybe I can drop you off somewhere so you can hitch a ride going your way."

"That would be awesome. I really thank you from the bottom of my heart. It's really nice to finally meet one good soul around here."

"You don't need to thank me. You kinda remind me of a younger version of myself that I have lost along the way. It kinda brings me back and it feels nice."

I took out my wallet and tried to give him the remainder of my money – which was around forty dollars.

"Here ... For your trouble," I offered him.

"I can't accept that. It's no trouble at all," he politely declined.

"But I insist."

"Keep your money. You'll need it if your next driver needs gas money."

"Oh, okay! Thanks again!"

"Would you stop it with the gratitude! I told you, I like the company. Karma is going to pay it back to me some day anyways."

"Suit yourself."

"Are you ready to leave?"

"Give me about an hour to pack my bags!" I replied – laughing loudly.

He laughed as well and said:

"That's the spirit. Okay then ... Let's go."

We got outside. He locked the door behind him and we sat in his Versa. We drove about ten minutes west on Williston Road. He then pulled up into the Holliday Inn parking lot, made a U-turn and stopped.

"Well ... here you go," said James – pointing at the passenger door window – "That's I-89. It will take you directly into the Province of Quebec. You are bound to get some Quebecer family heading home from here. Just be patient. It could take a while. You crazy Canadians are really nice and polite, but don't take many hitchhikers. Must be your fears about Americans and their guns ... Hahahaha!"

I laughed as well.

"Listen James. I have one last favor to ask you. You don't happen to have a sheet of paper or a piece of cardboard and a pen lying around?" I asked.

"Well ... Lemme check."

He opened his hatchback trunk. There was a box there – the kind that holds stacks of paper for printers. He took off the box cover and handed it to me. He went back in his car, opened the glove compartment and took out a permanent black marker.

"Will that do?" he asked.

"It's perfect!"

I tore off the side of the box cover and I wrote a big "Montreal" with the marker on the rest of it. I gave the marker back to James and thanked him – yet again. He shook my hand, while saying:

"Good luck Kid ... and Godspeed."

He got back in his car and drove off. I thought to myself: "What a swell guy!" There are some people that come into your life for a brief moment and disappear forever afterwards. But these people have the ability, in a couple of hours, to bring back your faith in humanity.

I took my cardboard sign, got on the side of Williston Road and held it so drivers could see it. A ton of cars passed, but none of them stopped. I must have waited there for about an hour. It was hot and the afternoon sun was beginning to burn my skin. Plus, my arms were tired from holding up the sign.

Suddenly, a black Honda CRV pulled in the Holliday Inn parking lot and honked its horn. I turned around and the passenger made a sign towards me. I hurried to the SUV – which had a Quebec license plate. The girl in the passenger seat pulled down her window and said with a heavy French-Canadian accent:

"If you want, we can take you as far as St-Jean-sur-Richelieu."

"Perfect!" I joyfully replied.

I hopped on the CRV's back seat as the driver made a U-turn in the parking lot, got back on the street and immediately took the ramp heading north on I-89. The driver and the passenger were two gorgeous twenty-something girls. I had noticed that they were French-Canadians, so I spoke to them in French. It had been three years since I had spoken any French at all, so I was a little rusty – even though I had done my entire pre-college education in that language.

They asked me where I was from, what I was doing in the states and all. I replied without giving too much detail – staying a little evasive on the whole story.

Forty-five minutes later we arrived at the border. I was kind of scared about what border authorities would say – I had been out of the country for three years. The customs officer asked us for our passports. I hadn't checked, but I was in luck, it was still good for two more months. I hadn't thought of that, but I would have been really screwed if I had stayed there. He asked the two girls where they were from and where they had been to. The driver told him that they were both from St-Jean and that they were coming back from Cape Cod where they had spent a couple of days. He then turned to me and asked the same questions. I told him I was from Montreal and that I had spent the last three years with friends and family in New England. He asked us if we had anything to declare. The girls just had a couple of souvenirs and I – evidently – had nothing at all. He gave us back our passport and let us pass. "Well, that was easy," I thought to myself. Canadian customs are really less picky than American ones. We drove another half hour north and finally arrived in downtown St-Jean. The girls left me at the bus terminal. I tried to give them gas money, but they refused and went on their way to their respective homes.

I found an ATM machine – because I only had American currency on me – and took out some money. I then went to the ticket counter and bought one. Twenty minutes later, I hopped on the 400 bus – direction: Montreal. The bus made a slight detour in Chambly and, an hour and a half later, I was back on the Champlain Bridge with the Montreal skyline welcoming me back. I felt a huge pinching in my stomach. I was anxious about what the future would hold for me, but I was kind of glad to be back home.

I got off at Montreal's Bonaventure bus terminal – on the corner of Mansfield and Saint-Antoine Street. I then went to subway station – which was located directly underneath the bus station. I took the Orange line, made a transfer for the Green line at Lionel-Groulx station and then made my way to Jolicoeur. I was finally home after all this time. I thought it would have been harder to come back – with all the bad memories – but it kind of felt good and heart-warming actually – like a mom's home-cooked meal. I knew exactly where I would go. I walked down Jolicoeur Street, made a right on Laurendeau and, later on, a left on Cardinal Street.

I arrived at my destination. I knocked on the door. I heard footsteps coming nearer and, when the door opened, I said:

"Hey Mom! Missed me? …"

Return of the Prodigal Sons

I

"EAMON!!! My baby!" shouted my mom – so loud that the people on the street turned to see where that scream had originated from.

She jumped on me and hugged me really tight without loosening her grip for a very long time.

"Mom! You're smothering me!" I said – trying to grasp my breath – slightly pushing her away from me – without much success.

She finally loosened her grip and let me in her home.

"What are you doing here? I never expected you to come back. Things were going so well for you."

I explained to her all that had happened. She was turning whiter and whiter as the story went on. When it came to the part of me running away from an arson scene, she bitch-slapped me – without even thinking about it. She stared at me with an incredulous gaze – dumbstruck with the story I was building up – and of the slap she had just given me.

"I'm so sorry, Laddie!" she said.

"It's okay, Mom. I kinda deserved that! I made really stupid choices and ended up being such an asshole. I still can't believe that I'm back home. With the fire and the false identity, it's still a shock to me that I made it across the border. I'm glad to be safe though. The only thing that pisses me off is that I lost everything. I'm not talking about my possessions; that's just material stuff. I'm talking about all my writings. My laptop and hand-written notes burned to hell in that fire and, with it, all the progress I had made on my novel. I can't believe that I have to start over again from scratch."

"The only thing that matters is that you are safe and home!"

"I'm glad to be here. But ... Mom ... Tell me you kept all those drafts I sent you!"

"Of course I did. You are my pride! I could print the pages you sent me if you want to start again."

"Well ... The Miranda and fire thing kinda sucked the life outta me. But on the way back, I started to have new ideas. Just hold on to those pages. I may want to take it up from a different angle."

"Suit yourself... I will print them anyways them in case you ever change your mind."

"God I missed you, Mom!"

"I missed you too, Laddie ... Hey! Did you hear that Tom's mom passed away?"

"No, I haven't!"

"Yeah ... She passed away last October. I went to the funeral even though I didn't know her very well ... you know ... outta respect."

"Was Tom there?"

"Yes, he was. We had to postpone the funeral to give him to fly back from Edmonton. But after the burial, he told me that he thought of volunteering to be shipped to Kandahar. I really hope he didn't do something stupid like that! You know he keeps sending me letters addressed to you in case you came back."

"How the hell did he know I left the country?"
"Well ... I told him!"
"You did what?!?"
"I knew you would never make peace! So I'm trying to make peace for you until you change that pig-headed mind of yours."

"Just let it go Mom! You don't know everything. You only know what I have told you. Anyways, I don't want those letters. You can throw them away"

"But he just lost his mom and he may even be risking his life in a war zone by this time. Maybe you should stop being so selfish and give him some slack."

I was in shock. I had never thought of it in that perspective. I had been too self-centered to realize that I may never see Tom alive again. I was so much in treason mode that I had never put myself in Tom's shoes. Of course, he was a prick and an asshole to have done what he did, but I was pretty sure he had paid his pound of flesh since the last time I saw him.

"You're right, Mom. You were always so full of good advice. I missed you so much!" I replied – bowing my head.

"I missed you too, Son," she replied – hugging me again – my weakened bones aching from so much love.

I stayed at my mom's place for a couple of days. I used that time to find a job and an apartment. My mom insisted that I stay with her – but I had my pride – I couldn't overstay my presence at her place. I must have sent out about fifty resumés during that short period of time. The only place that called me back was the Cage aux Sports in LaSalle. I had never thought about that, but if you leave the country for more than six months, your whole identity slowly erases itself – like Marty McFly in *Back to the Future*. I had to reapply for healthcare and social security. I really hated those *Nineteen-Eighty-Four* social imprints. I had overstayed my time in the US and now I had to fight to get my rights back as a Canadian and a Quebecer. I had always hated bureaucracy, but this was just so infuriating. I had to "prove" that I was a goddamn Canadian citizen – which was so friggin' obvious.

With that said, I had found a job washing dishes at the Cage aux Sports. Sometimes, they would ask me to prep up the vegetables that would be needed later on. I had been a chef at Truants' Tavern, but I couldn't put that on my resumé for references – since I was paid under the table and had no green card and all. I was back to square one – even further back if you ask me.

As I reflected on my life, it felt like if the last three years had never existed – three years down the drain. I was doing the exact same job as before I left, I had no novel on the way, I wasn't registered in school anymore and I had no girlfriend nor any friends – for that matter. Even Andrew wasn't there anymore. He and his girlfriend Lisa, had bought a house together on the South-Shore, in Brossard. Lisa was four months pregnant with their first child – I was so happy for them. The only thing I still had was most of my inheritance money. So I went to Ikea and bought furniture, dishes, utensils, pots and pans for my empty apartment. I also had to buy all those everyday things from the grocery store like spices, sugar, aluminum foil, toilet paper, tooth paste, etc. I even bought myself a new computer. In two days, I had spent more than four thousand dollars. My mom had offered to give me some of her things, but I politely declined. I didn't want to take away anything from her that she would have to buy back. I spent that week assembling furniture that I'd had delivered to my new second-story apartment on De Biencourt Street – near the corner of Laurendeau.

When I was all settled in, I felt kind of lost. I really hadn't much to do outside of work. I tried to write, but nothing good came out of it. I had the blank page syndrome – yet again. It was the middle of the summer and it was hot. I went strolling around Montreal, alone. Downtown was squirming with people from locals, to outside visitors who were here for basic sightseeing or a festival. You see, Montreal is a city where – from June to August – festivals are incessantly succeeding one another – comedy, French music and Jazz being the three most popular.

At night, I went bar hopping from one venue to the other – like the Club Soda, the Foufs, the Petit Campus, the Absynthe or Brutopia – depending on who was playing that night. I avoided the Esco and the Katacombes in case I would run into Marla. I really got back to my punk, ska and reggae roots. I fell in love all over again with local bands like the BCASA, the Planet Smashers, Danny Rebel and the KGB, the Beatdown, the Sainte Catherines, the Brains, Hellbound Hepcats, East End Radicals and other Canadian bands like the Dreadnoughts, the Artist Life and, especially, the Flatliners. God I loved that band! I never missed a chance to see them anytime they would come in town. They had just released what I consider to be one of the best albums I had heard in my life: *Cavalcade*. I saw them one day – that summer – at the Underworld. It was a really cool show, but man was it hot – so hot that I was wet from head to toe and was suffocating. I even tried to go into the mosh pit, but I didn't even last a whole song – there was just no air to breathe in the middle of it. Still, it was just mind-blowing.

That whole summer was just shows after shows – which helped me to unplug my brain a little as I lost myself into the music. It felt quite good to finally escape the bad karma that had fallen onto me through those last few weeks.

II

In mid-August, I decided to enlist at Concordia University as a part-time student. Since I was over twenty-one, I could bypass college – I didn't have to go back to Dawson and restart over – which was a good thing. I didn't enlist in any particular program. I just took two courses for my own personal knowledge – and because I was so bored. I chose as courses: *Emigrants and Immigrants: Writing the Irish Diaspora* and in *The Creative Process*. I thought that maybe they would help me with my blank page syndrome. Twice a week, I took the subway back and forth from Jolicoeur to Guy-Concordia station. Both my courses were in the Henry F. Hall building, on the corner of de Maisonneuve Boulevard and Bishop Street. I was learning so much and absorbed everything the teachers said like a sponge. There was really a huge step between college and university courses. I was reading like hell and writing papers. It helped me focus on something else other than self-pity – finally a step forward.

Before or after my courses, I would sometimes go up on Redpath Street and make a right on Pine Avenue to hop on the trail that went up Mount-Royal. Although light years away from the Appalachian Trail, it still kind of felt good. It grounded me back to my roots and helped me make peace with the last three years. After the half-hour ascension, I would get to the Mount-Royal Chalet observatory and blindly stare the city's landscape – the Olympic Stadium with the HoMa slums surrounding it, the Montreal Port with its oil silos, Old-Montreal with its 18th century buildings and historical landmarks, the Golden Square Mile skyscrapers, the four bridges that headed to the South-Shore who were filled with almost non-moving vehicles jammed in traffic and, far on my right, my hood – enclosed between the Lachine Canal – central point of the old fur trade colonial economy – and the Aqueduct – the watery border between my soon to be gentrified quarter and the slums of Verdun.

On September 15th, I was coming back from work and had decided to stop at the Green Stop – the fast food deli on the corner of Jolicoeur Street and Monk Boulevard – under where my dad used to live. As I was standing in line, I noticed a familiar face standing behind me.

"Hey Noémie! Long-time no see!" I greeted her.

Noémie was my old lab partner from science class, back in high school. She stood 5'6", had long black hair with bangs – which stopped at the top of her glasses – and beautiful green eyes. She had these cute dimples when she smiled and sported really nice curves – even more than in high school. She stared at me trying to remember who was talking to her. I could see in her eyes that my face was familiar to her but couldn't pin-point exactly who I was. Then, I saw the spark and the smile that came with it. She unsurely asked:

"Eamon?"

"Hey! You remember me!"

"How are you doing? God, it's been so long!"

"I hear you! I'm doing okay ... 'Could be better. How 'bout you?"

"Same thing here."

"Hey, listen ... Ummm ... Are you busy right now? We could do some catching up?"

"Well, I kinda got to pick up my boy from the daycare."

"Oh! You have a child. I didn't know that."

"Yeah! He's two years old ... Well, almost three in a month. I was pregnant during prom, but it hadn't shown yet."

"Good for you! So who's the dad?"

"You don't know him. His name's Dan. But he's not in the portrait anymore ... Well, I mean we've been separated for a year now."

"I'm sorry to hear that!"

"Don't be ... Anyways ... It's ancient history ... I'm trying to get over it."

"Listen ... Ummm ... If you wanna grab a bite someday and catch up ... I would really like that."

"Oh, Okay! That sounds good. Here's my number. Text me and we'll find a time and place that suits us both."

"Perfect," I replied – while turning over and getting my paper bag containing my two hot dogs and poutine that I had just ordered a couple of minutes prior.

"See you around," said Noémie – as I was leaving.

"Sure will!" I replied – winking at her as I left the restaurant.

I couldn't believe my eyes. After all these years, I had finally had an almost date with that girl that used to drive me crazy. The tide was finally turning.

Noémie and I started to text each other a little, at first, but went a little crazy afterwards – constantly writing to one another – adding each other on Facebook – stalking her profile like a madman – liking every picture of hers on which I thought she was really pretty. She had posted a lot of pictures on Facebook ... and I mean a lot. But I figured out too late that she would receive about fifty "like" notifications in one night. I would look like a crazy obsessed guy. But I was relieved when I received tons of "likes" myself for my pictures.

After a month – on Thursday, October 7th – she had finally agreed to go on a real date with me. I had found out that she was a huge Montreal Canadiens fan too, so we decided to go to the Cage aux Sports where I worked. She lived in Ville-Émard, but worked in LaSalle as a secretary for a notary. She had studied to be a paralegal, but she had never found work directly in that field – settling for a receptionist job, which she hated, but it paid the bills. She met me after her work. She had her ex taking care of her boy until the next morning. It was perfect because she only worked every two Fridays and I didn't work either the next morning. I had had to reserve a table because it was the Habs' season opener against the Toronto Maple Leafs – the place would be packed – I was glad I wasn't working that night.

We sat down and ordered some drinks and our food. I ordered a beer, but Noémie ordered a Coke – she had actually never taken a sip of alcohol in her life – her mom being an alcoholic and a junky – we had that in common – referring to my dad. We talked and talked about everything and nothing. Our orders arrived a while later – I always ate chicken quesadillas at the Cage – that evening was no different. Noémie, for her part, had ordered a simple burger and fries.

"So, what's the deal exactly with your ex?" I asked.

"Well, we were dating and all, about five years ago. We had split up for about three weeks, when I learned that I had become pregnant. He came back to me and everything was going sort of good. Of course we had our ups and downs … like every couple. He found me controlling and obsessive, but he was always lying to me and I never really trusted him. Last year, I caught him cheating on me. Well, actually, I didn't catch him in the act, but one of his exes, with whom I had become friends, spilled the beans that she had slept with him once and couldn't cope with the guilt anymore. She also said that she wasn't the only one; that he was bragging about it to his male buddies. I was so furious that I threw him out. He's still trying to deny his cheating to me ... at least the extent of it. The problem is that he was not the first guy to cheat on me, so you can guess that my self-esteem was not very high to start with. He destroyed what was left of it. I never really liked myself, but now it's even worse. Plus, my pregnancy screwed up my belly and my breasts. I can't even look at myself in a mirror without almost crying."

"Are you kidding me? You're gorgeous. Those guys are just assholes who don't get it ... Can I confess something?"

"Sure ... Go ahead."

"I had a huge crush on you in high school, but I never had the courage to ask you out because I thought you were way out of my league."

"Oh! I never noticed!" she replied – somewhat in shock.

"I have always been good at hiding my feelings."

"You are flattering my ego, but it still doesn't change the perception I have of myself."

"Time will heal that. Once you start to see yourself for who you really are ... kinda like I see you ... you'll have the world at your feet."

"Awww! You're so sweet."

We kept on talking while slightly watching the game – we weren't really following it – too much absorbed in our conversation – not noticing that Montreal had lost 3 to 2 to the goddamn Maple Leafs – it's almost as painful as getting beaten by the Bruins. By the time the game was over, I had her hand in mine – and butterflies in my stomach. We paid our respective bills and she said:

"Listen, my sister and some of our friends are playing pool at the Skratch ... Wanna join them?"

"Sure!" I replied – happy the date wasn't over but also sad because I had hoped that she would have suggested somewhere more "intimate".

We took her car and drove a little further down Newman Boulevard.

When we got there, she introduced me to her sister and her friends. They seemed really nice. I was a little shy because I didn't know anyone – but God her sister was hot! – she kind of looked a little like Noémie, but somewhat different at the same time – and she was way more open and forward towards other people. I started to imagine myself with Noémie AND her sister – an instant hard-on. But I quickly brushed that idea off – I kind of felt like Tom for a second and that gave me goosebumps – and not good ones – kinda like when Sideshow Bob gets a rake in the face.

We spent the remainder of the evening talking and shooting pool. I kinda sucked but I still was better than Noémie, so it was all good for my semi-macho self-esteem. After two hours of pool, the others wanted to grab a bite. She asked me if I wanted to go with them. I agreed – although I was starting to be a bit tired. I got back into Noémie's car and we headed to the Tim Horton's about a block further west – on the corner of Newman and Shevchenko Boulevard. I ordered a simple coffee while they ate donuts – as we all just sat in the restaurant talking and talking.

Around 4:00am, my eyes were drowsy. The group decided to head back to their respective places. Noémie turned to me and asked:

"What do you want to do? You want to call it a night and head back to your place or do you want to come to mine?"

Like I would pass on this opportunity! My answer was, of course:

"I would love to see your place!"

Once again, we got in her car and we drove off to her place – a second-story apartment on Beaulieu, between

Allard and Raudot Street – near the Monk subway station. When we got there, she showed me around and asked me if I wanted anything to drink. I politely declined the offer.

"Hold on ... I'll go put on my pajamas ... I'll be right back," she said – leaving me kind of perplexed on the kind of sleepover invitation that was offered to me.

I took no chance and played along. I took off my socks and jeans – keeping my t-shirt and boxers on. I slid under her bed sheets and waited for her to come out of the bathroom – half-expecting lace and stockings – which would have been such a dream come true. But – to my demise – she came out wearing a camisole and sweatpants. She got under the sheets – next to me – and we talked, talked and talked some more – my eyes closing by themselves. I was fighting to stay awake. I found her so beautiful that I didn't want to miss one moment.

Around 6:00am, she said:

"Oh boy! It's really late. I am so going to pay for the lack of sleep later on."

She closed the light and wished me goodnight as the sun was rising. I wished her a good sleep as well and approached to finally kiss her. She reciprocated, but it was really not what I had expected. It was really quite good and all, but, at the same time, very short and expeditious. She then turned around in a sleep-like position. I did the same – taking her in my arms and spooning – gently caressing her arm and hip. The feel of her skin and the smell of her perfume was driving me mad. I had such a hard-on, but tried not to let her know I was this aroused.

Her alarm clock rang five hours later. I was a little comatose, but it was nothing a good coffee couldn't fix. We got up, got dressed and had breakfast. She didn't drink coffee, so she had none at her place. She had to go get her son before 1:00pm, so after breakfast we talked a little. As I was ready to leave, I kept waiting for her to kiss me good-bye. But since there was no move coming from her part, I came closer to kiss her. It was like the previous night, really good, but short – like her heart was not really into it – or that she was ashamed or something. I let it pass on the account of first date awkwardness.

I left on foot and headed to my place, which was really not far from there – about a short twenty minute walk. Finally, when I got back home, I crumbled on my bed and fell asleep again for another four hours.

When I woke up, Noémie had texted me saying that she had a great evening and all. Also, she apologized for her behavior concerning my advances – at least concerning my "hopes" – giving me the "it's not you, it's me" routine. It was bizarrely the first time I actually believed it. She told me that she had always hated her body and, because of that, she always had trouble being with someone skinnier than her. She wrote that the night before, she had wanted to go further, but just couldn't do it. I told her that she was crazy to think that; that in fact she was just a beautiful girl who had gone out with the wrong people; that she should see herself as I saw her. She was flattered, but apologized – I didn't push it further. We stayed friends though. We texted each other a little less, but still often. She came to watch hockey at my place a couple of times – where I would make these killer nachos for the occasion – talking for hours and barely watching the game – always having this unspoken sexual tension between us. Nothing ever happened though. At least I had made a good friend along the way.

III

All through this time – from before my departure from North-Woodstock to this cold December day of 2010 – I had continued to chat with Shelly. We kept in touch at least once a week. She had finished her B.A. in communications and her dad had gotten her a job working for the enemy – the Boston Bruins – in their public relations department. They were having a terrific season. She called me on December 15:

"Hey Buddy! How are you doin'?"

"I'm doing okay … Nothing great, but I can't complain … What about you?"

"Well, I'm in Buffalo tonight. We're playing the Sabres. But tomorrow night, we'll be at the Bell Center. I was wondering if you'd like to come in our box to watch the game?"

"Are you insane?!? Of course I wanna go!" I almost scream at her – out of pure joy.

"The only thing is that's it's a Bruins box for the night, so don't you come wearing a Canadiens jersey or get too emotional if Plekanec or Cammalleri fill the goal."

"You gotta be kidding?!"

"No, I'm not. I'm doing you a favor. Plus, I miss you, dipshit. So, you play by my rules … Understand?"

"Yes Mistress … As you wish, Mistress."

"God, you're such a pain in the ass sometimes. Hahahaha!"

"Yeah! I love you too, Shelly!"

"OK, I'll meet you tomorrow in front of the Bell Center around 5:00pm. Be there!"

"Of course I will! God! I have never seen a live hockey game. You just made my day … Hell, you just made my year, Lady!"

"Hahahaha! Glad to hear it. Anyways, I gotta go. I got work to do before the game tonight. See you tomorrow … Kisses! … And, by the way, I hope Lucic will bruise a couple of your players!"

"Shut your mouth, Wench!"

"Hahahaha! See ya!"

"Yeah! See ya!"

I hung up the telephone, harboring a huge smile.

The next day, I called in sick at my workplace – fake coughing and talking like I was on the verge of dying from having a huge fever. My boss wasn't too happy that I was missing work – a Montreal vs Boston game always packed the place up.

I prepped up that afternoon – taking a shower and making myself presentable. At 4:00pm, I walked to the Jolicoeur station and took the subway up to Bonaventure. The station is a focal point in Montreal. It connects the central bus and train terminal with the 1000 La Gauchetière – Montreal's po'boy Rockefeller Center – and the Bell Center – home of the Montreal Canadiens. In downtown Montreal, you can get around almost everywhere without setting foot outside – using the subway lines and various tunnels – which is really practical come winter time.

When I got out, I lit a cigarette and walked to the Bell Center's main door. As I drew closer, I saw a pretty redhead waiting and looking around. I walked up to Shelly and yelled:

"Hey there, foxy momma!"

"Eamon!" she screamed – jumping into my arms and hugging me.

God she smelled good!

"How are you doing?" she asked.

"I'm doing well! How about you? God you look great!" I complimented her.

"You're just saying that ... But you're sweet ... You sweet talker, you!"

"You don't know how much it means to me that you invited me!"

"Glad I could do this for you. But it was more to please myself than you. You see ... Being on the road all the time, I don't have many friends to talk to. Messenger can only get you limited human contact. I wanted to see you, but I'm working tonight. So I put one and one together and got you a place in the box. But you do have to cheer for the Bruins though."

"You only said that I couldn't wear my Habs gear. You never said I had to root for the enemy!"

"Ah, come on!"

She got close to me and whispered in my ear:

"I'll make it up to you later on ... Don't you worry about that!"

I instantly turned red and was prepared to accept anything. For all I knew, I could've found myself handcuffed, hanging from the ceiling, with a gag ball in my mouth, without even noticing how I got up there.

"Anyways, they're going to win the cup this year," she finally added.

"Blah, Blah, Blah! Boston hasn't won anything since 1972. During that time, the Canadiens have won seven cups."

"Care to put a wager on that? ... Let's say the fifty bucks you stole from me last time?"

"You're on! It's gonna be easy money ... yet again!"

"You're so full of yourself!"

We got into the Mecca of North-American hockey, got up a couple of escalators and got to the Boston Bruins box. She presented me to everyone there, including her dad. I felt small in my pants with all these NHL big shots surrounding me.

"'You hungry? Everything's free ... Including beer," asked Shelly.

"Hell yeah! I never turn down free food anyways."

The game started about an hour later. It was a real fast pace game. The box was quiet after the first period because the Canadiens were up 3 to 1. I was secretly grinning and was having this inner sadistic pleasure. Shelly knew I was having a blast and playing the comedy of being falsely offended by the score. She looked at me with a glacial look. I winked at her and blew her kisses. She was livid. But the game wasn't over. There were two more periods to be played.

At the end of the second period – as I was eating my second nachos order and drinking my third beer – the score was now 4 to 2 – it could still go either way. When Lucic made it 4 to 3, with five minutes to go in the final period, I started to get nervous. But Carey Price held the fort and the Canadiens finally won the game. I was ecstatic inside but let out a: "Goddamn it!" just to please Shelly and her co-workers.

After the game, she had to leave for an hour to take care of the post-game press conference. I spent that time pacing in the Bell Center corridors, looking at the pictures of the team's rich history. I had told Shelly I would meet her in the Cage aux Sports – that was located on the ground floor – around 11:30pm. I got there around 11:00pm, ordered a beer and watched sports highlights and news on the giant screens all around.

Shelly arrived around 11:40pm – looking tired.

"Is everything okay?" I asked her.

"Yeah, yeah! It's just that two games in two nights are always hard on the system. But the upside is that we're only leaving tomorrow morning. I have a room at the Marriott, just here on the corner. You wanna join me?"

"Yeah, sure! Of course!"

I thought to myself: "Wow! A hockey game and a five-star hotel! I'm so lucky!" Being with Shelly, on top of that, was just icing on the cake. On our way to the hotel, I gladly ranted about the Bruins' loss and she kept punching me on the upper-arm. That girl could throw punches! But it didn't stop me. I was on cloud nine.

We entered the cheese grater shaped Marriott Chateau Champlain and took the elevator up to the 26th floor, to where her room was. It was very spacious and luxurious – well at least for my social standing. I went to the window and looked at the incredible view that laid before my eyes. A city at night is just breathtaking – illuminated skyscrapers – ant-like people squirming through the snowy streets – the rotating light of the Ville-Marie making circles around the Golden Square Mile – the Saint Lawrence River as a black hole sucking all the light – except for the ones from the bridges to go athwart. It was like urban poetry to the eyes.

"Are you coming?" asked Shelly – getting me out of my visual trance.

I turned around and hadn't even noticed that she had undressed herself and was waiting for me on the bed, only wearing lace panties – her fiery red hair half-covering her voluptuous breasts.

"Oh! I'm coming all right!" I replied – overwhelmed to have sex for the first time since I had left New Hampshire.

I undressed at a very fast pace – like my life depended on it – and jumped on the bed – like a clumsy WWE wrestler – almost bouncing off the bed upon my landing – as Shelly was laughing her ass off. I crawled between her legs and started to kiss her to shut her up.

That night we made love several times. I was like a machine and she was insatiable. Everything was perfect – the right key to unlock lust and passion. We were perfect together. It just pissed me off that she didn't see that. For her, it seemed that I was just some good friend she could fool around with when time came. For me, she was more than that. I honestly thought that she could be the one. So I took everything she threw at me, like a goddamn junky. At least I'd have a piece of her for a short time, although it felt like dusk in the Arctic – the last rays of sunlight before another six months of darkness.

The next morning, the hotel wake-up call drove me out of sleep way too early – but I could sleep it off later at home. Shelly and I got up and got dressed.

"Listen Shelly" – I told her in a shy voice – "We need to talk …"

"I know what you're going to say and please don't. I don't have time. I have to hurry up. I have a charter plane to take with the team to get back to Boston."

"But …"

"No buts Eamon. You know I really like you and all. But you and I have different lives and want different things in life. You're a real sweet kid, but I'm just starting my career and I'm always either in Boston or on the road with the team. I don't really have time for a relationship. It's not you … It's me!"

Oh God! The *it's not you it's me* routine again.

"Okay. I understand," I replied – melancholic. "And do you have other guys like me on the side in other cities?" I shamefully added.

As the question left my lips, I regretted asking it.

"Oh, look at you, Mr. Jealous," she replied – like a little girl talking to a puppy. "Not that it's any of your business, but no I don't. You're actually the last guy I had sex with. Didn't it show last night?"

"I just thought I was THAT good."

"Well, you kinda are, but I made reserves for the months to come," she said – winking at me and adding: "I just don't have time for all that bullshit. You, I know and like … So it's easy."

"Are you calling me a slut?" I asked – falsely offended.

"Indeed I am. You're my little man whore!"

We both burst into a laughing frenzy. When we got our serious back, she kissed me and said:

"I'll try to come see you more often. I promise. Or you could get your friggin' driver's license and come see me you know."

"That would be an idea."

"Okay! I gotta run or I'll miss my plane."

"No problem!"

We left the room, got down to the lobby, where she checked out. We went outside and she hailed a cab.

"Well, this is goodbye," I said.

She kissed me on the cheek and replied:

"Be good now! And write to me often."

"Will do!"

She got into the cab and I said:

"Have safe flight …"

She smiled and closed the door. As the cab drove off, I added:

"… I love you" – without her hearing any of it. I heavily sighed.

IV

Christmas time came around. Andrew and Lisa had invited the entire family – at least what was left of it – to their home. Andrew had arranged for his mother to come pick-up both my mom and I in mid-afternoon. I was ecstatic to see him – it had been such a long time. It was a kind of warm December 25th and it wasn't snowing – so the roads were all clean. We only had a fifteen minute drive to do.

Andrew and Lisa had bought a 1970s bungalow in Brossard, on Bienville Avenue – near Milan Boulevard. We were the last one to arrive. Outside of Andrew and Lisa, only his sister Julie, with her new boyfriend, were there. I then realized that we really had a small family. As we entered, Andrew yelled:

"Hey lil' cous'! Long time no see!"

He walked up in a fast pace and hugged me with his Hulk-like strength – almost crushing my ribcage.

"Missed you too, bro," I replied – as the air was being pushed out of my lungs from his bear hug.

"Sorry!" he said, "I always forget how frail and weak you are."

"That I didn't miss, though," I sarcastically replied.

"Hahahaha! Welcome back and merry Christmas!"
"Thanks!"

I took off my boots and coat and got in the house.

"Hey Julie! How are you doing?" I asked my cousin – giving her kisses on both cheeks.

"I'm doing great! I'd like you to meet Charles, my new boyfriend," she replied.

"Nice to meet you," I greeted him – shaking his hand.

"Same here," he replied.

Andrew put a beer in my hand and said:

"Here you go! I bought IPA just for you."

"Oh! You remembered! Thanks!"

"Don't sweat it! Cheers!"

We clunked our bottles together.

"So tell me everything!" he said.

"Do you have five hours to spare?"

"Hahahaha! No, I don't. Summarize it in a PG-13 story, so that our moms' ears won't bleed."

I laughed. I told him the basic story leaving out details – especially the arson part.

We sat at the table for supper and had a traditional Irish Christmas meal – consisting of a roasted goose, stuffing, mashed potatoes and plum pudding half-drowned in whiskey. My belly was full and so was my heart. It felt really good to see my entire family and knowing that I had people that loved me and could rely on. I kind of had forgotten that when I left Montreal. I was seeing everything so darkly, back then, that I had put away the basics – family is always there to pick you when times are gloomy. That supper kind of recharged my batteries.

On the way back home – half-drunk on the backseat of my aunt's car – my mind was racing a hundred miles an hour. I started having all those ideas for a novel.

"Hey, Mom! Do you have a pen and a piece of paper?" I asked.

"I don't know, lemme check," she replied – searching through the rubble inside her purse like an archaeologist looking for the missing link.

It took so long that I said:

"Forget it Mom, we're home in two minutes."

"Sorry Laddie!" she replied.

"Nah! It's okay."

They dropped me off first and I said:

"Thanks for the ride, Aunty. Have a great Christmas you two!"

"Aren't you going to kiss your mother?" my mom asked.

"Yeah! Yeah! Sure Mom!" I replied – leaning over to kiss and hug her.

"I love you, Laddie!"

"Me too, Mom! Thanks for being there!"

"No problem! It's my job as a mom!"

"Yeah! But not everyone as a mom as great as you."

She smiled and I could see a tear building in the corner of her eyes. She closed the passenger-seat car window and they rolled off into the night. I climbed the stairs to my apartment, got in, threw my coat on the sofa and sat in front of my computer with two bottles of wine, a glass and an ashtray – embarking on a long night of writing.

I ended up crumbling drunk on the sofa, six hours later, exhausted and mentally drained. I was woken up by the telephone. It was my boss at the Cage. I had totally forgotten that I was working at noon that day. I got up – not bothering to change – and rushed to my workplace. My boss wasn't too happy. I don't know if it was only because I was late or because I stunk like a goddamn hobo and that my tongue was red and purple from all the red wine I had drunk the previous night.

"I'm sorry Mr. Townsend. It won't happen again! I promise."

"I sure hope not! Now get to work. You're behind on your prep. There's a game against the Islanders tonight so we may not have a lot of people. But still, you better hurry up."

"Will do, Sir!" I replied – getting straight to work – still a little woozy from the night before.

At least, I finished at 5:00pm, so I went back home – tired. I laid on my bed and was pissed because I couldn't sleep. My head was again rushing with ideas. So I mixed, in a tall glass, a lo-cal Rockstar with Jack Daniels and went back to writing until the early hours. In two nights, I already had twenty pages down. The ideas just flowed naturally from my brain to the tips of my fingers. I was just out of touch with reality. I had cut myself off from the outside world – with the Sainte Catherines' *Dancing for Decadence* pounding in my earphones on repeat mode. I was proud of myself. It was like an epiphany. It was the first really good stuff I had written since that day when Miranda discovered I was a fraud.

Two weeks later, I went back to school – this time taking three new courses at Concordia –*The Novel, American Literature from 1914 to Mid-20th Century* and *Post-War Canadian Fiction*. I was learning so much, it was uncanny. Since I was reading and doing essays for those courses and working full time in between, I didn't have as much time to write my novel as I would have liked. I had cut down going to shows as well. I just didn't have time anymore. I wasn't seeing anyone and had no friends whatsoever. I was like a hermit who got out once in a while. The only contact I had with the outside world was when I was chatting with Shelly and Noémie. It was going to be my life until the end of the semester in late April and I was okay with that.

End of April, I had rendered every paper due for school, did all my exams and was finally off for the summer – well from school at least. I had had a great run and my grades were averaging around A-. I was ready to get back out in the world – even though Shelly was being a sore winner when the Boston Bruins eliminated the Habs in overtime on game 7 in the first round of the playoffs – ranting and flooding my Facebook wall with Bruins publications – "Go fuck yourself!" and "Get bent bitch!" were my only two friendly answers to this tragedy. I had thought of going to see her in Boston, but I was scared to cross the border – in case there was a warrant on my head for the arson – not knowing if Miranda or her dad had pressed charges about that. I didn't want to take that chance and rot in an American jail and be some inmate's bitch. So, every time she would suggest that I come down to see her, I made up a stupid excuse not to go. When the Bruins came into town, I was always working or had a class, so I couldn't see her – and that pissed me off.

On May 3rd – early in the evening – I was writing a couple of pages more of my novel on my laptop. It was good to be out of school because I had more time to finally dive into it. It was pouring rain outside and thunder storms were pounding across the sky. It had been hot and humid the last previous days – more than it usually did this early in May. Suddenly, the doorbell rang. At first, I wasn't sure because I had my earphones on and was listening to the Dreadnaught's *Polka's Not Dead* on my I-Pod. I took off one earphone and waited. The doorbell rang again – so I put my music on pause, put down my I-Pod and went to answer the door. When I opened it, I saw a man – soaked from head to toe – wearing a military uniform and cap, relying on a cane to stand up.

"FINALLY! ... TOM HAS COME BACK TO MONTREAL!"

I turned from white to red in seconds, clenched my hand into a fist, swung my arm and hit him straight in the face as hard as I could. He went flying and fell – back first – on the balcony's metal railing. I looked at him – he seemed in pain and shock – and said:

"Eamon 3:16 says I just whipped your ass!"

V

I approached Tom and presented my hand to him. He took it and I helped him to get back up. He was limping, so I bent to fetch his cane and handed it to him.

"I kinda deserved that, I know. But I think you broke my nose!" he said – holding his nose and sniffing.

"You don't know how long I have waited to do that! But don't worry, it's out of my system now. Wanna come in?"

"Really?! Of course I do! Thanks!"

He got in – relying on his cane to walk – and went to sit on the couch.

"Like your new place!" he said lighting up a cigarette.

"How the hell did you find me?" I asked.

"Your mom. 'Was there about twenty minutes earlier. I didn't know you were back in town."

"I didn't know you were either … When did you get back?"

"Last night ... 'Stayed in a motel on St Jacques. It was a cheap, but real nice. 'Called myself a hooker. Man she was nasty. The things she did with her mouth. Oufff! She had these huge natural t…"

"God! You haven't changed at all, you douchebag! 'Still the same motherfuckin' Irish asshole!"

"Why fix it when it ain't broken."

"I'm not sure about that ... What the fuck happened to your leg?"

"Got ambushed by Talibans in Kandahar. Dodged the bullets, except the two that ended up in my foot. My bones down there are in shambles. After two weeks in the infirmary and rehabilitation in Germany, I finally had my ticket out of the army."

I found out about a month later – when he was drunk as hell – that he had, in fact, shot himself in the foot because he couldn't stand life in a war zone anymore.

"Glad you're alive!" I said.

"Yeah, me too. I'm happy to see you, Bro. And I'm really sorry about what happened. I was drunk and ..."

"I don't want to hear about it ... Ever. Let's pretend like it never happened. If you can do that, you and I are gonna be good ... Understand?"

"Of course! No problem here ... Hey! 'You got anything to drink?"

"Sure! Whattaya want? Water, Pepsi, Beer...?"

"Got any whiskey? And some ice for my nose?"

"Like I said, some things never change."

I went to pour him a glass of Jack Daniels and get an ice pack for his nose, but when I came back, I saw him open a bottle of medicine.

"What are those?" I asked.

"Painkillers ... Morphine," he replied.

I handed him the glass and he downed two pills with a shot of liquor.

"I ain't no doctor, but I'm sure you shouldn't be drinking while on morphine."

"Well ... I'm not operating heavy machinery ... that is outside from my cock. Hahahaha! No, seriously, my foot is killing me and it's the only thing that numbs the pain."

"As long as you know what you doing."

"No ... I actually don't know what I'm doing, but it beats the hell from not doing anything. At least I get some relief."

"So what's your plan now?"

"I have no friggin' idea whatsoever. My mom passed away ... You must have heard about that?"

"Yes and I'm really sorry for you."

"Thanks ... I'm okay now ... But I took it rough when I buried her. I even had the stupid idea of volunteering to be sent to Afghanistan after that. Anyways, like I was saying, I can't go there anymore and I really don't have any friends ... Well, outside of you, of course ... All my stuff is in a storage place I rent. I don't have any place to go ... You think I could crash here until I find my own place?" he asked – downing another sip of whiskey and looking at me with puppy-like eyes.

I inhaled and exhaled heavily, looked at him in desperation and replied:

"Yeah, okay! ... But I only have one room though."

"It's okay. I can crash on the couch. Sure beats my improvised bed at the Patricia outpost in Nakhonay."

He took another gulp of liquor and added:

"Thanks dude. It really means a lot to me what you're doing. I'll never forget it."

"Don't sweat it. The only thing I ask is that you keep it clean and, for the love of God, don't bring any hookers or one-night stands here!"

"Where would I go?"

"I don't know? To their place or a goddamn hotel room ... Just don't bring 'em here ... Understand?"

"Sir! Yes, Sir!" he yelled.

"OK, Private Joker ... Cut it out!"

It was kind of fun – at first – having Tom around again – it drove me out of my isolation. Plus, Tom was the bible when it came to finding anecdotes to put into my novel. He didn't do much moving around – because of his foot – so we mostly stayed home and talked a lot.

"So how was it back there?" I one day asked him.

"Like you would expect any war zone to be ... Maybe worst. It wasn't like facing a regular army. The enemy could be anywhere and could be anybody. You always had to watch your front and your back for ambushes or IEDs. The entire country is filled with landmines that would rip open our humvees like they were made of cardboard. We were trying to help those poor bastards who, at the same time, were resenting us. It was a really weird feeling, like they didn't understand that we weren't the enemy. Thirty years of civil war and religious extremism will do that to a nation. We tried to train the local police and army, but they have a different mentality, which is mostly based on ancient medieval tribal laws. Let's put it this way: it was hell. I'm just glad to be home; I was going crazy out there."

"But why the fuck did you volunteer in the first place?"

"Like I told you, my mom had just passed away and I was kinda lost. I thought that if my little contribution could change something, it could buy back some of the wrongs I had done in my life ... and that includes you. But the first time I got fired on and saw civilians and army buddies getting blown up, I regretted my decision. But it was already too late."

"I think you paid your pound of flesh. You don't have to feel guilty anymore for what you did to me ... And, for what it's worth, I'm really sorry about your nose."

"It's fine, it's been three days now. It's gonna heal crooked I think. But the booze and morphine help the healing process," he replied - winking at me - gulping vodka directly from the bottle.

He had downed an entire bottle of Jack and of Captain Morgan since he had set foot in my house. I watched him drink and I think he had noticed my concern. He said:

"Don't worry, I'll buy you new ones."

"It's not really the bottles but your drinking that concerns me."

"Well, this world sucks. You can't even imagine the horrors I witnessed all in the name of ... Of fuckin' nothing. People are fighting to push their truth with their combat boots to try to justify their military looting."

He took a long pause and added:

"I guess you're right. You were always like my good conscience, this angel watching over me, trying to prevent me from doing stupid things ... But not managing to prevent all of them ... That one's on me though."

"Damn! Afghanistan made you into a deeper person. I had never really heard you talk like that."

"I think I must've aged fifteen years in the few months I was there ... So what about you? Why did you leave the country? What made you wanna come back?"

"Same thing as you, but with no blood on my hands. I don't really wanna talk about it."

I was getting a little tired of telling the same story over and over. Plus, I knew Tom would keep interrupting me and would want details about my sex life with Shelly and Miranda. I did not want to give him that satisfaction. And on top of that, I was pretty sure he would have high-fived me for burning down the house. So I kept the entirety of my time in North Woodstock to myself.

Tom would really leach on my attention. I think he was bored or something. Once I set foot in the house, I was screwed. I couldn't even write anymore. So I would pretend to take a summer course. But, in fact, I was running off to write in hiding. If it was a sunny day, I would go to the Quai-de-la-Tortue Park in Verdun and sit on the pier. If it was raining, I would go to the Marie-Uguay House of Culture, on Monk Boulevard, or simply ride the subway from one end to the other. I never knew why, but the subway always inspired me – must be because of all the people getting on and off. I liked making up stories around what I imagined their lives could be like. Anyways, through that process, I had managed to get another twenty pages down.

VI

In the middle of the night, or early morning – depending on how you look at it – of June 16th, I was woken up by a phone call. I tried to find my phone – a little lost of having been sucked out of sleep in the middle of a dream. When I finally found it, I looked at the time – it was 3:30 am. I answered my phone – half-asleep:

"Hello?"

"YOU OWE ME FIFTY BUCKS, BITCH!!!!!!" screamed Shelly – so loud that I had to take the phone off of direct contact with my ear.

"You're kidding, right?"

"Nope. 4-0 ... Game 7 ... Bye bye Canucks, HELLO STANLEY CUP!!!!"

"You woke me in the middle of the night to tell me that?!"

"Shit! I forgot about the three-hour time difference between Vancouver and Montreal. Sorry!"

"It's okay. I'm glad to hear your voice, even if that means I have to hear you gloat."

"And you won't stop hearing me 'till next November ... Hahahaha!"

"It's gonna be a long summer!"

"You better believe it, Old Sport."

"I like your Gatsby reference."

"I knew you would! Anyways, I gotta go. There are still celebrations here, but we got a private place. We didn't want to piss off the Vancouver people. Some of them even rioted after our win. We're leaving later on. It's gonna be wild at Logan when we land tomorrow morning. I'll have a lot of work to do."

"I'm sure you will ... Well, it was nice ..."

"Hey ... Wait! I'm going to Quebec City to see my mom in three weeks. Wanna meet me there and catch up?"

"That would really be nice. You're gonna laugh at me, but I've never set foot in Quebec City before."

"There's a first time for everything ... Good, then it's settled. I'll write to you to fix the exact date."

"Perfect! See you then."

"See ya ... And don't forget my fifty bucks ... Mouhahahaha! Now go back to sleep ... Kisses"

"I won't! Kisses!"

I hung up the phone and went back to bed with a smile on my face, not because the Bruins had won the cup – that pissed me off big time – but because I was going to see Shelly.

A couple of hours later, I woke up and went to the living room. Tom was already up. He was sitting on the couch in his boxers – my laptop on his lap and a cigarette hanging from his lips. He turned his head in my direction and said:

"Dude! 'You workin' next Tuesday night?"

"No ... why?"

"NOFX are playing at the Metropolis with Old Man Markley and Teenage Bottlerocket!" he replied – puffing out smoke from his mouth.

"'Could be nice."

"Whattaya mean: could be nice? It's NOmotherfuckinFX ... it's gonna be legen ...wait for it ... dary"
"But what about your foot, dude?"
"Nothing a little morphine won't numb. But you gotta come because I already bought the tickets."
"What if I had something else planned?"
"You would have canceled for your old buddy right here."
"You're such a douche"
"Yeah! But you like me that way!"
He exhaled another puff of smoke and added:
"By the way, I put them on your credit card."
"Wait ... What!?"
"Yeah! Your wallet was lying on the table. I thought you wouldn't mind."
"I do mind! I don't mind for the tickets. I just mind that you just took it without asking me first."
"Hey! You were sleeping. Plus, I wanted to hurry before it was sold out."
"That's not the point ... The point is ..."
"Okay, okay! I get it! Sorry! Geez! I'll ask next time before taking anything from you. Don't get so bitchy. You're not my girlfriend you know."
"And you're a guest here ... So try acting like one!"
"Okay, dude! Chill out ... I got it, I told ya! ... I made some coffee if you want."
"Yeah ... Thanks!"

Five days later, we walked down to Jolicoeur station, took the Green Line train down to Saint-Laurent station and then walked to the Metropolis – which was just around the corner. The place was packed – they had sold all the twenty-three hundred tickets for the show. Tom was really hyped. He couldn't stop talking – mostly about "the good old days" – when we were younger. It felt good to do something out of the house with him for once. This was our first show together in four years. Tom said:

"Man! I really missed this. There's not much entertainment in Edmonton or Kandahar."

There weren't many chairs for him to sit down, so we stayed up – until a nice guy saw Tom leaning on his cane and offered him his place. I stayed standing up – I never liked to sit down during shows – I prefer to move and jump everywhere. Normally, Tom and I would be somewhere in the moshpit, but he couldn't do that anymore – at least not for the next couple of months ... or years.

Teenage Bottlerocket and Old Man Markley were awesome, but when NOFX came on, all hell broke loose – and I mean that in a good way – it was just mind-blowing. It was everything you would expect from a NOFX show: classics, covers, five songs in seven minutes, an hour of music and half an hour of talking where Fat Mike and El Hefe would insult each other and people in the crowd and putting on bras that some girls threw on stage. One word: Epic. The only downside was that they didn't play *The Decline* – the greatest punk-rock song ever – eighteen minutes of pure magic. I went into the moshpit a couple of times – feeling bad for Tom – but I couldn't pass on the opportunity.

After the show, Tom and I went to grab a beer at the Foufs – which was only less than a block east from the Metropolis – on Sainte-Catherine Street.

"That was some show, bro!" said Tom.

"Yes, it was!"

Tom put his Saint-Ambroise Pale Ale half in the air and toasted:

"To renewed friendship. I deeply missed you. You were always like a brother to me."

I lifted my beer, clunked his and said:

"To friendship and family".

He looked me straight in the eyes and I could see all the sadness, loneliness and the gratitude he felt.

At one point, I was almost certain that he was going to cry, so I changed the subject:

"Wanna shoot some pool?"

"Yeah, sure! Why not?"

Since he came back, I was seeing a totally new side of Tom that I had never seen before. I didn't know if he had matured or if the army had fucked him up. Sure he was his old self most of the time – a cocky loudmouthed player – but there were other times – like that night – where I actually saw a lot of sensitivity in him. After all these years, he finally let his guard down and opened up. I think seeing him like that shook me up because he emptied the pool table in just two turns – limping around it between each shot. We played about three games and I got slandered during each one of them. After I "cried uncle" and admitted my defeat, he took his cane and we walked back to the subway and headed home. I would always cherish that night as one of the best ones I had had with Tom in my entire life.

VII

"Hey Tom! ... I'm leaving for Quebec City," I told him – at the last minute.

"What?! Why?" he asked.

"I have three days off, so I plan to visit the city."

"What's your sudden interest in Quebec City?"

"Well, I've never been there and I figured it was about time."

"Cool! Can I come?"

"Well ... Ummm ... You see ..."

"Hahahaha, I'm just messin' with you. I don't wanna visit that right-wing city ever again ... Lots of bad memories ... So what's her name?"

"What're you talking about?"

"Oh, come on dipshit?! I know you ... What's the name of the lucky lady?"

"Ummm ... Shelly."

"I knew it! Hahahaha! Got a picture?"

"I'm not showing you her picture ... Forget it!"

"Oh, come on! You know I never back down ... I'll either flip through your phone while you're sleeping or beat the crap outta you 'till you show me."

I knew he wasn't bluffing. So I took out my phone, flipped through the pictures, found one of Shelly and showed it to him.

"There ... 'You happy now?" I said – annoyed.

He grabbed the phone out of my hand and looked at her picture.

"Dude! You're kidding me, right?"

"No why?" I asked – scared he knew her – or something worse.

"Bro! She's fuckin' hot! Even I could never get a girl like that!" he replied – drooling over her picture – "You lucky dog! Damn. Does she have a sister ... or better ... a hot mom?"

"God, you're sick!"

"Hahahaha! You know me ... Where did you meet her? Does she have a special government grant to date retards?"

"Get bent Tom!"

"Hahahaha! No seriously ... How did you score a girl like that? Man! She's WAY outta your league ... Even mine for that matter! If such a thing is even possible."

"We carpooled to the US four years ago and we stayed friends."

"Friends?!"

"Yes ... She made it clear that, with her career, she didn't have time for a serious relationship."

"Hey, you got the best of both worlds."

"You know I want more in life than that."

"Yeah, I know ... You're a hopeless romantic!"

"And you're just hopeless ..."

"Wait ... Where did I hear that before?"

"The Bouncing Souls ... *Hopeless Romantic*."

"Oh yeah, you're right ... So what does she do for a living?"

I hesitated for a couple of seconds. Tom asked:

"Is it that shameful? What ... She's a stripper? A hooker? A deputy for the Conservative Party? A convict in an all-women prison? Yum! I could see them stripping each other out of their orange prison uniform."

"God you're sick! And they don't wear orange uniforms in Canada!"

"It's a shame if you ask me!"

"No ... It's none of that ... It's even worse than that!"

"Oh my God! She's a serial killer?!"

"No ... She's ... a public relation's agent for ... Ummm ... the Boston Bruins!"

Tom pushed me and said in shock:

"Get outta here! I knew she had a flaw somewhere for going out with you! Leave this apartment right now. I've faced the Talibans, but this is just unacceptable to me. How could you do this, you traitor?! I don't know if I can ever talk to you again now that you are sleeping with the enemy."

We then stood there staring in each other's eyes – impassable. It didn't take long for us to break out in tears laughing. Tom finally got some seriousness back into him and said:

"Seriously, Bro ... I wish you the best of luck ... You of all people deserve it ... Go get her Tiger."

"You are really just a little too fond of quoting popular culture."

"What was that from? I have no idea!"

"Spider-Man ... Mary-Jane ... Ah! Forget it!"

I took my backpack, bro-hugged Tom and – before going out the door – I turned my head and shouted:

"Don't do anything stupid!"

As I was going down the stairs, Tom replied:

"Always! Mischief managed!"

"You're doing it again!"

"What am I quoting now? ... Hahahaha! I'm playing with you ... That one was on purpose."

"You're such a dick."

"Yeah, I know!"

I walked to the subway, took the metro up to the Bonaventure station and wallowed through its subway halls until I reached the Montreal Central Train Station. I had decided to take the Via Rail line instead of a regular bus – I had never taken a train in my life – well that is outside of the subway, of course. I paid for my ticket and boarded the middle wagon. About fifteen minutes later, the train departed east on the tracks. During the entire trip, I found myself writing – missing most of the scenery along the south shore of the Saint Lawrence River – I was too deep into my novel to notice anything. Sometimes, I would get nicotine rushes and would stare out the window and look at the trees and rivers along the way – blindly staring at the Saint Lawrence Valley's beauty. But it wouldn't take long for me to plunge back onto my laptop and start typing again.

After a three and a half-hour train ride, I finally arrived at the Quebec City Central Station – which is located in Lower Town, near the port. As I got out, I looked around for Shelly, but she was nowhere to be found. So I lit up a long overdue cigarette – gazing at the surrounding scenery – being not too impressed – Quebec City was kind of looking like any other North-American city. The train station – on the other hand – was astonishingly beautiful. As I finished my cigarette, I saw, on my left, fiery-red hair approaching from afar. A small grin instantly lit up my face. Shelly came up to me and said:

"Hey laddie!"

"Please don't ... My mom calls me that."

"Oh! I'm sorry ... 'You doin' okay? How was the ride? Where's my fifty dollars?" she asked – so full of herself.

I looked at her and she had that cocky satisfied glare in her eyes. I handed her a Mackenzie King, sighed in despair and replied:

"It was okay. 'Gave me time to write a little."

"Well, good for you. What do you wanna do?"

"I don't know? It's actually the first time I'm setting foot in Quebec City."

"Okay ... Well ... We'll do the virgin tour ... You know ... For first timers."

"I'm not stupid, I got that!"

"Just in case. Follow me. Hope you got some good walking shoes."

"My Doc Martens should be fine."

We spent the afternoon walking through the Petit-Champlain quarter and then uphill to Upper Town – beyond the walls surrounding Old-Quebec. My first impression changed drastically after that. Upper-Town was breathtaking, with its 17th and 18th century architecture, little restaurants, European-like hotels, the Chateau Frontenac and the various churches. We then went outside the walls – still in Upper-Town – along the Citadel and the Quebec Parliament building. For supper, she took me to the Grande-Allée Tavern located on East Grande-Allée – on the corner of de la Chevrotière Street. We sat on the terrace – where she ordered a Tavern Grilled Cheese and, I, a smoked meat poutine with a pitcher of IPA. As usual we talked and talked – both of us having the verbal diarrhea syndrome. She was rendering all her excitement of the Stanley Cup win in Vancouver and the parade in the streets of Boston that followed. I knew she was rubbing it in, but I didn't care – I let her have that moment. Plus, she was so beautiful with all that glitter in her eyes as she was telling her stories. As for myself, I mostly talked about Tom – a subject I had always kind of avoided with her. She listened to my entire story with great attention and was in shock at this persona I was describing to her.

"How can you be friends with such a guy?" she asked.

"He's like family ... The brother I never had. I don't know ... I have this gut feeling that I have to look out for him. We've been through so much together. Part of the reason I am the person I am today is due to him. He's a tender but broken human being. But you can only find that out once you break through his armor. Outside of that, he just looks like an obnoxious womanizer ... But I know better."

"If you say so," she replied – with not much conviction in her tone.

After dinner, we went walking again. She told me she had rented a hotel room because she wanted us to have some privacy outside of her mother's home – which was located in Charlesbourg – a suburb of Quebec City. I welcomed her initiative. She had rented a room at the Krieghoff – a small hotel boutique on Cartier Avenue.

Later on that evening, we got up into the room but, bizarrely, we didn't have sex that night. The strangest thing about that was that I actually liked it. We talked, cuddled, took a bath together, kissed a lot and spooned until we fell asleep. For once, I did not feel like a piece of meat. For once, I thought I was breaking through her reluctance to be with me. For once, I was having a couple-like evening instead of a "friends with benefits" one. Even if it didn't go anywhere else, I finally had that one night I had dreamed about. I felt like such a girl thinking that way, but who gives a rat's ass. Like Tom always said: I was a hopeless romantic.

The next morning, I woke up a little before Shelly did and I watched her sleep – she looked so peaceful and calm as opposed to when she was awake – I always had trouble placing a word through her cute verbal diarrhea. My heart was pounding, trying to escape my chest. That's when I realized she was actually the one – THE one. The only problem was that she didn't see it that way. So – although my heart was yearning for her – my head was trying to get me to cut the shackles that strapped me to her and try to move on with my life – which was easier said than done – having never met anyone more interesting or more beautiful in my life. I had had two serious relationships, but they could never live up to the one I barely had with Shelly – even though we only had spent minimal time together.

She then woke up, we kissed, got dressed and went downstairs to have breakfast at the little café that was part of the hotel.

After breakfast, we headed to the Quebec City Aquarium – in Sainte-Foy – for about two hours. I always liked to see animals from all around the world – although I found it sometimes inhuman to keep them locked up for our selfish amusement. We then headed on foot to the Domaine-des-Retraités Park – across the highway leading to the Pierre-Laporte Bridge. I never understood why, but I had always been fascinated and amazed by bridges. I just found them beautiful. We strolled along the riverside park – hand in hand – serenity through silence – just gazing at the tree patches landscape and the Saint-Lawrence River fauna acting out its daily routine. We sat down along the riverbank – blindly staring at it all. It reminded me of the times where Miranda and I used to sit near Gordon Pound or Eliza Brooke along the Appalachian Trail. I suddenly felt kind of nostalgic. After a while, Shelly drew me out of my daydream and we headed back to her car and then back to the hotel room where she screwed my brains out for three hours. I was out of energy and we fell asleep.

The next morning, I had to get back home and Shelly drove me to the bus station –I didn't want to take the train this time. I kissed Shelly goodbye and asked:

"When will I see you again?"

"I don't know, I'm going back to Boston soon. Free agent season starts July first. It's gonna be hell. Although I don't think we'll be very active on the market this year, winning the Stanley Cup and all, we have a pretty good base."

"That's it ... Rub it in my face again!"

"Every opportunity I get, I take ... Hahahaha!"
"Okay ... Well ... I'll see you around then."
"Of course! Take care of yourself, sexy!"
"Yeah, you too!"

I turned around, left to get my ticket and hopped on the bus. It was a boring ride back. Highway 20 is not the most inspiring road. I tried to write a little, but I didn't have much inspiration that day. I was tired and, I didn't know why, but the trip left a sour taste in my mouth. Maybe it was the feeling of having a one-way relation with Shelly.

I got to the Montreal Central Bus Terminal – near the Berri-UQAM subway station – took the subway and walked the couple of blocks back home in a robotic fashion. I was all in my head, thinking, and I didn't even notice how I got back home – being on some sort of automatic pilot. I unlocked the door and stepped inside. Tom laid on the couch, a long stylish Asian-looking pipe lying on the floor next tom him.

"TOM!" I said loudly.

He didn't even budge. "Ah fuck it!" I said to myself. I went to my room, which was pitch black, and turned on the light. I jumped when I noticed there was a naked girl in my bed, foaming at the mouth. Her arm was elastically hanging in mid-air with a used up syringe lying on the floor beneath it. I shouted, to myself:

"OH, YOU GOTTA BE FRIGGIN' KIDDING ME!"

VIII

I walked up to her, carefully looking where I was setting foot – making sure I didn't step on anything dangerous. I put two of my fingers on her carotid to see if she was still alive. There was a pulse – a faint one. I hurried out of the room and yelled out:

"TOM!!!!!!"

Still he didn't budge.

I went into the kitchen, filled a pitcher of cold water and threw it right in Tom's face. He opened his eyes and mouth in shock and angrily said:

"Dude! What the fuck?!"

"Why the hell is there a naked girl in my bed? ... She's half-alive, unconscious and foaming at the mouth!"

"Oh God! That stupid bitch! She's O'd-ing on us. Call an ambulance fast!" he replied – dizzily getting up, a little out of breath and going into my room.

I called 911 as he tried to slap her back to reality – without any luck.

"What the fuck happened here, Tom?" I asked – annoyed.

"I met these two girls at the RV bar last night and brought them back here. We had this intense threesome. It even turned into this kinky roleplay where I ... "

"Tom, goddamn it! I don't care about that! What the fuck happened exactly?!"

"I was getting there ... Geez! ... Anyways, one of them left after a while and the other fell asleep in your bed. My foot was hurting from all the standing up while I was doing doggy style and all, so I came to the living room and smoked a little of the opium that I had managed to smuggle out of Afghanistan. But I seem to have passed out on the couch. The rest is out of my knowledge. This girl seems to have shot up not so long ago. She would be dead otherwise."

"God, Tom! What were you thinking bringing strangers over here?! You promised not to fuck any girls in my home!"

"I promised not to do it while you were there! Anyways, they both had boyfriends and neither of us had any money for a hotel. I just couldn't pass on the opportunity. Do you see how hot this girl is? The other one was even hotter! She had these huge b..."

"Junkies foaming at the mouth, dying on my bed, don't turn me on ... God! You piss me off!"

"Chill out a little! It's not like she advertised that she was a junky. I had no idea!"

"You didn't notice the holes and bruises on her arm?"

"Well it was kinda hard while I was fucking her from behind and her friend's ..."

"Ah, fuck you! It's really not the time to make jokes or brag, you dipshit!"

"I'm just saying ... Geez! I had no idea."

In less than ten minutes, the ambulance had arrived. One of the two guys gave her an adrenaline shot and she started to cough, while the other asked us what had happened.

"I don't know ... I wasn't here. I came in about twenty minutes ago from Quebec City and found her like that," I replied.

Tom for his part invented this bullshit story – not to look bad or getting the cops to come back and search my apartment.

"We spent the night together, we watched movies and all and I fell asleep on the couch and she probably went into the bedroom and shot up I don't know when," he half-lied.

They strapped the girl on a stretcher and were about to take her out, when one of the paramedics asked us:

"So, which one of you is coming with us?"

"Not me! I don't even know who she is!" I replied – turning to Tom.

His answer was obviously selfish:

"Well, she kinda has a boyfriend. So when she comes back to her senses, she's bound to call him and I don't want him to beat or worse kill me. So that's a no for me too. Plus, I don't even know her last name."

The ambulance guy looked at him in disgust and said:

"Yeah... Just watching movies, hein?! Looser!"

He then turned around and they both left with her on the stretcher. For one of the rarest of times, Tom actually looked like he had remorse for his actions.

"Eamon! I'm really sorry, you know!" he plaintively said.

"Never again! Do you hear me? Or you'll be out of here in no time, without even touching the floor with your feet! Understood?" I replied – pissed.

"Yeah ... Sure!" he shamefully acknowledged.

"Now clean up this mess and don't leave anything lying around. I don't want to catch AIDS or hepatitis ... And wash my sheets for God's sake! I'm getting outta here. I don't wanna see your goddamn face right now ... And by the way, since when do you smoke opium?"

"Like I said, I smuggled some out of Kandahar ... It's so easy to get down there. It helps me to numb the pain I have from all the horrors I saw and the guilt of killing other human beings and seeing my buddies die. There's not a day that goes by that I don't regret enlisting in the army and volunteering to go there!"

"I told you so! But that doesn't mean you have to slip into a path that leads to self-destruction and drag me down with you along the way. Anyways, I'm outta here! Don't wait up ... I need some air. When I do get back, the place had better be spick and span!"

I stormed out of there before Tom had time to reply.

I walked without stopping, heading west, without any clear direction of where I was going. I just strolled on and on – hands in my pockets – along the north shore of the Canal until I hit the Lachine Canal National Historic Site – the western entrance of the old gateway through Montreal. I sat on the waterfront, took off my shoes and soaked my feet in the water as if it could cleanse me of all my past sins and my misery.

A little while later, I got back on LaSalle Boulevard – along the Saint-Lawrence River bank – and started to walk back home. I kept thinking of Shelly to keep my mind from wandering to the O'd episode that had just happened in my apartment. The harder I kept thinking about Shelly, the more depressed I got. I was screwed.

I walked back along the riverside park – half-noticing where I was – being in this parallel universe – sometimes drawn out of my daydreams by police cars and ambulances rushing to LaSalle Hospital. It took me about four and a half hours getting from my home and back. It had only seemed like a fifteen minute walk to me in the end.

By the time I got back to my apartment, Tom had gotten the whole place shiny like a brand new dime. I had left for a long walk to clear my head, but I came back with it being fuller than it originally was.

From the time he had set foot at my place, I had never seen Tom so helpful. I could have gotten used to all that guilt that was devouring him. Unfortunately, I was never the one to abuse of any situation. If I could help my fellow human being, then I would do so.

A couple of days later, Tom came back from God knows where and said:

"Dude! You'll never believe it! I met this girl right off the streets. She was waiting in a line, just before me, at the drugstore. She said her name was Noémie. I did one plus one from what she told me and all those pictures you kept in your room and used to jerk off to."

He was saying all that while searching through his Facebook contacts on the living room laptop.

"Is this her? ... Your old lab partner?" he asked.

I was in shock. It was high school all over again – Tom getting all the girls I couldn't even dream of having. I was pissed. But fate intervened, for once, in my favor. Tom said:

"She's really hot! Although a little young for my taste ... But hey! Who's to complain? The weird thing, though, is that she seemed to like me, but not so much at the same time. I tried to make a pass at her and she coldly turned me down. It had never happened to me before. I was in shock. I'm used to getting all the skin that I want. But this girl's different somehow. It's like she's broken or something."

I internally laughed my ass off and said:

"I don't know what to say man! Maybe she's oblivious to all your bullshit ... Like she's immune or something!"

"Nanh! I think she's just a tease ... It shows!"

Noémie was light years away from a tease. She was a real regular girl-next-door type – the kind of non-superficial girl Tom was not used to. As I entered my room, I said to Tom:

"Maybe she's just not into douchebags!" – closed the door behind me.

I knew Tom would be boiling with rage and incomprehension. As I let myself fall down flat on my bed – smiling in an argument winning grin – I knew for the first time that Tom was not this holy sex god that everyone thought he was. For the first time, I pitied the fool instead of envying him.

That night Noémie texted me:

"I think one of your friends came on to me today :S"

"Yeah, I know! He told me about it."

"What did he tell you?"

"That he found you real pretty ... You see, I told you ... But that you blew him off."

"Thanks! But, yeah, I did. He's really not my type!"

"Did I ever tell you that I loved you ...Hahahaha!"

"No ... But I'll take that as a compliment!"

"It is ... Actually! You have no idea how you just made my day!"

"Hey listen. When the season starts, we should really get together, you and I, to see a game somewhere!"

"Of course ... It's a date! ... Well, not really a date ... Just some friends getting together for a hockey game."

"Are you ashamed to call it a date?"

"Well :S With the way our last meeting went ... I just don't want to lead you on or anything ... I know you just want to be friends and everything."

"You're cute ... I appreciate that! It's going to be a no pressure "date". I like those. I don't like to be pressured into something or being too openly courted."

"Don't worry ... I'll always be a true gentleman!"

"I know you will. It's in your nature. You're a genuine nice guy; a classic romantic."

"Stop it! You're gonna make me blush."

"No need to blush. I like the way you talk to me. It's good for my self-esteem. Maybe you need glasses, because you're the only one who sees me the way you do."

"Well maybe you just don't notice it or the other guys just don't manifest themselves."

"Maybe ... But I'm not there yet in my life, so I don't really care. I just like being appreciated and found beautiful ... Well, outside of douchebags who hit on everything that moves ... Well ... Like your friend there."

"He's harmless. I'm starting to think he has a lack of self-esteem which he compensates by screwing anyone or anything."

"Wow! That makes me feel special!"

"You are! He just doesn't know that ;)"

"Well ... I'm not interested."

"And I would suggest you stay the hell away from him. He's not for you ... Hell no ... Not for you!"

"Thanks for the advice! Well ... See ya! xox"

"Yeah ... See ya xxx"

It was not for her own good that I suggested that, but for my own good. If anyone should go out with her, it was me.

I felt a little cheap somehow. I had feelings for two girls at the same time – Shelly and Noémie. But that didn't stop me. I found that they both fit in different spheres of my personality. They were two very different girls, but similar at the same time. Both of them had long hair, greenish eyes, a passion for hockey and killer curves that made me drool – that's all I needed. The rest was just what made them special and unique in their own respective way. But the way things were going – even though she didn't want to get into a relationship – I felt that I had a better chance with Shelly than I did with Noémie.

IX

At the end of the summer, I had gotten back to Concordia and had taken two other courses – *Introductory Creative Writing: Prose Fiction* and *Quebec/Montreal: Writing in English*. I was actually looking forward to the second one where we would study authors writing about my hometown, about the life I was leading. Those courses would maybe help me get some ideas, some inspiration.

In early September, I went to that class after work – I had gotten my boss to bend my work schedule so I could attend university. The teacher was awesome and I was learning so much. But that was not the only thing that I appreciated that evening. There was this girl in class – two rows to my left – that caught my eye. She was astonishingly beautiful. She had short black hair, these incredibly sky blue eyes, wore a black and fluorescent Disney t-shirt and a short black skirt. She had a bridge and septum nose piercings and tattoos everywhere – a half sleeve I had noticed exceeding her t-shirt and her entire left leg. She had small breasts but had a nice round butt – at least I thought she did from what I had noticed when she got up to leave class. I followed her a little through the corridors leading out of the building. I was not stalking her or anything – I just found her pretty and she was going the same way as I. When she exited the door, we went separate ways – she made a left and I made a right to head to Guy-Concordia subway Station.

When I got home, I wanted, for once, to talk to Tom about the girl from my class. But he was nowhere to be found. I was a little disappointed, but it gave me some time to write a little. My class and the sexy tattooed girl had given me some inspiration. I was writing like a machine and drinking tons of red wine.

By the time Tom had gotten back home, I had three pages down and was really drunk. When he got through the door, I drunkenly stuttered:

"Hey douchebag! I wa … was … waiting for you … t … to get home. Guess what?!!!"

"'You drunk bro?"

"Slightly … But that's not the p … point … Bro! I b … beat you!"

"Beat me to what?"

"I saw the sexiest girl today!"

"Sober up and we'll talk afterwards."

"N .. No …Nooo! Dude! I mean this girl is hot! You don't understand! She's a g … girl in my class and she's tattooed and pierced everywhere!"

"You saw her naked?"

"Eh nooo! I j … just … met her tonight."

"So how can you tell she's tattooed and pierced everywhere?"

"Ahhh Forget it! I just guess she … she is. Anyways she's hot. So where were you?"

"I went to see a show. But I had to leave early because my foot was killing me. It pissed me off because the Beatdown were amazing … As always. I know you said that you wanted me to get a job and move out someday, but, dude, it's really painful!"

"I ... I understand ... Don't sw ... sweat it."

"Thanks Bro. I'm gonna take a bath and smoke a joint. Want any?"

"No thanks. If I take any ... anything else, I think I'm gonna be sick."

"Hahahaha! You pussy! More for me! Anyways, you should get to sleep. Aren't you working tomorrow mornin'?"

"Wha ... What?"

"Yeah! Tomorrow's Thursday. You always work on Thursday mornings."

"Fuck, I forgot! Damn, I'm gonna be a mess."

"Hahahaha! Good luck!"

As he turned on the water, I went to bed. I tried to sleep, but my head was spinning like hell. I felt like I was going to be sick, but tried to fight it. After about twenty minutes, it was just too much and I ran to the bathroom. As I swung the door open, Tom yelled – blowing out marijuana smoke out of his mouth:

"Dude! What the fuck!?"

I lifted the toilet seat and vomited the surplus of red wine I had chugged down that evening.

"Dude, you're disgusting! God!" he said.

"Says the guy who was passed out on opium and had a girl O'd-ing in my room," I replied – while going at it again with my offering to the porcelain god.

"Do you have to make so much noise when you're barfing? I don't think they heard you three blocks down."

"Go fuck yourself, Tom!"

"Nanh! I got hookers doing that for me. Hahahaha!"

"Well, maybe if you didn't spend .... Wahhhhhh-hhhhhhh! .... God, I'm going to die ... If you didn't spend so much money on alcohol, drugs and hookers, you'd have some for rent. I'm starting to be tight. I'll be behind rent this month."

I was feeling a little better, so I flushed the toilette and sat down on the tiles – my back to the wall. Tom replied:

"I don't tell you how to live YOUR life!"

"Well, I'm not leaching off of yours."

"Dude, that's harsh ... True, but harsh. Listen, we could make a "rent and grocery" pot and when I get my veterans check, I'll pitch money in before I spend it all."

"That would be great, thanks."

"And I think I could get some extra money as well."

"Do I really wanna know how?"

"Well, it's kinda better you didn't ... For your own safety."

"Then I definitely don't wanna know. As long as you chip in, we're alright."

"Cool ... Co-co-cool!"

"You started watching *Community*?"

"Yeah! Relaxes me when I'm high!"

He lit another joint and said:

"You should really get some sleep. You look like hell, bro."

"Yeah, you're right. Good night!"

"You too."

I got up and went to bed and fell asleep easily – now that most of the poison was out of my bowels. The weirdest thing though was that the next morning, I was in top shape and full of energy. Karma had given me a free pass this time.

A week later, I was ecstatic to go to class again. Fate would have it that the teacher gave us an assignment to do in teams of two. I didn't know anybody, but I seized the opportunity. After class, I walked behind the sexy tattooed girl and said:

"Hey there, wait up!"

She turned around and said:

"Yes? What can I do for you?"

"Well ... We're in the same *Quebec / Montreal* class ..."
"Yes, I have noticed."
"Yeah ... Ummm ... I was wondering if ... Ummm ... You would like to do the assignment ... like together ... That's if you ... Ummm ... haven't found anyone yet."
"Well ... Sure ... Why not?! I'm Pam by the way."
"Eamon ..." I shyly replied.
"Nice to meet you. Wanna grab a coffee ... or a drink ... and talk about it?"

She caught me kind of off-guard – not imagining that it would be so easy.

"Sh ... Sure!" I stuttered back, "Like right now?"
She laughed and replied:
"Well ... That's if you don't have anything else planned."
"Actually, my schedule's wide open. A beer would be nice."
"Do you know any good places? I'm from Laval and I just come downtown to go to my courses and work."
"Well, there's this nice pub, two blocks down, on Crescent Street, called Brutopia. They have really good beer and awesome chicken quesadillas."
"I'm not really hungry."
"Me neither ... I was just saying."
She smiled and added:
"Okay ... So ... Lead the way."

We then walked down to Brutopia. She wasn't much of a talker and I was kind of shy to break the ice. Maybe sitting down face to face would make it easier than swarming across the busy Montreal crowd. We got up the stairs to the pub, got a table on the terrace and ordered some beers. I then broke the ice:

"So, tell me about yourself."
"Whatcha wanna know?"
"Well, where are you from exactly? What do you do outside of school? ... You know the basic stuff."

"Well ... I live in Pont-Viau, Laval, with my dad. University's costing me an arm and a leg and my dad can't really help me outside the fact that he lets me live with him for free. I work part-time at the Concordia student co-op and I earn just enough to pay for tuition, books and bus fare. Outside of that nothing much."

"How old are you?"

"I'm 24 ... How about you?"

"I'm 22 ... Well, 23 in little more than a month."

"Okay ... So what about you?"

"I live in Côte-Saint-Paul, near the Jolicoeur subway station and work full time at the Cage in LaSalle. I live alone ... Well, used to live alone ... I have a friend who's in a bad patch and I'm letting him crash on my couch until he gets his life together."

"That's very noble of you."

"Well, we've known each other since high school and he's kinda like family to me. In fact, I'm kind of the only family he has left. Anyways ... Outside of that nothing much ... In my spare time, when I have any, I mostly go to see shows and write ... I'm kinda trying to write a novel. That's why I'm taking these courses, part-time as a free student, to help me structure everything and get some inspiration. What about you? What do you wanna do with your B.A.?"

"I have no friggin' idea. I started with the same intention as you, but found out I had no real desire to pursue in that branch. But I had invested so much time and money, I didn't want to drop out after a year and a half ... So I stayed on. This is actually my final year. At least I'll have a diploma. After that it's all blank. I don't know ... Maybe do a master's degree or something in I don't know what yet."

"Oh, okay!"

I turned around and saw a familiar face.

"Hey Danny!" I greeted him.

"Hey Eamon, man! How're you doing?" he replied.

"Pretty good! Whatcha doin' here?"
"I'm doing a set later on."
"For real?! That's awesome! I didn't see the rest of the band."
"Patrizio's here, but the other guys should arrive soon. Well … I gotta prep up. See you inside later?"
"Hell yeah!"
"Cool … See you later, Man."

I turned back to Pam and asked:
"Do you like Reggae music?"
"Yeah … Sure. I'm not too familiar with it though."
"That was Danny Rebel who just walked in. He's amazing. Wanna stay for the show?"
"Ummm … Sure."

Later on, we went inside as Danny Rebel & the KGB were starting their set. I was singing and dancing my ass off to two-tone ska and rocksteady reggae as Pam was sitting down looking a little bored. In between two sets, I asked her:
"Aren't you enjoying this?"
"I do … I love it! I'm just not the expressive and dancy type. I basically lose myself in the music and switch my brain off."
"Okay! Cool!"
"But you're kinda cute, fully into the music and all!"

I turned red of shyness. She had actually said that I was cute. We stayed through the entire show. I was sweating and was out of breath from all the dancing and singing. After the show, I talked a little with Danny when Pam came up to me and said exasperated:
"Fuck! I just missed the last subway. And by the time I get to Henri-Bourassa by night busses, there won't be any of them left in Laval and I don't have money for cab fare."
"Well, you can always come sleep at my place," I suggested.

"If you don't mind ... I would like that."

"Of course I don't mind. We better hurry though, I think the bus passes soon."

I bade Danny farewell and we were on our way out. We walked to the corner of René-Lévesque Boulevard and Bishop Street. We were in luck because the bus was just two corners down the street. We hopped on the 350 and, a half hour later, got off on the corner of Jolicoeur and Laurendeau Street – just three blocks from my place.

I opened the front door really quietly – not to wake Tom up. But as I entered, I noticed that he wasn't there.

"Oh good, my roommate's not here. We won't have to whisper," I said to Pam.

"Oh, okay. But I'm getting kind of tired. Where do I sleep?"

"Ummm ... I have no idea where Tom is and he may come back later on. We can share my bed ... If that's okay with you?" I suggested – not knowing how she would take the proposition.

"Yeah, sure!" she replied – in a more joyful tone than I had expected – tides were turning I guess.

When we got to my room, Pam took off her pants and socks and got under the covers. I did the same and closed the light.

"Good night!" she said.

"Good night!" I replied.

After a couple of minutes though, I got the courage to say:

"By the way ... I find you gorgeous and very attractive. You're a real nice girl."

"You are cute yourself, you know!"

Following those revelations, there was a minute of awkward silent. Then, I turned my head in her direction and our lips met. It rapidly turned into a lusty dance of kissing, fondling and groping each other's bodies. A few minutes later, she was between my legs giving me a blowjob – then making a 180 degrees turn to 69 me. Her moaning was driving me crazy. We then had sex – changing positions every time she came – which averaged about every two or three minutes. It was uncanny! I had never seen a girl cum so fast and so often. And every time she came, she would crisp her body – banging her fist on the bed – biting and scratching me – sinking her nails into my skin until I winced in pain. I tried my best to hold in my own pleasure because it was too awesome. But in the end, I just lost it and exploded.

When I came back to my senses, she laughed a little and said:

"Did you just have a heart attack or an epileptic stroke? Hahahaha!"

"You're not the first girl to ask me that …" I replied – regretting having said that at the very moment the words left my mouth.

You cannot talk about other girls you had sex with while still being "inside" another one. She noticed my discomfort and said:

"Don't worry! I'm not a virgin either. We all have a past. You're not the first guy I had sex with this year … For what it's worth you're not even the first guy I had sex with this week."

At that moment, I realized that I had just met a girl who had even less social skills than I did. In the past, I would have been shocked if a girl had said that to me. But I kind of didn't give a rat's ass at that point. I think Tom was starting to rub off on me – or maybe I had been burned so often that I was starting to protect my feelings and just go with the flow. Then it hit me:

"Fuck! I'm working in five hours!"

"Ohhh!" she replied.

"Don't worry. I'll go to work in the morning and come back later. You can stay here as long as you want."

"Okay. Thanks!"

I didn't know that she would take that literally.

X

The next morning, I turned off my smartphone alarm quickly – not to wake Pam up – and quietly left the room – taking my clothes with me. I got in the living room and was startled by Tom:

"Nice show last night, bro! You got a screamer there. Her moans were so sexy that I had to jerk off hearing you two going at it!"

"God, Tom! You're fucking disgusting!" I replied – annoyed.

"Hahahaha! I'm friggin' kidding you! I would never jerk off thinking of you ... Yuk! But promise me that if you get rid of her someday, I can have her!"

"It wouldn't be the first time you'd take my sloppy seconds!"

Tom was in shock. His awed faced rapidly turned into a grin and then a laugh. He said to me:

"I finally made a man outta you! Nice uppercut you just gave me. You're now a real Irish sonavabitch!"

I laughed at what he had just said and started to get dressed. I was suddenly interrupted by Tom:

"Dude! Look at your chest and arms. You're full of scratches and bruises everywhere. Did you get into a fight club or is this the screamer's work? Well, if it was a fight club, you couldn't talk about it, because, you know, it's the first rule ... Hahahaha!"

"No, I did not fight anyone and by the way ... her name's Pam."

"Pam what?"

I was in shock. I smiled at Tom and replied:

"You know ... I have no fuckin' clue what her last name is!"

Tom forced me to high-five him and took me in his arm, falsely weeping:

"My son! You're growing up to be just like Papa Tom. I'm so proud of you!"

"Hahahaha! You're such a dick! You know that?"

"Yup! Proud graduate of Dicksville University!"

"Finally! You graduated something. I, too, am proud of you!"

He smiled and gave me the finger.

"Love you to, Bro! But I gotta get going or else I'm gonna be late for work," I added.

I finished getting dressed, got my coat – it was starting to get cold on mid-September mornings – and left. As I passed the door, I stuck my head back in and said to Tom:

"Hey! By the way ... She is tattooed and pierced everywhere ... and it's MAGNIFICENT!"

He threw a couch cushion at me and said:

"Get to work, you Irish motherfucker!"

The next few weeks, Pamela Schroeder – I had learned her last name by then – and I were always together – seeing shows, movies, art exhibits and going to restaurants. Of course, since she didn't earn enough money, I paid for everything. I had more money than her because I hadn't touched most of my inheritance. I didn't want Tom to know that because he would leech off of me even more.

But I was starting to think that Pam took advantage of me a little. She knew I was generous and never tried to stop me when I took out my wallet. I even paid for her winter semester for crying out loud. I just couldn't say no to her – like she had bewitched me or something.

On top of that, she was leaving more and more stuff at my apartment without me really noticing – starting with a toothbrush and then some lady products like perfume, conditioner and tampons. I had now even given her a couple of drawers in my highboy. The electricity bill started to skyrocket due to the fact that she took about three to four baths a day – only staying in them for about five minutes. She ate all the time, but only small portions, so there was a lot of leftover food thrown out. I was washing three times the amount of clothes that Tom and I used to wash – combined. On top of that, she was kind of a slob – leaving her clothes and dishes lying around – to the point that even Tom – who wasn't the cleanest of guys – was starting to get fed up.

Pam and I had been going out for about five months and she now was practically living int the apartment. One day, Tom came to me – while she had a class and I was home – and tried to have some sort of intervention with me:

"Dude!!! Your "girlfriend" is such a bitch!"

"Be careful with whatcha say, Tom! I won't accept you badmouthing Pam," I warned him.

"I'm not badmouthing her. I'm just stating facts!"

"And calling her a bitch is called what?"

"Okay, I got carried away with that one ... But wake up, man. She's taking control of your life. You're paying everything for her. She's going to ruin you. She's a slob and a leech. You're not the same since you started seeing her. Your grades have gone down, you're taking a lot of "sick" leaves from work, we're never hanging out together like we used to and you barely ever talk to Shelly or Noémie anymore. Did you know that Shelly even messaged me on Facebook because she's worried about you?"

"She's just jealous that I'm with another girl."

"Dude, wake up! She's poison for you."

"But I really like her!"

"I'm sure you do Bro ... She's one hot woman, but, dude, she's using you. You do know she is seeing other guys ... and other women?"

"Now you're just making that up!"

"I'm ninety percent sure. Once you leave the apartment, she's always on her cell phone, texting. The other day, while she was in the shower, she left her phone on the coffee table. She received a text message and I checked, you know because I don't trust her. It was pretty explicit bro. It wasn't just texting ... it was sexting!"

"It doesn't prove anything!"

"Dude, wake up! It's not the first text message I happen to fall upon. I bet you fifty bucks that in the next two weeks, she's going to ask you to move in and will want to get rid of me."

"Hell, I, myself, am trying to get rid of you! ... Hahahaha!"

"Fuck you! Would you be serious, please? ... For once this is not a joke, but a fair warning. She's going to take you down and suck your personality out of you and replace it with what she wants you to become."

"You're paranoid, dude!"

"Fifty bucks! I tell you. Fifty motherfuckin' dollars! That's how sure I am."

"Don't worry. I'm a grown man. I can take care of myself. You know you will have to move out eventually ... whether she's there or not."

"Well at least my conscience is clear. I did my job. Hey! You wanna go out somewhere? Seems like ages since we did anything!"

"I can't. Pam has this course where she's way behind and I offered to help her. I gotta do a five-page paper for her by tomorrow. She's in way over her head this semester."

"God! You just proved me right!"

"Not at all! I'm just a good guy. She was in need and I offered ... That's all! She didn't pressure me into anything."

"That's your problem. You're too much of a good guy that people trample over you and you say thank you."

"Oh! You mean like you?"

"That was really cold. I'm leaving for the night before I start to knuckle back some sense into you. So ... Good day!"

"But ..."

"I SAID GOOD DAY!"

He took his flask, grabbed his cane and stormed – limping – out of the door. I was kind of pissed at him. I didn't know if he really had my interests at heart, or his own. I thought he was just afraid that he would lose his place both literally and figuratively. But it wouldn't even take a week before I lost fifty dollars ... again. Karma's one messed-up gal.

Pam and I were alone in the apartment. We were sitting on the sofa watching an episode of *Parks and Recreation* when she said:

"Eamon, Baby, can we talk?"

I paused the episode and replied:

"Sure! What's on your mind?"

"Well, I was thinking. We've been going out for more than five months now and I think that it may be time for me to officially move in with you. I'm always here anyways. Might as well make it official. What do you think?"

"Well ... Ummm ... What about Tom?" I replied – trying to buy some time.

"His foot seems to be getting much better. Don't you think it would be time to push him out of the nest? He needs to learn to live on his own. It's not that I don't like him, but don't you think it's about time that you didn't hold his hand anymore?"

"Well … Ummm … This is a shock … Let me think about it …"

"Think about what? It's time to take this to the next step, no? I feel that our couple needs to move forward and not be in a stalemate. Whattaya think?"

"Well … Ummm … I have a question for you … But don't take this the wrong way … I just want to know exactly what I'm agreeing to."

"Yeah, sure! You know I'm an open book."

"Well … Ummm … I know we never said we were exclusive and all, but have you been seeing other people since we met."

"Well …Ummm … Of course not. I'm not a slut!"

For the first time, I doubted her – having Tom's earlier warning in the back of my mind. Plus, she had hesitated a millisecond to respond and her tone sounded a little fake. But I still wasn't sure if it was Tom who was playing with my head or Pam that was playing with my heart. My first answer was a simple:

"Well … Ummm … It's a big step … Can I have a short time to think about it for real … Please?"

"Okay! Sure … Hey! Whattaya wanna do tonight?"

"I don't know. I thought we would stay home and watch *Parks and Rec.*"

"I felt like going out. I have this friend who's doing an art expo in a gallery on the Plateau."

"That could be nice! I love art!"

"She's a conceptual artist. She does amazing work! You wouldn't even believe it! She hit a rough patch in the last few years. She had a child and she had no resources. The father is M.I.A. She had a real downward spiral. But now she's trying to get her head out of the water. It's actually her first expo since, I don't know, about four years."

I didn't know why, but I had a bad feeling about that. I asked the question – to which I dreaded the answer:

"What's her name?"

"She goes by the artist name *Yellow*, you know, because she's blonde. But her real name is Marla … Marla Tillman."

I was in shock! My face became ghostly white – to the point that Pam asked me:

"Are you okay baby?"

This was all too much for me. Tom was right all along. And on top of that, she was friends with Marla. It was the slap in the face I needed. I looked her straight in the eyes and said:

"You gotta go!"

She looked at me perplexed and asked:

"What's wrong? Are you okay? You look like you've seen a ghost or that you are going to be sick!"

"Just go!" I said – somewhat angrily.

"Okay Baby! But for how long? I'm worried!"

"Frankly, my dear, I don't give a damn! I never want to see you again … Go! And take all of your things or they'll end up in the garbage!"

"What the fuck is wrong with you all of a sudden?! You can't just throw me out like that!" she replied – her voice getting louder and her face getting red.

"Why not? You're just a leeching, lying bitch who wants to take advantage of me and …"

That's when she slapped me out of rage. I looked at her in a psychopathic way – like Gomer Pyle in *Full Metal Jacket* during the bathroom scene. I think she got scared and said:

"I'm really sorry! I didn't mean to hit you."

"Leave before I call the cops."

"Baby, I'm sorry!"

"LEAAAAAVE!!!!!!! NOW!!!" I screamed at her.

She then really got scared. She quickly assembled all her things and left the apartment – heavily sobbing.

I stood up from the couch, got to the kitchen, took the bottle of Jack from the pantry and gobbled it up. Before

I felt like I was going to pass out, I took a pen and paper and wrote: "Here's your fifty bucks, you piece of shit … Love Eamon". I took the note, with a fifty-dollar bill I had hidden in my room, and left it on the coffee table for Tom to see. I drank on the sofa watching *Parks and Recreation* – alone – laughing my ass off to Amy Poehler and her gang in all their awkwardness. At one point, I blacked out – falling unconscious on the sofa. It was the last thing I remembered from that evening.

XI

It had been three days and still I had no news from Tom. I was starting to be worried. I was wondering if I had pissed him off with that whole Pam story. I was feeling guilty and the absence of Tom wasn't helping. I had dropped out of university – not wanting to fall face to face with Pam – and it pissed me off. That was seven hundred dollars down the drain. I had become a good escape artist when things went sour – I had learned that about myself.

In the middle of the afternoon, I received a call from an unlisted number. I answered it and – to my great surprise – it was Tom.

"Bro! You gotta help me, like right now!"

"What's wrong?" I asked.

"Don't ask questions. Just fill the backpack that we both have the exact same one, with a bunch of clothes and go to Bonaventure. Then walk south to the corner of St-Antoine and de la Cathédrale Street. When you see me get there, take the same bus as I: the 36 West. Act as if you don't know me, please! I have someone following me … I think. Maybe an undercover cop or something. I'm talking to you from a payphone at the Montreal Central Bus Station, near Berri. So, on the bus, I'll go sit in the back and you'll stand up in front of me. Put your backpack next to mine. Get off at the corner of Monk and Jolicoeur Street and take my bag instead of yours. I'll head down to Angrignon station and, I don't know, maybe go play pool at the Skratch or something for a while and then come back home when I'm sure I'm not being followed."

"Goddamn it, Tom! You gotta be fuckin' kidding me?!?"

"Dude! I'll totally make it up to you!"

"Okay! But this is the first and last time you pull a trick like that on me!"

"I promise! Now, hurry up!"

"I should be there in about half an hour tops."

"Thanks! You're a life savior!"

I hung up the phone, packed the bag he wanted me to bring and left to take the subway up to Bonaventure and then head to the meeting point.

I waited about ten minutes unsuspectedly and innocently looking around me to see if I would see Tom anywhere. He popped out – turning the corner about a block west of me – heading in my direction. I did as he had told me and just pretended like I didn't know him. We both waited in line for the bus – which arrived about five minutes later. We both got on and, as planned, I headed in the back of the bus and so did Tom. He sat down and put the bag in front of his legs. I, for myself, stood up in front of him, holding the horizontal pole – putting my backpack next to his. The entire ride long, I played on my phone to prevent me from ripping his head off.

When it was time for me to get off, I took his backpack instead of mine and exited the 36 bus on the corner he had planned and started to walk home – which was just a couple of blocks North – subtlety turning my head from time to time to see if anyone was following me. I was relieved that the coast was clear. I finally got to my place. As I climbed up the stairs, I took one last look around. I was the only one on the street, so I got in my house and locked the door behind me.

I sat down on the couch and reflected on the dilemma that was in front me – to open or not to open the bag … That was the question. Tom had wanted me to keep out of his business for my own protection. But I was always the curious type, so this was an itchy situation. Curiosity finally got the best of me and I decided to open the bag. I was in shock. There was about seven or eight big blocks of hashish and a bag of a brown substance which I figured was either heroin or opium – most likely the second one. I was so mad at Tom and I wanted to punch his little snot-nosed Irish face until his mom wouldn't recognize him anymore. How could he impose this on me? How could he bring this shit into my home? There must have been more than a couple thousands of dollars worth of shit in there. I tried to find a place to hide the drugs. The only place I could think of was the empty drawers of my highboy – the one Pam had emptied three days earlier.

I came back on the couch and just smoked one cigarette after another – blankly watching episodes of *30 Rock* – not really remembering anything. After four hours, I heard someone unlock the door. Tom came in the apartment. I stood up and screamed:

"Are you out of you fucking mind?!"

"Calm down … I can explain!"

"You better! Although there is not a lot of explaining to do. You got a lot of drugs in my home, you crazy piece of shit!"

"Yeah, I know and I'm sorry. I didn't want you to get involved into all of this."

"Where were you the past three days?"

"I made a trip to Ottawa. I have a friend in the military who got his hands on this. It's really easy to smuggle this shit out of Afghanistan like I told you a while back. I just thought I could make some extra money and help you pay for this place. I don't like that you feel that I'm leeching off you. But I'm sorry that I put you in this situation."

"I'm pissed ... But I'll get over it ... Like always! By the way, your fifty bucks has been lying on the table for the last three days."

"What fifty bucks?"

"The bet we had ... You were right!"

"Geez! I'm sorry bro. I saw it coming, but I didn't want you to get your feelings hurt. You're the most decent and sweet guy I know. You don't deserve all the shit that's been coming down on you."

"Don't try to slither your way out of this with your smooth talkin'. And by the way, asshole, half of the shit that has been happening to me is because of you!"

"Yeah, I know! How do you think I know you've got such a big heart? ... Hahahaha!"

"I hate you, Motherfucker!" I replied – bro-hugging him.

"Love you too, Bro!"

He sat down on the couch, lit up a cigarette, looked at the TV screen and said:

"Hey, *30 Rock*! That show's awesome. I love sitcoms. Plus, Tina Fey is really hot!"

"She must be like fifteen years older than you!"

"That's what I'm saying! She's hot! She has everything. She's funny, intelligent, a good writer and she's gorgeous. You can't ask for more."

"You never change!"

"Why should I? I can't help it that I like older women. In my defense, I never had the drama you have with your emotionally immature twenty-something girls."

"I hate it!"

"What?"

"When I'm winning an argument and you always have the uppercut line to knock me out!"

"Hahahaha! You have some good ones in ya ... You just hafta have more confidence in yourself."

"Maybe you're right. But coming back to what we were talking about before, you gotta get rid of the drugs fast. I don't want any more of this here. Once you get your own place, I don't give a damn. But this is still my place."

"Yeah, I know! You're right. Hey ... Once I'm done moving this shit ... You think you could get me a job to where you're working?"

"I don't think that it's the best of ideas."

"Oh, come on! You know I work well in a restaurant. I'm a goddamn machine!"

I knew he was right, but it's his outside of work lifestyle and his attitude that I had a hard time with. But maybe this could get him on the right path somehow. Plus, by working at the same place as I, it would occupy him not to do some crazy stuff. And on top of that, I could keep an eye on him.

"I'll see what I can do. I'll talk to my boss. But first, you gotta move this shit outta here. Only then, will I talk to him," I replied.

"You've got my word. By the end of the summer, all this will be gone ..."

"End of summer?!?"

"No ... the drugs will be gone within a couple of weeks. But I will have made enough to last me until September or October. By then, my foot should really be better."

"Well, I really hope so. What a stupid move to shoot yourself in the foot!"

"It's always better than being court-martialed for desertion."

"You've got a point there."

So this is how I met Tom Murphy. The most self-centered, obnoxious, Irish douchebag that ever crossed my path. But still, he was my best friend ... He was my brother. And you don't let family down even if they screw you up.

XII

"… But that chocolatier was nowhere near as nasty as that squirter I had a MMF threesome with a couple of weeks ago!" Tom bragged.

"You never told me about her," I replied.

"I sometimes do that. I dress up good and go on the prowl for MILFs."

"A kitten hunting cougars … I've seen it all now!"

"Hahahaha! Good one, bro! By the way, I would really like to thank you for this job. For the first time in since forever, I feel like I'm doing something outta myself."

"No problem. You kept your end of the bargain … I kept mine as well."

It felt good working with Tom again. It brought us even closer. It reminded me of when we worked used together at Dilallo's. It also brought me back to the years I spent working with John at Truant's Tavern. Although it was all a sham, I missed those guys back in New Hampshire. It's really fun when your co-workers are also your friends. It makes the work experience more relaxed and entertaining.

That evening, Tom was a friggin' machine – even though he was on a mix of morphine and liquor hangover. It was uncanny what that guy did to his body. It was even more uncanny how he had managed to still be alive with all the shit he had done and the people he had pissed off.

The next day, I got a message from Shelly asking me if she could come to my place for one or two days the next weekend. We had restarted messaging each other like crazy – I constantly apologized to her for the entire Pam debacle. She didn't give me much grief and I had a feeling that we were getting even closer than ever. Usually, around that time, she'd be really busy with work – with all the pre-season training camps. But that fall, the hockey world was on hiatus. Failing to reach an agreement with the Player's Association, the owners had decided to put their teams on lockout. Shelly still had to work, but she had way more time on her hands. She wanted to spend the weekend with me and I wasn't one to complain. It was actually the first time that she was coming to my place.

That evening, Tom came to my room and said:

"Dude! I have something to ask you. But before you say no, please hear me out."

"I don't like when you start your demands like this."

"It's nothing illegal, don't worry. You remember that chocolatier girl?"

"How could I forget ... You keep bragging about her."

"Anyways, we're planning to meet again."

"Good for you. But what's that gotta do with me?"

"Well, she has a husband, so we can't go to her place and I don't have any money for a hotel room ..."

"I see where this is going and my answer is no ... You're not bringing a girl back here! You remember how it ended last time?"

"Yeah! But this time it's different. She's not a god-damn junky. You won't even know she was here. You have a class Thursday and all. I was hoping we could crash here for two or three hours. You won't even know that she was here. Come on bro! I'm begging you!"

I sighed and caved in:

"Fine, you whining baby! But no bullshit! And I want the place to be exactly as I will leave it!"

"Yeah, yeah! What can go wrong dude? She only has three hours and, after that, she needs to get back to her home before her husband comes back."

"Hey, come to think of it, are you still using my Tinder to talk to her?"

"No. I never use it more than once. I chat with them a little and then get their email address. That's when I tell them I'm not you. Half of them tell me to go fuck myself. The other half don't give a shit and just want to jump my bones ... You know since I'm way hotter than you."

"Get bent, asshole!"

"Hahahaha! No, it's them I want to bend over!"

"You're such a misogynistic douchebag!"

"I'm not misogynistic ... In fact, I love women way too much, that's my problem ... And by the way, you're the one that had Tinder on his phone, not me!"

"First of all, you don't have a phone and, second of all, I haven't met anyone. I just wanted to talk to women and get to know them. Maybe after that who knows? But my interest died down since Shelly's back in my life big time!"

"That snobby Boston girl who keeps leading you on and dropping you when she gets what she wants. She really doesn't have high standards from what I can tell."

"First of all: Fuck you! And second of all ... I really feel that this time it's different. She doesn't talk to me the same way she did before. It all coincided with that Pam situation. We were barely speaking anymore and I guess she got afraid of losing me. At least, something good may come out of all the money I lost with that leech. It may have been a nice investment in the end."

"God! You're such a positive goody-two-shoes! You should write a self-help book instead of that novel. By the way, how's it going with that?"

"In circles ... I keep rewriting everything. I'm never satisfied. It's progressing, but way slower than I had expected. The courses I take have both a good and a bad influence on me."

"Whattaya mean?"

"Well, they give me inspiration and ideas, but the more I learn and read, the more I find that what I previously wrote is goddamn garbage!"

"Ah! The artist angst!"

"Talk to me about it!"

"So, Thursday you won't be here, promise?"

"Yeah, yeah! You goddamn pervert! You couldn't have found one that was not married?"

"Come on! They're the best kind! No strings attached and they never spend the night. Plus, they don't care that you are sleeping around because ... well ... that's just what they're doing."

"You're a pig, you know that?"

"Yup! A sexy Irish pig!"

"So ... I gave you what you wanted ... Can I ask a favor from you in exchange?"

"I knew you had something behind your mind when you agreed. How long will you want me gone?"

"Well, at least Saturday evening."

"OK, that seems fair. I'll try to find myself some sugar mommy that will keep me for the evening, or maybe the night, for a five-course Irish meal. But I will need your phone though."

"You can't be serious?"

"Dead serious ... You want me out? That's the price!"

I threw my phone to him and added:

"Why don't you create your own profile? I won't need mine anymore. I'm not a dating site guy. It's just not for me."

After he agreed to do so, I left him in the living room, went to my bedroom and started reading a new book for one of my courses. Since the Pam debacle, I had decided to change University – so I wouldn't bump into her. I was now a McGill University free student. I registered in *Studies in Literary Form: Autobiography and the Novel* and *Irish Literature* courses. The first one was really the one that appealed to me – being about what I was trying to write – autobiographical fiction.

When I came back from my Thursday night course, Tom was lying on the sofa, only wearing boxers, smoking a cigarette and drinking Jack directly from the bottle while watching the ALCS.

"Dude! You look tired!" I said to him.

"Yeah! That girl's one sexy, feisty and insatiable MILF. I thought I was a nasty and kinky guy. Bro, you have no idea! I felt like a virgin compared to her!"

"God! Is such a thing possible? Hahahaha! Glad you had fun. Now *Purell* the hell out of the living room. I'm not sitting on that couch until you clean it first."

"You're right... You better not. Her squirts even passed through ..."

"God Tom! You never heard the saying: A gentleman does not kiss and tell?"

"Yeah, but I ain't no gentleman."

"I know that. But there's such a thing as too much information!"

"Okay, okay! Don't be such a prude!"

I turned to look at the TV and asked:

"So, who's winning?"

"Detroit's destroying the Yankees. Feels like a sweep. It's a good thing, 'cause I hate the goddamn Yankees."

"Yeah, me too."

"Hey, by the way ..." – he reached for something at his side and threw it to me – "Here catch! ... Happy birthday, fuckface!"

I caught the thing. It was a gift.

"I can't believe you remembered that it was my birthday today! Even I had forgotten!" I replied – touched.

"Shut up and open it!"

I opened the packet. It was NOFX's latest album *Self Entitled*. Tom added:

"Hope you'll like it! It came out about a month ago."

"Thanks, Bro! I'm really touched!"

"Come on! It's nothing. If I had had more money, I would have given you so much more."

"You know me … I'm uncomfortable with expensive gifts. It's the fact that you thought of me that I appreciate the most."

"And that's not all. I found a place to go on Saturday night. I'm going to this rich cougar's house in Westmount. She recently got divorced and she wants a young stallion for the night … An all-you-can-eat Irish buffet."

"Well, good for you!" I replied – half-happy I would be alone with Shelly, but half-discouraged about his behavior.

The next morning, Tom and I went to work. It was just another regular day. Since the hockey season was on hiatus, there were a little less clients coming in – meaning a little less preparations to make for supper time. I was so hyped to see Shelly again. It had been more than a year since the last time I had seen her. I kept smiling and singing all day. Tom started to sigh and said:

"Give it a rest, dude! All this happiness is starting to drive me crazy. I think I like you better when you're bitter and sarcastic. You're less annoying."

"You can't say anything to ruin this day. It's just a beautiful bright and sunny day!" I replied – harboring a huge smile.

"Dude! It's pouring buckets outside! And they are forecasting rain all weekend."

"I don't care. It's still sunny for me!"

"Oh God! You're such a sappy romantic. It makes me wanna puke!"

"Maybe it'll rub off on you some day."

"I sincerely doubt that and hope it never does!"

"You've got a soft spot somewhere I know it. You've built yourself this armor that makes you untouchable. But everything and everyone has a weak spot somewhere. Just look at the Death Star. You're just afraid to lose yourself and open up; too scared to get hurt some day."

"Maybe ... Who knows."

"See ... I'm getting to you!"

He threw a piece of cauliflower at me and said:

"Stop talking like a shrink and playing games with my head."

I laughed because I knew I was right. His refusal for real human contact was just a defense mechanism.

"So, what time is your girlfriend's supposed to arrive?" he asked.

"First of all, she's not my girlfriend ... Well, at least not yet. Second of all, I have no idea ... Somewhere after supper ... Maybe around 7:00pm."

"Okay ... So after work, I think I'll go see a movie, before meeting my cougar, and leave you two alone."

"Thanks, bro! I appreciate. What are you going to see?"

"I don't know yet. Maybe *Dredd*. I hope it's better than the awful one with Stallone."

"I heard it kicks ass and that it's fuckin' violent."

"You just sold me then! ...Hahahaha! I'll eat here after work and just go next door afterwards."

"Okay ... Cool. Thanks again."

"You know, it would be fun to have money for some popcorn and a Pepsi!" he added – in a childlike way.

"What are you, like, twelve years old and asking your dad for an allowance?"

"Hey, I'm doing this for you. Add another twenty and I won't come back until the middle of the night."

"You suck, you know that?! This is extortion" I replied – handing him forty dollars.

"Nice doing business with you, my good man."

"Go fuck yourself!"

"Maybe I will! It all depends if she's a screamer like the last one you brought home!"

I threw a whole carrot at him and he yelled:

"Dude! That stings!"

"I thought that the army had toughened you up, you sissy."

"I got soft living with you. I guess you're right, you are rubbing off on me."

I laughed and flipped my middle finger at him.

XIII

As I got home, I hurried up to take my shower, put on some clothes and perfume – knowing the one I wore drove her crazy – so I put a lot of it – but not too much at the same time. The doorbell rang and I hurried to ring her in. She came up the stairs – looking as gorgeous as ever.

"Hey there!" she said, "It's been a long time!"

"Indeed it has! I'm glad to see you and that you finally came to my place after all these years," I replied – all too happy.

"Well, it's a pleasure. But you got Gary Bettman to thank for that."

"For once, I agree with one of his decisions! Hahahaha!"

She smiled as I let her in and took her coat.

"Wow, you smell good!" she added.

"Thanks! I knew you'd like my perfume. You always had."

"For real?" she replied – quizzical.

"Well, you've never said it before, but I could see it in the way you always had your face on my neck."

"You're cute! … So, this is where you live?"

"It's not much, but it's home. You want something to drink?"

"'You have any red wine?"

"Sure I do … 'Comin' right up!"

I went into the kitchen and served us some drinks. When I came back, Shelly was sitting on the sofa. I had forgotten to tell her not to sit there. I sat next to her – a slight feeling of disgust – her presence rapidly changing that though.

"So what have you been up to lately?" she asked.

"Like I told you on Facebook, I'm taking two courses at McGill, I'm still working at the same place and …"

"Yeah, that's right. You've already told me all of that … I'm sorry. I guess I'm just a little nervous," she shyly replied.

"Nervous? But, why?"

"I don't know … I feel like things have changed between you and I. With the thing that happened with that girl you dated … Pam … Well, for the first time, I was afraid to lose you. I guess I'd always took you for granted. Even when you were with that Miranda girl, I never really believed that you would spend your life with her. Something was off between you two. I always knew that you would come back to me one day."

I saw this coming a mile away, but I faked confusion.

"You're sending me mixed messages here. Didn't you say you didn't want to be with someone and focus on your career?" I asked.

"Well, I thought I did. I was sincere. But it gave me a slap in the face when I saw that you were really slipping away from me and moving on. I thought I would never see you again and it was like a wake-up call."

I was shaking all over from excitement. I wanted a verbal confirmation of what I was hearing – that I was not imagining things – even if it sounded clear to my ears.

"What are you implying here exactly? ... So I don't get the wrong idea."

"Well ... Ummm ... I would like to try that long distance thing, even if I'm still not sure about its feasibility. But I told myself: Hey! What have you got to lose? 'Might as well try it. So, here I am!"

I was speechless. I sat there, dumbstruck – unable to move or say anything. She looked at me waiting for an answer, but no words would come out of my mouth. She looked like she was getting scared of my response.

"So? What do you think?" she asked.

"Hell yeah! You have no idea how long I've been waiting for you to say that to me!" I replied – overwhelmed with joy.

"Great! But don't get too ahead of yourself. I said I was willing to try. For the rest, we'll figure it out along the way. Like I said, I never did this long distance relationship thing."

"Well, I'm more than happy to be your guinea pig. And in the meantime, I could try to apply for a green card and all. Do things legit this time. You know writers can write anywhere and every city needs a good assistant chef. Plus, with the money you make, I could enroll into Harvard."

"Wait! ... What??!"

"Hahahaha! I'm joking. You should've seen your face!"

"Come here and kiss me, you turd!"

"I'm not sure I want to, since you're insulting me."

She took me by my t-shirt collar, dragged me to her lips and started kissing me. It was even more passionate than ever.

After an extensive make out session, she started taking off her clothes.

"Maybe we should go into my bedroom, we'd be more comfortable," I suggested – remembering really well that there were still maybe some chocolatier fluids in the couch cushions.

"You're so square. Live a little!" Shelly replied.

"Trust me! You don't want your bare skin touching these cushions. Remember ... Tom lives here!"

"What? Yuk!" she said – jumping off the sofa – "You could've told me that earlier!"

"Well, I wanted to. But you had already sat down before I could warn you."

"I'll have to burn those clothes tomorrow! But now, help me take them off!!"

That night we made love. I'm not talking about sex, but love – sweet, passionate, intense and slow love making – kissing and caressing each other all through it. I had been waiting for this moment for so long, that I tried to make it last as long as possible. She trembled under my slow and deep grinding. We had to change position a couple of times, because I didn't want this to end ... ever. It was so intense – like nothing I had previously experienced.

After I came, I collapsed on the bed, but my mind was elsewhere – somewhere between heaven and nirvana. She turned to me panting and cuddled. She passed her hand through my hair and asked:

"So, how's my little epileptic doing?"

"Better than ever!" I replied – all too happy.

"You're cute!"

"And you're so goddamn gorgeous. That was amazing. Where did you hide that all those years?"

"I could ask you the same, sexy!"

We kissed some more and then spooned until she fell asleep. Well, I guess she was sleeping, because her breathing was different. For myself, I just couldn't fall asleep – being too goddamn excited with what had just happened – my mind spinning about a hundred miles an hour.

About half an hour later, I heard Tom walking into the apartment. I slowly and quietly got out of bed – making sure I wouldn't wake up Shelly. I put on my boxers and got out of my room – gently closing the door behind me. Tom was startled to see me – he was even more surprised when I jumped in his arms.

"What the fuck are you doing, dude?" he asked.

I took a step back and replied:

"I was right, bro! She wants more than casual sex once a year with me! She wants to try this long distance relationship!"

"Wow! I never saw that coming. I guess I was wrong about her!"

"Yes, you were!"

"I just missed you having sex, haven't I? ... I shouldn't have had that third drink after all."

"How do you know I just had sex?"

"Well, you always have that glow ... Like an Ethiopian being given a poutine for the first time. Plus, your chest is still full of red spots. You always get red sports on your chest when you have sex."

I felt a little ashamed for I don't know what reasons. Tom saw the shame on my face and said:

"Don't be ashamed, bro! I'm rooting for you! You should get rid of that Judeo-Christian guilt that sex is dirty. It's not! It's the most beautiful thing in the world!"

"No ... Shelly's the most beautiful thing in the world!"

"God! You gotta stop talking like a girl or I'll have to smack some sense into you!"

"Hahahaha! Sorry ... I'm just so happy ... You wouldn't understand."

"I do understand. From what you told me, you've had that girl under your skin from day one. I'm so happy for you, bro. Your happiness means a lot to me."

"Thanks!"

"But tell me something ... What the fuck are you doing here talking to me about it? Go back there and spoon her round butt with her big breasts overflowing out of your hands. Now get back to bed! Dr. Murphy's orders!"

"Sir! Yes, Sir!"

So I went back and slithered my way under the sheets – slipping my body between the curves of Shelly's body. I was finally happy.

The next morning, I awoke and Shelly was already up – I hadn't noticed that she had left the bed. When I got out of the room, the air was filled with the smooth and tasteful perfume of pancakes and bacon. I got to the kitchen and she was standing in front of the stove, flipping pancakes, only wearing one of my t-shirts and black Brazilian-cut panties. Tom heard me come in. He turned his head in my direction and said:

"Dude! You gotta marry that girl! If you don't, I will!"

Shelly replied:

"I don't do interracial."

"I'm not black!" replied Tom.

"First of all, we say African-Americans and second of all, they are Homo sapiens too ... So, the same race. I was saying that I don't date Neanderthals!"

I laughed and said to Tom:

"You're right! ... I am gonna marry this girl!"

Tom replied:

"I changed my mind. I don't want you both ganging up on me. It just wouldn't be fair!"

Shelly then added:

"From what I've heard ... Since when do you turn down being ganged up on?!"

Tom looked resourceless and overpowered. I was almost rolling on the floor laughing. Tom had finally met someone even more obnoxious than him. This was priceless. Shelly was really the one for me. Plus, she was an amazing cook. Her pancakes – well, crepes – were so goddamn delicious.

After breakfast, I took her on a Montreal sightseeing tour – like she had done with me the last time we saw each other in Quebec City. We spent the next two days roaming through the Montreal Museum of Fine Arts, the Redpath Museum of Natural History, the Pointe-à-Callière Museum, the Biodome, the Botanical Garden, the Insectarium, Old Montreal, climbing up on Mount-Royal and shopping in the thrift shops and second-hand book and record stores on Saint-Denis Street and Mount-Royal Avenue. On top of that, I made her the grand tour of my hood, between the Aqueduct and the Lachine Canal – showing her where I grew up, all the places I lived and played. We ate a Bock Burger at Dilallo's and went to drink a beer at Magnan tavern. It was just a magical two days. We held hands everywhere we went and kissed all the time.

On Monday, it took me all my inner restraint not to say the three words I had wanted to say for such a long time. The most beautiful thing in the world actually came from her mouth first. We were skipping stones on the Jolicoeur Street Bridge – over the Aqueduct – when she said the *I love you* I had longed for such a long time.

Time flew so fast, it was crazy. I didn't want her to leave. But she was working the next day. Although the players were in lockout, the public relations team had to make constant press releases about the evolution of the negotiations and all. Just before supper, I had to let her go.

"Are you sure you don't want anything to eat before you leave?" I asked.

"No thanks, I'm still full from those burgers we had at that place where you and Tom used to work. If I'm ever hungry, I'll just do as always and get something out of the value meal menu at MacDonald's."

"God I love you! You know that right?!"

"I've known for a long time. I just had to lose myself into you and accept that this could be it."

"I'll try to come join you as soon as possible!"

"I'm already counting the days."
"Have a safe trip back home sweetie!"
"I will. I promise!"

We kissed like forever before she headed down the stairs from my apartment. I watched her head for her car – which was parked about five houses down on the other side of the street. I kept blowing her kisses every time she turned around and she kept pretending to catch them in mid-air. We looked like two fourteen years old – puppy loving each other. If Tom had seen this, he would have kicked my ass for the next month. I watched her get in her car and drive away with a melancholic loving heart. Karma had finally made a pass at me for me to score the winning goal. I got back in the house with a new hopeful feeling in my heart – a new non-dystopian future for my love life.

As I got back in, I tried to talk to Tom, but he was making himself dinner with earphones over his head, listening to the music on his I-Pod. I tried to get his attention, but the music was so loud that he couldn't hear me – so loud, that I could hear what he was listening. I thought to myself; "Fuck it! I'll talk to him later!" I then went into my room to catch up on my university reading. Since Shelly had been here, I had neglected my school work, but I was determined to catch up with everything by Tuesday night.

I laid down on my bed and started to read Frank McCourt's *Angela's Ashes* – for class. Suddenly, the doorbell rang. I yelled; "Tom! Could you get the door?!" When I saw that he didn't hear me, I got up and went to unlock the downstairs door. I was hoping that it would be Shelly – that she had forgotten something, so I could give her another kiss. I opened the door and it turned out to be a man that I didn't know. He was tall, about six feet three inches tall, weighed around 250 pounds. His head was shaven with a nasty cut on top of his cranium. He was wearing a brown leather coat and stone washed jeans. He came up to the door. He looked like a friggin' monster.

"Can I help you?" I asked.

"You Eamon?"

"Yes ... Who's asking?"

"You fucked my wife a couple of days ago and I'm coming for payback!"

"What the fuck are you talkin' about?"

He then pulled out a 69 Smith & Wesson and pointed it directly at my skull. He added:

"I had my doubts, but I never would have thought that she would actually do this to me. So I looked through her phone and saw she had registered on Tinder. I looked through her conversation and there you were: Eamon! A snot nosed little punk wanting to fuck a married woman. I couldn't believe my eyes, so I started following her. Last Thursday, she came to this very place to meet you and I knew that she had been lying to me. I loved her so much and I still do ... But you and her have to pay for what you made me go through. I won't let a young asshole like you ruin the best thing that has ever happened to me without answering for your actions. She was mine and you can never take her away from me!"

At that point, I had wet my pants and was shaking. I could see Tom in the kitchen, deep in his thoughts making supper with the Flatliners bursting through his headphones. I started to cry and said:

"This is a big mistake. It's not what you think. You don't have to do this! Just leave and we'll both forget this whole incident."

"You think I can forget you screwing my wife. You think I can forget that a little motherfucker like you came into our life and threw away twenty years of marriage. Well you're wrong, you little turd! She's already gone and you'll be joining her in hell, asshole!"

I looked him straight in the eyes, weeping, and pleaded to him:

"Please, don't do this!"

"Well, you should've thought of that before you started fucking my wife!"

I saw a tear run down his left cheek and then I heard a loud bang. Pain ran through my entire body as I fell to the floor. I heard another gunshot and a large thump, like something tumbling on the porch. The last thing I heard was Tom yelling out my name – his running footsteps drawing nearer to me. Then everything went black ...

Epilogue

George Stroumboulopoulos: Hi! Welcome to *Tonight*. This week we are receiving Montreal's upcoming author, Tom Murphy, who has been receiving critical acclaim for his first novel *The Lachine Canal Chronicles*. How are you doing Tom? Nice to have you on the show.

Tom Murphy: Thanks for having me George.

George: So tell our viewers a little about your novel.

Tom: Well George ... Ummm ... It's kind of a hard to talk about. It's based on the true story of my friend Eamon Jovanovski who was murdered a little less than two years ago. Oufff! It's always hard to get back to that fateful night of October 21, 2012.

George: It's okay, take your time.

Tom: Well ... After his death, I went into a really rough patch, drinking and doing hard drugs. I finally got my act together and started to seek testimonies from everyone who knew him. He had been writing a novel of the same title for some years now. Living with him, I had access to all his drafts and his mom was good enough to hand me earlier writings he had done.

George: So you are telling us that you have compiled Eamon's writings and assembled them all together.

Tom: No, that's not it. I read everything over and over again, but didn't copy a single line. I inspired myself from his writings and, like I said earlier, with testimonies of the people who were the closest to him. At this moment, I would like to thank Shelly Sullivan who has been such a great help in all this adventure. In the end, the novel is a biographical fiction about my best friend's life. I tried for several months to put myself in his shoes and tried my best to re-enact the most significant parts. Most of them, I was there to testify the events that took place. But, like I said, I had a lot of help from close ones and previous incomplete draft writings I have found here and there. I tried to remain as true as possible to the persona Eamon embodied; his hopes, dreams, mentality and all.

George: Aren't you afraid that some people would accuse you of leaching off a tragedy for your own personal gain?

Tom: No ... Not at all! In my heart I know I wrote this book with as much integrity as I could. For the people who have read it, they will notice how I portray myself and will understand that all the work I did in the past two years is in no way for personal gain. You could say that I come up as a friggin' asshole in the book. I can honestly say that I was a real bastard at that point of my life. I am now trying to make amends for all the wrong that I have done. I know that all this will never bring back Eamon. But at least, I hope that he did not die in vain. That somebody will recognize himself in our twisted lives and do something about it. If I am able to influence at least one reader out there who has lived the things Eamon and I have and tries to do something about it, then my work here is done.

George: So this novel has been some sort of therapy for you?

Tom: Hell yeah! It's actually the first good thing I did in my life.

George: So Tom, what are your plans for the future?

Tom: Well, I'm thinking of writing a sequel to *The Lachine Canal Chronicles*. I'm still in the process of thinking how to make to story progress. I'm also thinking of writing a screenplay for the first book. I had everything in my head since day one. So Mr. Scorsese or the Coen Brothers, if you're listening have your people call my people!

George: Well this is all the time we have. We'd like to thank Tom Murphy, the author of *The Lachine Canal Chronicles*, for his openness throughout this interview. Next week, we are welcoming a great …."